T0363448

WORD HUNTERS

WAR OF THE WORD HUNTERS

NICK EARLS &
TERRY WHIDBORNE

UQP

First published 2013 by University of Queensland Press
PO Box 6042, St Lucia, Queensland 4067 Australia
Reprinted 2017

www.uqp.com.au
uqp@uqp.uq.edu.au

Typeset in 11/16pt Horley Old Style by Jo Hunt
Printed in Australia by McPherson's Printing Group

Cataloguing-in-Publication Data
National Library of Australia

Earls, Nick, 1963- author.
War of the word hunters / Nick Earls ; Terry Whidborne (illustrator).

Earls, Nick, 1963- Word hunters ; 3.

For primary school age.

Whidborne, Terry.

ISBN (pbk) 978 0 7022 4959 4
ISBN (pdf) 978 0 7022 5075 0
ISBN (epub) 978 0 7022 5076 7
ISBN (kindle) 978 0 7022 5077 4

A823.3

University of Queensland Press uses papers that are natural, renewable and recyclable products made from wood grown in sustainable forests. The logging and manufacturing processes conform to the environmental regulations of the country of origin.

While stories build from words, it's true,

The words themselves have stories too.

Who dares to read? Who dares to look?

Who dares to hunt within this book?

'**L**IKE THIS,' GRANDAD Al said as he lunged forward with his sword. The tip stopped a millimetre in front of a button on Will's shirt and stayed perfectly still. 'That's the thrust. If you put your legs and your body into it, you'll add at least 50 centimetres to your reach. Any time we land in Europe between 300 and 1500, it's one of the most useful moves you'll make with a sword. Anyone know why?'

Will took a step back, put his hand up to the wooden blade and turned the sword away from his body. Alan Hunter had a point to make and it would be all too easy for him to forget he was holding a sword to someone's chest.

The rest of them had no idea why the thrust was so useful, so Grandad Al went on. 'The Romans liked swords and they knew how to use them. They used the thrust and you should be ready for it before the year 300. The Saxons and the Vikings preferred axes, which meant they tended to hack with their swords.' He lifted his sword and chopped the air with it, first from the right and then the left. 'Same as their axe action, and that's what they're expecting in return. That's what their shields are ready to block. If we're up against them, the thrust will be a surprise most of the time. It comes back by the 16th century, though, so remember that.'

Lexi felt sweat in her hair. She waved her hand in front of her face to get rid of a fly. 'Camping with Grandad Al' – that's what this medieval warrior boot camp had been called when it was put to their parents. The scars on her arm from the Battle of Hastings were fading, but still pink, and her memory of the fight hadn't faded at all. She tried to make herself take in the tactics her grandfather was talking about. She wanted to reduce the idea of battle to tactics for as long as she could, and not to think about it as a clash of unwashed bodies, axes splintering shields, the black specks of arrows in the sky, falling, hundreds of them. She tried to picture thrusting and blocking – calculated moves – rather than being caught in the middle of chaos.

Grandad Al flipped the sword over, caught the blade and gave the handle to Will. He knelt down, slid his left arm into the straps of the round shield that was lying on the ground and picked it up, along with another sword in his right hand.

'Okay, this is what you have to look for,' he said. 'I'm a Saxon or a Viking and I'm assuming you are, too.' He nodded at Will. 'So I'm ready to hack with my sword or axe and to block you doing the same. You might want the other shield.' He lifted the edge of it with the toe of his boot and tipped it over towards Will.

Will picked it up. 'Are we—'

'No. This is a demonstration. Slow motion. So, my blade will come down like this—' He moved into the action. 'From here I can only do a kind of forehand – I don't know what they called it. So Will can block that.' Will moved his shield to cover. 'Then I'm ready for the same from Will, so my shield goes here.' He moved it to check Will's likely blow. 'But if Will drops the point of his sword and thrusts—' Will did as instructed. 'See the space? See how I'm not covered for that at all? He can go straight to the abdomen from there. If I'm wearing chain mail – and I probably won't be – he can go for my thigh, for the femoral artery.' He lowered his own sword to show where the artery ran. 'The thrust to the abdomen should put them out of the fight right away. The femoral artery might too, but if it doesn't, blood loss will do it within a minute or so.'

The two of them worked through the moves again in slow motion, as Lexi, Al and Mursili watched, knowing that their turn would come soon.

'Spears are another thing to look out for,' Mursili said as Will lunged again. 'If we're fighting an army with spears – the kind for holding and jabbing, not for throwing – they might be more ready for the thrust with the sword. So, 3,000 years ago, the thrust will not surprise. And the swords will be

short. Bronze bends if it's too long. So did Hittite iron, even though it was supreme in its time.'

Mursili had been googling to see what had gone wrong in Hattusa all those years ago, but too much time had passed and the damage had been too great for there to be good records or a clear answer. The Kaskians had wrecked the place and done nothing with it. The waste of it all was more than he wanted to think about.

Al was starting to wonder how he'd remember everything he needed to, particularly if an ancient warrior was coming for him in a battle. He could picture Hastings, too, and the Norman with the mace who had wounded Lexi. He could see it differently now. There had been a chance, as his shield blocked the mace, to thrust. The Norman was exposed.

But the thrust would stick a sword in a man's stomach. In battle it wouldn't be a theory, or a blunt wooden blade in a national park two hours from home. It would wound someone, and maybe do more than that.

Back over the hill they'd pitched two tents in the campground, which was no more than a cleared area beside a track. Mount Barney was a wilderness park, so there were no amenities. Tomorrow they would climb the mountain and it would take all day, but this afternoon's schedule was all about fighting techniques.

Grandad Al had brought padded clothes, and Viking and Roman style shields as well as the swords. It had taken two trips to the car park, 20 minutes down a fire trail and through a paddock, to bring all the gear in to the camping ground.

Alan Hunter had known this time was coming and he'd had years to plan for it, without anyone noticing what he was doing. He had looked into fencing classes and the protective gear fencers wear, but the techniques weren't right for medieval battle, the weapons weren't enough like an arming sword and the outfits didn't give the right kind of protection.

But his grandchildren, and now this team of word hunters, needed to be as ready for battle as anyone could make them. So, while the dictionary had been dormant in the late 20th century, he had thought through the battles of the past and worked out as precisely as he could what they would need when a word next sent them into history.

It was summer and Lexi and Al would soon be 13. They were survivors already, but not warriors yet. Will was the closest to that and, at 20, he was a good age for it, too, even if he was technically 110. Which was nothing on Mursili, who had been born more than 3,000 years before and managed not to look a day over 35.

At least Mursili could handle a sword, even if it was in an ancient kind of way, and shoot a bow, and ride. He had been a Hittite boy before he'd become court librarian, and all those experiences were part of a standard Hittite boyhood in the 1190s BC.

And now it was time to put the padding on and start fighting. Grandad Al lifted the gear out of the bag.

'I know it's hot,' he said. He had a motorbike helmet in each hand. 'We'll only do five minutes at a time. Who wants to go first?'

There was a pause and then Will said, 'Me. I'll give it a try.'

'And me.' Mursili swaggered across to Will and drew himself up to his full height, which put his head at the level of Will's chest. 'You probably don't need the helmet, but your femoral arteries are in grave danger, let me tell you.'

Lexi picked up a spare sword and imagined a shield on her other arm.

'What if one of them's coming at you from here?' Al said to her. He was over to her right, and he made a move in her direction. She lifted her sword to block his imaginary axe swing as she turned.

'Good.' Grandad Al clapped his hands together. 'You two work on the theory, while these two get the gear on. And, Lexi, if Al's swinging something big at you, like an axe, just try to deflect it, rather than take the full force of it with your sword. Your choice is right, though. Use the sword if you can't get the shield there in time. And focus on the defence. You won't get to attack if you don't defend. And remember, we're not there to win these battles. It's about staying alive.'

Al swung again and this time Lexi's shield arm was ready.

'So you're a Viking or a Saxon?' She couldn't really picture Al as either, but that wasn't the problem. She turned to her grandfather. 'What if he was a grey-robe with a sword? How do they fight? Are they like everyone else from whatever time it is, or—'

She wanted the answer to be yes. She wanted Grandad Al to know, and something to be certain about the people who seemed to want to kill them.

Her grandfather looked at Will, who shook his head.

'I don't think we know,' Grandad Al said. 'We don't know if they're gathering in some of the times we go to, or if they're being sent through time to find us. We might not be the only time travellers.' He couldn't help looking past her through the trees, checking. 'None of us has seen them after 1648. And they didn't take my pegs then.' It sounded like two bits of good news, but it didn't amount to much. 'We have to assume the worst. That they know who we are, they know what we do, they know most of what we know and if they've got swords, we should expect them not to be surprised by the thrust.'

Lexi nodded and tried to pretend that she hadn't wanted a different answer. Her friends from school were on their way to Madison Bond's house for a sleepover. They would play music till late, eat junk food, and take a thousand photos of the whole thing. Not a second of the evening would be spent discussing sword-fighting techniques. Sometimes it seemed to Lexi as if she had to be ready to ride into battle against the entire past, just to keep the present as it was – to make sure iTunes existed, and phones. As well as the English language and perhaps most of the people she knew.

She poked at the ground with the wooden sword. 'So can I have the next fight?'

'So much better with stirrups,' Mursili said. He was built like a jockey, and now he was riding like one.

He turned the horse and started it cantering again. The axe in his hand was beginning to feel heavy. Al kept the target moving. It was two hay bales in a wheelbarrow, with a hat on top.

Through the trees beyond Mursili, he could see the house he was trying to get used to thinking of as Grandad Al and Grandma Noela's. He and Lexi had two sets of memories now – that was how Grandad Al had put it, though it wasn't as simple as that.

They had true memories of their own lives that were now wrong, because they'd saved their grandfather in 1648 and sent him back to his own time. Now he had always been in their lives, but only pictures proved it to them. And he and Grandma Noela had lived at Brookfield for two years. Lexi and Al had visited dozens of times and yet never visited at all. In the lives they remembered, Grandma Noela was alone and still in her old house.

'You'll have both sets of memories in there, I think,' Grandad Al had told them. 'But your brain can't accept that, so it won't bring one up. That's my best guess.' He shrugged. 'We weren't built for this – for time travel or for what it can mean if something changes – but it's what we've got.'

Grandad Al and Grandma Noela lived next door to the Franklins, who had horses. There was nothing coincidental about that. Al and Lexi could hardly believe how well their grandfather had planned it. One way or another, he had the makings of a medieval military training camp in place, without it being visible to anyone. Hiking and climbing had always been in the family, so the trips to Mount Barney were no surprise. He'd had two things in mind when looking in real estate agents' windows after Noela and he retired – neighbours with horses and a place with a workshop almost as big as the house.

After they moved in, he befriended the Franklins and became the most obvious person to care for their horses whenever they went away. And, over time, he turned the workshop into exactly the place he needed it to be. Grandma Noela talked about 'men and their sheds' and imagined him down there painting toy trains. Instead he made shields and swords, padded jackets and targets and he tried to imagine every past conflict he might face with his grandchildren, when they became word hunters.

When he took them to the shed for the first time, it reminded them of only one thing.

'Best looking workshop I've seen since the 5th century,' Al told him.

'If only,' Grandad Al said. 'I could do with some of those scrolls.'

There were three pairs of light stirrups on one bench and he was working on two more, for Will and Mursili. Like every word hunter, Grandad Al had his own packing list, but his had more than 50 missions behind it and then 30 years of planning.

Stirrups would give them an edge in Europe for 800 years. Stirrups arrived in the 7th century, but the solid saddle

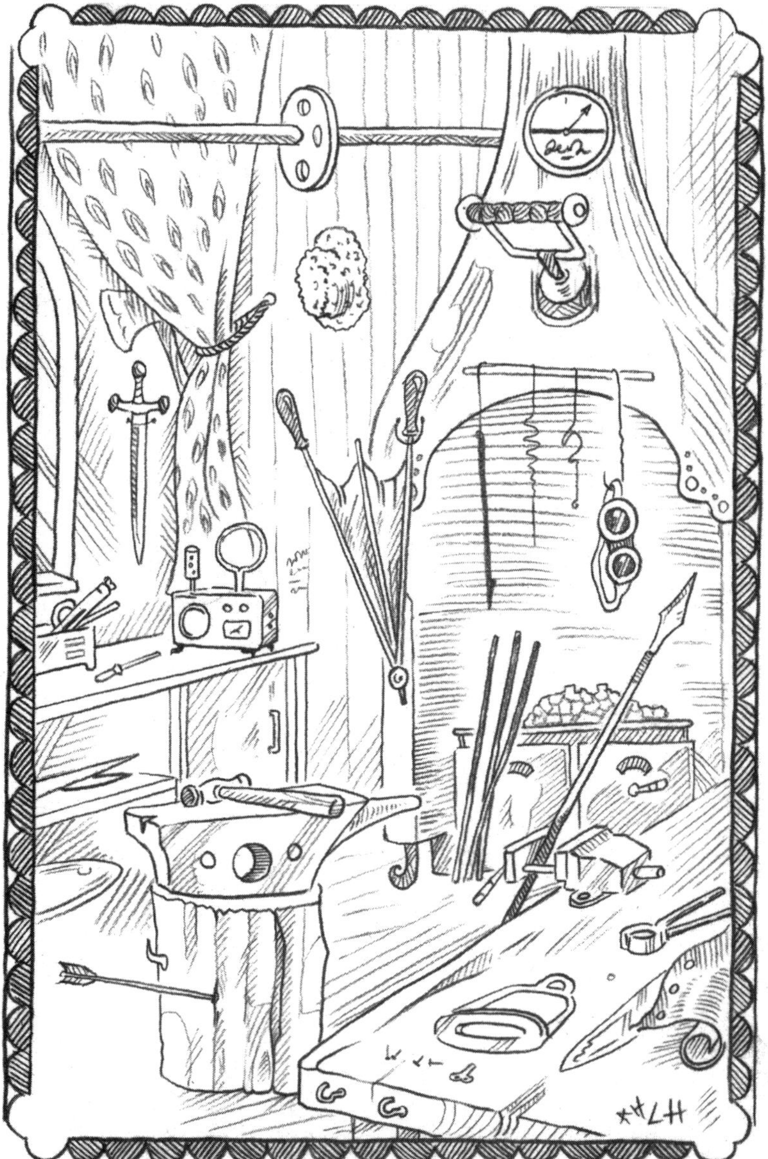

they required if they were to work came long before, with the Romans. If the word hunters could ride well enough, they had a chance of outriding someone far more experienced, who didn't have stirrups.

With the Franklins out of the country, they had their opportunity to practise.

Mursili urged the horse into a gallop. He wanted to ride one day without a battle plan in mind and for the sake of riding, but for now he had the hay to focus on. Al moved the barrow back and forward and the bales rocked from side to side. Mursili made small corrections to his line, talking to his horse the whole time.

With only metres to go, Al pulled back hard on the wheelbarrow, but Mursili was ready and leant out from the saddle, swung the axe and felt the heavy head thump into the upper bale, jerking the handle from his grip.

'Nice one,' Lexi said, and clapped.

Mursili gave a small bow and drew back on the reins to turn the horse, before they reached the end of the yard. He followed the arc of hoof prints around and rode back towards Al.

Al picked up the axe from the ground.

'Yeah, nice one,' he said, as he handed it back to Mursili. 'I still don't get how you didn't have a saddle – how no one worked that out before the Assyrians.' He couldn't help himself – he'd double-checked Grandad Al's research and found that the first saddle was a fringed cloth used by Assyrian cavalry a few centuries after Mursili's time.

'Oh, please. Until two weeks ago you could hardly tell a horse's face from its bottom!' Lexi laughed, so Mursili kept going. 'I hate to think what would have happened if we'd sent you in here with a bucket of carrots. That Assyrian remark is where a small amount of googling can get you into trouble. You should talk to the man.' Mursili tilted the axe head to point to himself. 'Have you seen a Hittite horse? Tiny. Well – small, anyway. We could ride them as kids, but their backs couldn't take the weight of an adult. Great for pulling war chariots, though, and we wrote the book on that. Literally. I had it in my library. By Kikkuli of Mittani, master trainer to

King Suppi I. Google that one, my friend. People talk about it all over the net. And it's there because of you. You helped save it from the Kaskians, remember. So thank you for letting the world know that the Hittites were in fact the first great horse trainers. If we'd had bigger horses—'

'And you know I love the history, too,' Grandad Al said before Mursili started going on about the Kaskians. He took the reins. 'But we don't want the Franklins to turn up while you're still in the saddle. They're only skiing in Japan for another week—'

Ye:

definite article, an older written form of 'the', brought about by substituting 'y' for an earlier letter of similar appearance. Only persists in forms such as 'ye olde', 'ye loste letteres'.

& MORE

L EXI TOOK THE first shower after horseriding. Al was always made to shower last, since he never came out quickly and often used up all the hot water. He'd heard every dull joke from his father about him dissolving, or Christmas coming, or Al having shares in the gas company. It was easier just to go after everyone else.

He stood in the kitchen eating handfuls of nuts. His mother was making herself a cup of tea.

'You know, I think it's really nice that you and Lexi give your grandfather so much help when he's looking after those horses,' she said. She jiggled the tea bag up and down.

'Yeah, well, we do get to ride them.' Al wondered what she thought went on at the Franklins', or in Grandad Al's workshop. She had no idea. Sometimes he wanted to say something like, 'He's training us for war, you know,' just for the shock value.

'Still, it's a lot of work. I'm not sure why he told his neighbours he'd do it.' She lifted the tea bag out and dropped it in the bin. 'It's good that he's got you there, too, for all the heavy lifting and bending and things.'

'Yeah.'

Grandad Al was such a faker. He walked around with a stoop and managed to look as if he wasn't up to much. And yet, if a horde of Vikings with battleaxes attacked the house, Grandad Al would see them off, one at a time at the top of the stairs, while their father would lock the family in the bathroom, dial triple 0 and talk to the operator in a hopeless squeaky voice that'd sound like a practical joke.

Al tipped up the nut jar. There were a few left in the bottom, but there was mostly salt.

His mother stopped her teacup halfway to her mouth. 'Go easy on those. You'll spoil your appetite.'

'As if.' He emptied the last nuts into his hand, set the jar down and left the kitchen.

The shower was still running in the bathroom as he walked past and opened the door to his room. He noticed the glow right away. It had been weeks since the last time, but there was no doubt now that it was there. Another word in the dictionary had been triggered, and that called for another trip into the past to save it.

He shut the door behind him and went to his desk. He cleared away the mess on top and opened the dictionary carefully. 'Ye'. It wasn't even really a word anymore. He wondered if they could let this one go, tell no one, but it was impossible to guess the consequences. So they would have to go anyway, and save a word that for a hundred years or more had only been used to mean that something was hokey and pretending to be old.

There was a scuffling sound from Doug's cage. Al turned to see a beady stare directed his way.

'Don't worry,' he said to him. 'You were my next step.'

He unzipped the top of his backpack and set it near the cage. 'Well, maybe not next step, but you're part of the plan. I'll put you in there just before we go.'

When he heard Lexi come out of the bathroom Al opened his door.

She was about to tell him the bathroom was free, but he got in first. 'It's gone off.'

The way he said it told her exactly what 'it' was.

'Okay.' She glanced down the corridor and then followed him into his room.

'Do I at least get to have a shower?' He shut the door behind her.

'Why? No one before the mid-19th century's going to care. You'll fit into most of history better if you stink. Which means you'd fit in really well right now. What's the—' She took a step towards the desk.

'I'm going to have a shower. You get the team together. It's a weird word.' He shrugged. 'I haven't looked for where it might take us yet.'

After Lexi called him on her mobile, Grandad Al called the landline and told their mother that she and Al had forgotten something, but that he was on his way out now and would drop it over.

'Your grandmother's been baking again,' her mother said. 'And you know she thinks it's a waste not to eat it when it's fresh. Grandad's in a bit of a hurry to go somewhere, so he wants one of you to meet him out the front. He'll have the pie in his car.'

When they heard Grandad Al pull up, Lexi went down the front steps while Al snuck out the back way with their packs and the dictionary. He met her at the gate. Grandad Al, Mursili and Will were all standing next to the car with their packs at their feet. Grandad Al was stuffing his old orange towelling hat into his before zipping it shut.

Lexi laughed. 'I can't believe you're bringing that.'

'It's my lucky hat.' He made out that he was offended.

'Lucky?' Will picked up his own pack and checked he'd closed it properly. 'You were a prisoner of the grey-robes for 30 years with that hat.'

Grandad Al unzipped his pack and put the hat on defiantly. 'You found me when I had this hat. That's the bit I prefer to remember.'

Al opened the dictionary on the bonnet and Mursili said, 'I've looked up "ye". I'm still the team librarian, even though I'm also a warrior now. There might be a 19th-century step first, since it came back then as a bit of a joke. Then I think it'll go to printers in the 15th or 16th, but I don't know who or where. Earlier than that it's all guesswork.'

Will laughed. 'It was already sounding like guesswork.'

'Hey, I didn't invent your crazy mixed-up language. Some trails go cold.' Mursili shrugged. 'Of course, if you'd been decent enough to hunt this word before, you might have something to offer on the subject. At least it doesn't seem to involve any wars. I know some people don't like words that drop us into battles.'

He didn't want to admit it, but he was one of those people. It had never been his plan to join them in the past, but Alan had talked about strength in numbers. Mursili had tried to run his line about being the cool tech guy who stays back at base looking things up on screens, but it hadn't worked. So he had trained as hard as he could and then, just in case, he had said a few quiet words to Tarhunt, the god of thunder and of war. And he had tried to put out of his mind the loss of the city of Nerik to the Kaskians. All the spare thick bread in the empire and dozens of oxen hadn't persuaded Tarhunt to change that.

Lexi took a closer look at the dictionary entry. There was very little light now, but the glow from the page was enough to read by.

'What do you think?' she said to no one in particular. 'I've seen "ye olde" before, on antique shops and things, but never "ye loste letteres". What's that about?'

She was sure someone would have an answer.

No one did.

'It's not one I've done before. It looks like an old spelling of "the lost letters",' Grandad Al said, 'but beyond that—'

'Maybe that's it.' Al leant forward to take a closer look. 'Maybe it's a clue and the earlier letter that looked like "y" was one of the lost letters.'

A bat flew by and the leathery flap of its wings caught him by surprise. His hand reached for a sword that wasn't there. He was about to leave Fig Tree Pocket for a past that might have anything in it – congresses, voyages, conflict – small moments that led to words despite themselves. He could feel the fight and the fear in himself already. But he'd never been more prepared.

'Time to go,' Grandad Al said. 'Your mother's expecting a pie. Who wants to— Mursili, what about you? You've never started one of these trips off before, have you?'

He turned the dictionary around so that it faced Mursili, who tried hard to keep his finger steady as he reached forward.

'Here goes not much—' Just as he thought it'd be a good idea to talk it all through again, his fingertip touched the portal and it opened wide with a flare of golden light and he felt himself sucked forward.

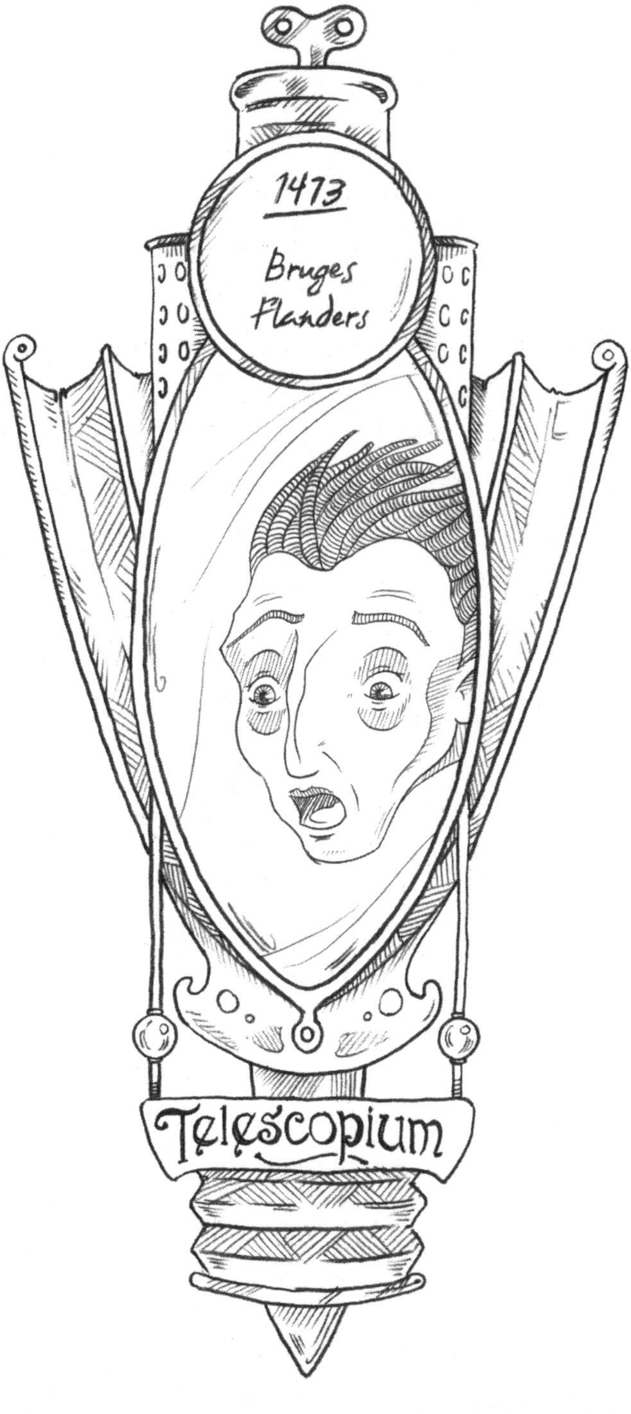
1473
Bruges
Flanders
Telescopium

$\mathcal{A}$s THE OTHERS braced themselves for a rush of small bumps, Mursili felt like he'd been thrown in a sack, dumped in the boot of Grandad Al's car and driven over a corrugated iron roof. Then came a lurch and a slower drop, a bigger unexpected bump and turbulence. Then pressure squeezed the air out of his lungs like toothpaste from a tube.

His ears popped and, just as he took in a huge breath, the sky cleared. Which was all fine except he was now thousands of metres above the ground and plummeting fast. The word hunters had told him all about that, but hearing it and living it were not the same. They all appeared okay, but he seemed to have taken every vowel sound possible and put them together into the loudest scream he could manage. He tried to fight his limbs into the flying posture they had told him about.

It was a total blur to Mursili as he tumbled, but they were falling over lush flat country, towards a town. The sea was ahead and to their left, and soon Al could make out a canal extending from it into a network of smaller waterways in the town. No 20th-century airport, no 19th-century factories. The town was oval shaped, perhaps on an island. It looked as if the canals went all around it, and then Al was sure he could make out the structure of a wall, with defensive points. There were red roofs and well-organised streets, but not the grid pattern of New York.

'The square,' Grandad Al called out, nodding towards it.

It was almost directly below them and offered a good landing spot, if they could avoid the market stalls that had been set up there. And the huge tower at one end of it, casting its shadow into the square like a giant sundial.

The word hunters tilted to a glide and Mursili stuttered after them, trying to pretend his scream was something else, as the hard ground came at them in a rush. There was a gap where two rows of stalls backed onto each other and the others found it, while Mursili dropped down onto a pile of English wool bales.

The trader looked around. At first he thought it was a bird, but then Mursili stood up. He stepped from the top bale down to the next one, and then the next, as if it was an entirely natural thing to do.

'Very fine quality,' he said to the trader as he reached the ground, rubbing some of the wool between his finger and thumb. He handed the pinch of wool to the trader, whose mouth was still gaping. 'I might get myself a bale or two of that. Later. I'll just rejoin my colleagues now.'

His colleagues had stepped out from behind the bales and were standing nearby, trying not to laugh. He wasn't sure if it was at the screaming, the landing or both. Probably both.

'Very soft spot to come down,' he said. 'I can recommend it for next time. And that sound I made in the air – just alerting Ellel, the god of the sky, that I was in the vicinity. Respect.'

'I just pretend it's like TV,' Al told him, in case it helped. 'Like I'm only watching the pictures and not about to be slammed into the ground. It always works out in the end.'

'Easy for you. You try watching TV when all you've got to go on for visual entertainment is 35 years of Hittite religious ceremonies. You're flying above New York at night then – *bang* – you're on the street. *Bang* – you're in an alley. *Bang* – there's a body next to the dumpster. Then you're in a lab. Then giant tweezers are removing a giant fibre. That's the first ten seconds and already you've been in six different places. At a Hittite ceremony you sit in one seat – or in your case, probably on a rough straw mat – for four hours. You know there will be a god on a platform directing the action.

There will be pestilence, smiting and sacrifices, and a nice song at the end. TV might be very clever, but if you think it makes sense—' Mursili noticed the fancy cuffs at the end of his sleeves. Everything looked different. The others were different, too. Just at this moment, however much they'd tried to get him ready for it, *nothing* actually made sense.

Lexi was wearing a long gown with full sleeves and an embroidered cap with a veil covering her hair. The others wore puffy-sleeved shirts with doublets and robes over the top, along with pointy boots and brightly coloured leggings beneath. Al's were yellow.

He turned to Lexi and pointed to her head. 'Before you say anything about chicken legs, I think Grandma Noela wants her tea-cosy back.'

'I'd totally wear this at home and you know it,' she said. 'It's cool if you take the veil off. On the other hand—' She started flapping her arms out to her sides and clucking.

'I'm getting the peg now.' Al swung his duffel bag down from his shoulder. As he loosened the drawstring, Doug blinked at the daylight and smelt the new air – sweaty humans, sheep, no sheep poo – odd.

Al pulled out the four pegs and rolled them around in his hand to see which one had activated. The other word hunters came in closer to read the details.

Mursili pushed his way forward. 'Please, let me. I've never— Ooh, Flanders, 15th century, interesting. Is the writing always in red?'

'We're dressed like the traders,' Will said. He was scanning the crowd, looking for signs, threats. 'We're something to do with the wool trade.'

The tower they'd seen from the air stood above the front of an imposing red-brick building that had a series of arched entrances at the level of the square. Most of the buildings around the square were red brick, with the bricks arranged to make patterns. All around them people were talking, bargaining, complaining about taxes and the crudeness of sailors and the quality of dye.

At the far end of the building with the tower, a canal came right up to the square and a ship was loading rolls of cloth. Beyond it, they could see windmills and the masts of other ships.

Then Al saw men in grey robes. He grabbed his grandfather's arm.

'Over there.' He pointed across the square.

There were eight of them, identically dressed and walking up some steps into a building. Will braced himself and looked for weapons nearby. Mursili stepped behind Grandad Al.

'Are they monks?' Lexi said, wanting to be right. 'Are they just monks?'

'I hope so.' Grandad Al already had a bale hook in his hand. It was a metre and a half long, and some kind of weapon at least. She hadn't even seen him move to pick it up. 'There's a cross above the door they're going into. I think you're right. Well spotted, though. Both of you.'

As Lexi watched each monk go into the building, she looked for signs of armour or weapons under their robes. But their hoods were hanging loose on their backs, their heads were shaved and they seemed to have no idea the word hunters were nearby.

It wasn't much relief to Al that the men were just monks this time. They might not be the next. There might be eyes on the word hunters right now, in this market. Until the grey-robes were tracked to their source and defeated, the threat of them would hang over every moment the word hunters were in the past.

Grandad Al set the hook back down, leaning it against a bale of wool.

'We have to carry something,' Will said. 'Let's take those monks as a warning.'

Before the others could say anything, he'd walked across to a nearby stall, taken off his felt hat and swapped it for an iron fire poker and toasting fork.

Will was the designated weapons expert. Grandad Al had studied battle tactics, but it was Will who had proven almost impossible to beat during training and who seemed able to make almost anything operate as a purpose-built weapon.

Even Al had eventually come around to the idea that he couldn't match Will when it came to weapons, and he'd started calling him 'the ninja' behind his back.

Will kept the poker himself and gave the toasting fork to Grandad Al.

'All right,' Grandad Al said, as he turned it over in his hand. It was solid enough. 'Good move, Will. Now we just need to swap Al's hat for a bag of marshmallows and find ourselves a fire.'

'Marshmallows?' Mursili said carefully. He pulled the chain that hung around his neck and the broken piece of Hittite tablet that translated for him came out of his shirt. He tapped it. Nothing became clearer. Some things simply had nothing close to an equivalent in Hattusa. 'These people have canals. They probably have marshes. Is it a kind of duck? A marshmallow.'

'No, it's—' Grandad Al had meant to lighten the mood, but Mursili had really got them there. 'It's a bit post-Hittite. We'll buy some when we get home. And you and Al can race each other to work out where the name comes from. It's not a duck. Now, someone somewhere around here is going to do something with "ye". Any ideas?'

'We need to find a printer.' Mursili felt as if he was back on sure ground. 'Late 15th century, someone's going to print it. We know printers were involved and the time's right.'

'But the word's English, isn't it?' Al wasn't so certain. 'Why would English printing be done in Flanders, which I'm pretty sure is Belgium?'

'The wool trade.' Will pointed out the bales all around them. 'English wool comes here to be sold. Maybe we need to find a wool trader rather than a printer. There'll be English people here. Let's find them.'

There were none in the first row of stalls, but in the second they met Thomas Wood from Lincoln, who sold English wool and bought lace, maps and eastern spices to take back to England with him. As he talked through his wares, all five word hunters waited for him to say 'ye', but he didn't.

When they asked about other English merchants, he explained that most were in the cloth hall – the large building with the tower – near the office of the Company of Merchant Adventurers of London.

'That'd be your best point of contact. Most of us are signed up with them.' He pointed to the main entrance. 'You're welcome to do business with me, though, if you've got the kind of thing I'm after. I'm loading now and there's room for some more. That ironwork you've got's not really it, though, if that's a sample. Not much of a market for imported pokers in England.'

They had moved only a few steps away from his stall when Lexi held up her hand. The others stopped. At the base of a wool bale, someone had written the initials 'JH'. She bent down and picked up a torn brown leaf that was tucked under the bottom.

'I don't know if this is—' She wondered if she was just picking up rubbish.

Grandad Al leant over and sniffed it. He thought about it for a moment. 'Will, what do you think?'

Will sniffed it, too. 'I think it's tobacco. A tobacco leaf.'

For a second Al was annoyed about not being asked to smell it, but then a wave of history hit him. 'Got it. It's 1473. There's no tobacco in Europe in 1473. That's why it's a clue. And why JH is one of us.'

'Good work.' Grandad Al rearranged the front of his doublet so that his peg badge could be seen clearly. 'Let's make sure everyone gets a good look at our badges. See if you can spot any of us nearby.'

Lexi and Al glanced at each other. Caractacus had said the initials gave lost word hunters somewhere to wait, but he'd said so much it hadn't really sunk in. The initials weren't just a sign that a hunter had been there before, or an indication that the word hunters were on track. They should wait each time for lost hunters to show themselves. That's why Grandad Al took the initials so seriously.

As they checked the crowd, he knelt down and slipped a blue ballpoint pen from a pocket inside his doublet. He wrote 'AH' next to 'JH' and tucked the tobacco leaf back under the bale, along with a paperclip he'd brought from home.

Al could remember meeting Will in Plymouth, and seeing him cross the room to get to them once he'd noticed their badges. There was no one doing anything like that here.

'That chest looks almost full,' he heard Thomas Wood say to one of his staff. 'Make sure you put one of Mr Caxton's notices on top before you seal it.'

'Caxton? The printer? The English printer?' It was out before Al could think twice.

The word hunters all turned to Thomas Wood.

'The printer? That's very flattering. I suppose he's a printer. He says he printed this.' Thomas Wood held up a sheet of paper. 'We're just trying to help him get started again.'

The sheet was headed 'The Recuyell of the Historyes of Troye'. Beneath that it said, 'A courtly tale newely turned to the English tunge. If it plese ony man to bye let hym send worde to Wm Caxton in Bruges and he shal have them good chepe. Soon in Westmonester'.

For Al, it felt like being six again and having to work out all the words from scratch. Is this what English was like before someone came up with the idea of spelling? Could this really be the work of William Caxton, England's first printer? And why wasn't he in England? There was no 'ye' on it. It might be an old way of writing 'the', but Caxton was already writing it as 'the'.

'I don't think he's made the book yet at all.' Thomas Wood seemed to think it was all a joke. 'Perhaps he needs some money coming in to make it, so he's selling it already. He was a good book *trader*, I'll give him that. Back when he was governor here. Of the Merchant Adventurers. Before the king had to come over here in a hurry.'

The word hunters tried to look as though they knew all about the king's hurry. Lexi and Mursili assumed one of the history nerds would tell them later. The history nerds had no idea.

1473 and the king had fled England not long before. Al looked around for some kind of clue, but all he noticed was that Doug had escaped from his bag. He was on top of the opened bale, scratching around and making a nest out of

the wool. Al grabbed him with both hands. Thomas Wood stared at Al, and at the rat he was holding. He wasn't at all sure what to make of it.

'Not a good look, Mr Wood,' Grandad Al said. 'Rats in your wool. Luckily we can get rid of this one for you.'

Al was already stuffing Doug back into his bag, along with the sizeable lump of wool caught in his claws.

'Um, thank you.' Thomas Wood parted the wool bale, looking for more rats.

'This Mr Caxton,' Grandad Al said. 'Is he anywhere nearby?'

'Um, yes.' Thomas Wood pointed past Grandad Al's left shoulder. 'Down that street, on the left. That rat was— it must have just dropped in there. Somehow.' The last thing he wanted was word getting around that his wool was infested with rats. 'I'd take you there myself, but I can't really leave my spot. "Mansion & Caxton" – you'll see the sign. If Caxton's started printing any books yet, do come back and let me know.' He laughed nervously. 'If he's got us all sending out these notices to our customers, I'd quite like to know there'll be a book at the end of it.'

Al wanted to set him straight right now. Not only was Caxton going to print a book, he was going to print plenty. He was going to take printing to England. He was going to change reading. He was going to stop stories being lost. Al had his comeback ready to go, word for word, and then he realised he'd read it on Caractacus's timeline of the English language. And he had a copy of that in his bag.

'Hang on a second,' he called out to the others as they left the market place. 'I've got something about that book. And Caxton.'

He put his bag down and rummaged around. The timeline was buried a long way down, but he found it. And there they were – two mentions of Caxton. One for setting up the first printing press in England in 1476, another for printing the Recuyell in 1473. So the first book in English wasn't the first printed in England, because it happened in Bruges.

'Good work,' Grandad Al told him. 'Looks like we're here for that book. The time's right.'

'But it said "the" on the flyer. Not "ye".' Lexi had noticed it as well. 'Are we too late? Has he fixed it?'

'I think we have to find him and see. Are you sure it said "the"?' Grandad Al hadn't seen it. Will and Mursili nodded. 'If it's him and he's fixed it already, somehow it lasts. Maybe it's not him. But he's just down this street. In fact—'

In the distance he could make out the sign, hung from a rod above a doorway – 'Mansion & Caxton', just as Thomas Wood had said. As they got closer, they could see smaller writing in Flemish below the names, and under that the words 'Makeres of fine bokes'.

'A printing legend maybe, but he couldn't spell to save himself. What's with that?' Lexi shook her head, then held up her hand. 'I know. I know the story. They didn't settle on spelling for another couple of hundred years, but don't tell me all the rest of you who weren't born in Hattusa aren't looking at that and thinking about what your teachers would have said.'

They stopped at the door, which was open.

Grandad Al took his hat off and ran his fingers through his hair. 'Time for an enquiry about the book trade, then?'

He stepped inside and the others followed. The place looked as if it was still being set up. One trestle table had what appeared to be two bales of paper on it and another had an angled board with boxes of lead letters set up across it. A man was working at a sturdier table that had a solid wooden frame over it, with a long fat screw holding a rectangular plate over the table's surface.

He turned when he heard them come in.

'You're from England,' he said, taking in what they were wearing. 'Traders. Very good.' For a moment it seemed all too easy and the word hunters didn't know what to say. 'William Caxton. Good of you to come. Colard, my business partner, is at a paper mill at the moment, but I'm—' He held up the letters T, H and E and shrugged. He had a beard and a floppy hat, and ink stains all down his front. 'I'm dealing with a bit of a typesetting challenge. But do come in. We'll have books—' He tried to find the right word. 'Soon. It's been quite a process.'

'Tell us more,' Grandad Al said, and Caxton did.

He put down the letters, wiped his hands on his apron and told them about the future. He pitched it to them, thinking they might be his first customers. The future was printed books – *his* printed books.

He had started trading in books from Germany, when he decided there was a market in England for printed Latin bibles. But no one was making books in English. He had been the governor then, and too busy to think of making them himself. He had also been secretary to Margaret of York, the sister of the English king, Edward IV, and wife of Charles the Bold, Duke of Burgundy and lord of Flanders.

'But that all came to an end, of course, when King Edward was overthrown.' He looked at each of them, trying to gauge their responses. He couldn't be sure which side they were on. 'I spent some time with him when he was here, before he reclaimed the throne. I think he's the man for printing. I think he sees what it'll do. But I was seen as too closely aligned with him then. No one in London would work with me. I couldn't bring wool over here and I couldn't take anything back. I went to Cologne, to see the presses for myself. I was part of the way into translating the Recuyell into English for the duchess when I left her service, and I wondered if there might be business in it. Books, I think, are about to change our world. How much does a good English book cost? As much as a farm. These? Printed books? They'll almost be free, by comparison. Soon even a merchant will have a library. It won't be left to kings and dukes and bishops. Soon, anyone of any means and even some without will be reading. Imagine that. And I'll be making their books. This one is just the first.'

He led them over to the frame he'd been working at on his printing press. Next to it was a pile of printed title pages for the Recuyell.

'What's a recuyell?' Lexi had to ask finally. No one was explaining it and there was no way to work it out.

Caxton reached out to the chunky letters of the word and touched them with his finger. 'There's no precise English equivalent. I'm hoping to introduce it to the language. I think it'll prove very useful. A collection, a compilation. Soon we'll all be saying it. Just remember you heard it here first.'

'What's making you start with a translation?' It had bothered Al since he'd seen it in Caractacus's timeline, but he'd never expected to have the chance to ask. 'Why aren't you doing something English?'

Caxton looked unhappy. 'Well, I wanted to do *The Canterbury Tales*, but the duchess—' He thought about how to put it. 'The Recuyell was written by the chaplain to the duke's father. You might say it's a family favourite. And this business takes some money to set up. I have her backing for a printed Recuyell. And if she likes my work the king will see it. And if the king likes it—' He didn't need to say the rest. There was no better source of money than the king. 'I hope to be making books in England soon, and books as English as they can be. So, this one's not Chaucer, but it's almost finished. It's translated and I've started setting the type, but—'

He left the printing press and took two steps to the table that had the type boxes on it. There was a note there, and he picked it up.

'You might see my problem.' He showed it to them, and then went on in case it wasn't as evident as he'd hoped. 'There.'

He pointed to it with an inky finger. In the note, instead of 'the', the duchess had twice written 'Þe'.

'I'm not going to tell her how out of fashion that is. Do you know anyone who uses the letter "thorn" now?' He didn't wait for an answer. 'And do you think the German typemakers make a "thorn"? Colard says I should just use "th", and I very often will, but it's clear that the duchess shall expect to see a "thorn" occasionally.' He ran his finger along the pen strokes that made the 'Þ' shape.

Lexi looked at Al, but 'thorn' was a mystery to him, too. He might be into history, but he didn't know everything. It was only since they'd found the *Curious Dictionary* that he'd learnt that '&' was once seen as part of the alphabet, and now here was something that looked like a 'P' gone wrong, but had the same name as a spike on a bush. It suddenly seemed possible that there might be a whole different alphabet that had slipped in and out of English.

'The lost letters,' he said quietly, so that only Lexi could hear him. It had been there at the end of the dictionary's definition of 'ye' – 'ye loste letteres'. 'Thorn' was the first of them. He wondered how many more there might be, and where they had come from.

William Caxton was back at the type bench, sorting through boxes of letters.

'It needs to be something with a tail below the line and a top above it,' he said to himself. 'We can be slightly modern about it – we can drop the ascender. Wait, there's a device – it's not a device, it's sloppy scribing, but—' He turned back to the word hunters, his hands grey with the residue of old ink from the lead letters. 'Do you know of Margery Kempe? A Norfolk woman. In the book of her pilgrimages, the thorn not only lacks the ascender, but looks almost like a "Y". Upper case.'

He reached for one of the boxes above the horizontal strip of wood dividing the sloped surface in two. He picked out a capital 'Y'.

'Seriously,' Al said. 'That's "upper case"?'

Caxton showed him the letter. 'Well, it's not lower case.' He reached into one of the lower cases and pulled out a small 'y' so that Al could compare them.

'Upper case' and 'lower case' – they were printers' terms, and actual wooden cases. Perhaps *these* actual cases, in Bruges, in 1473. Al wondered if they were the first to be called that in English.

'I can put the lower case "e" on top, see?' Caxton had already found the letter he needed and he held the two together between his thumb and finger, with the 'e' above the 'y'. 'It's pleasing enough. I suppose.'

A glow flared from the two letters as if they were melting. It lit up his dirty hand and his apron.

'I wonder if I might take a look at those in the daylight?' Grandad Al said, turning his hat over in his hand and holding it out. 'Old eyes, you know. And I do want to give everyone in London a thorough report. They'll be fascinated.'

'Yes, yes, certainly.' Caxton rubbed the letters on his apron to take some of the ink off before setting them on the fine felt of the hat. His luck was changing. These traders would be only the first. 'I'll just—'

He went back to the frame that had the first page of the book in it, and lifted out two 't's and two 'h's.

Grandad Al took only one step towards the window before offering the hat to Mursili. The letters had melted into a pulsing '& more' button.

Mursili touched it, delicately, but any touch was enough. Al had the activated peg in his hand, and he slipped it into the glowing opening that was forming where the button had been. He clicked the side levers into place and turned the key.

The room shook. The window misted over. A fog blew in the door and the floor fell away.

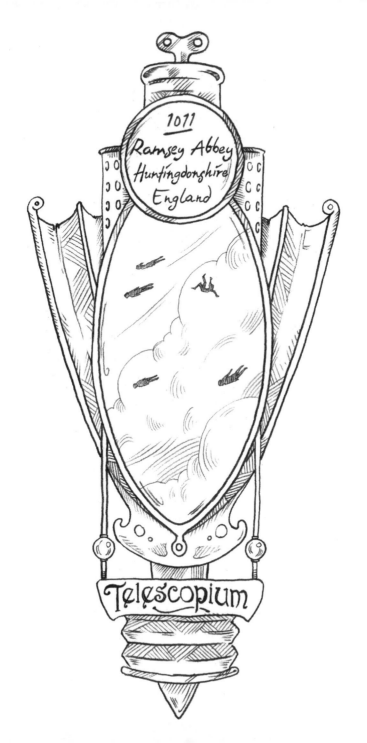

1011
—
Ramsey Abbey
Huntingdonshire
England

Telescopium

$\mathcal{T}$HERE WAS A swerve before the word hunters had even finished tipping forward into flight position, then a long clear drop. Just as Mursili had stopped bracing for bumps, they hit a big shudder. When they burst through cloud, he was tumbling and flapping every part of him that would flap. It only seemed to make things worse.

'Steady!' Will shouted out to him. 'Fall first, fly second. Don't fight it.'

Mursili stopped flapping. He went head over heels a couple more times and then steadied as the fog bank below rushed away from him. No, that couldn't be right. As the cloud bank above rushed away from him. He was upside down.

He stuck out one arm and his body turned.

Below them was a plain that seemed to be covered by grass, with patches of woodland here and there and only a few areas marked off as pasture or fields for crops. There were scattered houses and a village or two and, almost directly beneath them, the largest buildings in sight.

It all went past in a rush for Mursili, whose body kept turning. He fought too hard to fix it, then not enough and then, suddenly, he was facedown in wet grass. The others were standing around him when he rolled over.

Lexi laughed. 'You fly like a frog in a blender.'

Mursili looked shocked. 'You people put frogs in blenders? I thought you were supposed to be civilised.' He sat up.

'It's a—' Lexi didn't know how to explain it. 'We don't put frogs in blenders.'

The ground was swampy, but just ahead it rose like an island from the tall wild grass and on it stood a stone abbey, with a church and kitchens and sleeping quarters. They were all dressed as monks, in rough robes with rope belts, and sandals.

'We look like the enemy,' Will said as he adjusted his belt.

It was meant to be a joke, but they all checked around them for any threat. Near the abbey, two monks were ploughing a small field that led all the way to the edge of the marshy ground. Two others walked between buildings carrying something, but it was too far away to see what it was.

A lane led out from the abbey and curved past the word hunters. It was on a long strip of land barely higher than the marsh grasses, and they'd landed on the edge of it.

'Lucky,' Grandad Al said. 'It all looks all right from the air, but some of that would have been trouble to land in. I don't know how deep the water'd get, but all that marshland would keep the abbey pretty safe. It looks just like long grass, but you'd never get an army through it.' He turned to Al, who was already looking in his sack for the activated peg. 'Where are we? Norfolk? Somewhere like that?' He checked

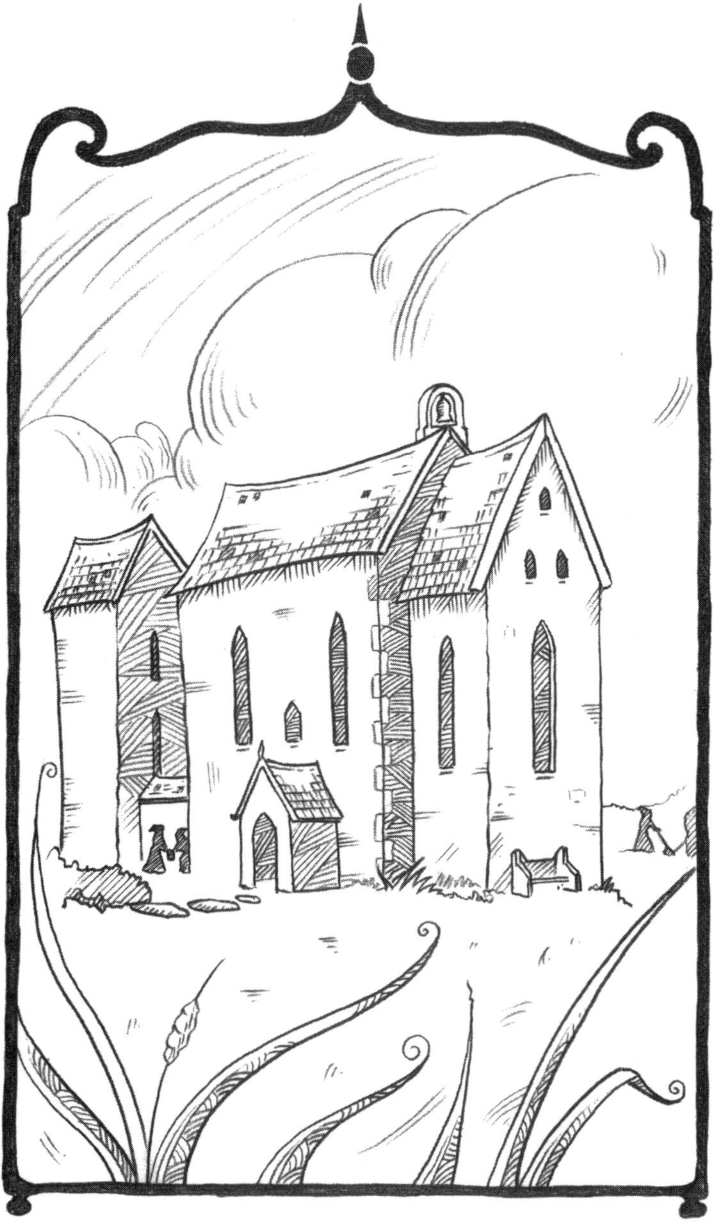

the writing. 'Anyone know Ramsey Abbey? Anyone got any ideas of what we're up for?'

'Never heard of it,' Will said. He looked at the buildings. 'As abbeys go it's not big, but these people have got money. That stone's come from somewhere. It looks like limestone and there'd be no chance of quarrying in these fens.' He pointed to the marshland. 'Caxton invented "ye", so we can't be here for that—'

'The lost letters.' Al almost spoke over Will. He reached into the sack to pat Doug, who was sitting in his nest of stolen wool and sniffing the air. 'Sorry. It's just— The dictionary gave "ye loste letteres" as an example, but it looked like a really bad one, since none of us knew it. Unlike "ye olde". So maybe it was a clue instead. "Thorn" is one lost letter. Maybe we're here for another.'

'Caxton kept "thorn" semi-alive almost by accident,' Lexi said, 'so maybe we're here for someone else who's keeping letters alive.'

'Maybe.' Grandad Al didn't seem convinced. 'Whatever we're here for, the abbey looks like the only inhabited place around. And if this is anything to do with writing, that's where it's likely to happen in 1011.'

'If we've got enemies there we could get stuck.' Will could see fenland to each side of the abbey. 'There might be only one way off.'

'So we should arm ourselves on the way in, and try not to let them block our retreat in case we need to use it.' Grandad Al looked around for any kind of weapon. 'There's not even a tree branch to turn into a walking stick. Will? Any thoughts?'

'They're farming. They'll have tools.'

Some ducks flew by, close to the ground. The breeze was cool and Lexi wondered if it might rain. From the height of the sun, she guessed it was late afternoon. She wished they didn't always have to think about being attacked – didn't have to *expect* attack and then, only once they'd left, be glad it hadn't happened.

'What about Lexi?' Mursili was looking at her. 'She still looks like a girl.'

Lexi glanced towards Al. 'Joan of Arc.' He'd explained it to her before.

'The monks won't see a girl,' he told Mursili, as he drew the cord closed at the top of his sack. He stood up and lifted it over his shoulder. There was some scrabbling around as Doug adjusted to the new position. 'When Joan of Arc wanted to check things out before a battle, if she dressed like a boy no one recognised her. People saw a boy. It'd probably be the same in Hattusa. If she dressed like a priest at a temple—'

'There were no women priests in temples.' Mursili almost recoiled at the thought of it. 'Assuming you mean the temples of male gods. A woman wouldn't dare—'

'Exactly. So if you saw a priest, you'd assume you were seeing a man.'

'Well, I would be.' Mursili stopped to think about it – women dressed as priests beneath the altar of Tarhunt, with the god above them holding three thunderbolts in one hand and an axe in the other. 'Goodness. It's as mad as a commoner making a wish on a holy day.'

Al was still processing their meeting with Caxton as they walked along the lane. Would printing have come to England later if the king hadn't been overthrown, however briefly, and Caxton had remained a powerful man at the duke's court in Bruges, bringing in English wool and trading books on the side? Al didn't know much about Edward IV. Other than him being the first English king to marry a commoner, Elizabeth Woodville. Two things about her had stuck in Al's mind. She was said to have heavy-lidded eyes, like a dragon, which totally rated as attractive in the 15th century, and she had met the king by waiting for him under a tree at a crossroads. And somehow that led to marriage. Different times.

As they got closer to the abbey, the monks in the field stopped working. One of them waved. He was tall and thin and the top of his head was shaved. He left his plough and came over to meet them.

'More pupils for Brother Byrhtferth?' He seemed happy enough to see them. 'All welcome. Even the late starters.' He looked Grandad Al up and down. 'He's just begun a lesson in the chapter house, behind the church. He'll be going until vespers.'

The word hunters weren't used to talking to men in grey robes, but this one seemed like a genuine monk. So far. Still, as they passed the church Will picked up a garden fork that was leaning against a wall, and Mursili took a stonemason's trowel from a spot where damage was being repaired. He checked the new mortar to see if JH, the word hunter from

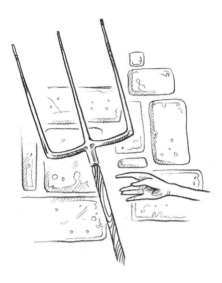

Bruges, had been there, but there was no sign of him all the way to the chapter house.

They could hear Brother Byrhtferth before they arrived, since the front door and the shutters over the arched windows were open. He was talking about the divine order of the universe, and how the study of numbers could make it clear.

The word hunters stopped in the doorway and he waved them in with a smile. He indicated some low wooden benches where they should sit. As they came in and took their places, his smile started to fade. He hadn't expected Will to bring the garden fork in and sit with it leaning against his knee, or Mursili to sit with the mason's trowel in his lap. They were rough, some of these pupils, and hardly knew inside from outside. But he told himself that, if God had called them, who was he to turn them away?

'With time divided into its atoms—' He went back to a table of Roman numbers on an easel and wondered if the new pupils had a chance of understanding any of it. 'And with each atom one 564th part of a momentum, we can compute the date of Easter flawlessly for centuries.'

Lexi wondered why anyone had made Easter so complicated, but it seemed to matter here. Like the monks with the plough, Brother Byrhtferth had his head shaved on top, so his hair hung like a floppy crown over his ears and forehead. The pupils, though, didn't have shaved heads. Maybe that was something that happened once you finished being a pupil. She counted ten of them, all sitting on benches.

None of them looked at the word hunters with any interest. Most stared at the table of numbers or the wall or the floor. They didn't look like a threat, despite their grey robes. She wanted to stop seeing danger everywhere that wasn't home. She knew Will and Grandad Al were watching them, too.

Another sheet of parchment or vellum was pinned on a separate easel to Brother Byrhtferth's right. It had a complicated diagram on it, with stars, moons and numbers, and angels blowing puffy clouds across fields of grain. Lines had been ruled linking pictures and numbers in ways that Lexi couldn't make sense of. She could see Al was staring at it, too, and getting nowhere.

'Ah, the harmony,' Brother Byrhtferth said, when he noticed it had their attention. 'So you see how it draws them together, the cosmological, numerological and physiological aspects of the world, all harmonious and one under God.'

Al saw one of the pupils stifle a yawn. They all looked hungry, like people who had come to be fed, but had to sit through the presentation first.

'God's harmony is all around us.' Brother Byrhtferth seemed to have hit one of his favourite themes. 'We only have to open our eyes. It's in the numbers. They're everywhere. I've put an alphabet in order, using God's numbers.'

Grandad Al sat up straight. 'I think some of us would like to see that.'

'Yes. Yes, certainly.' Brother Byrhtferth was already moving to a nearby bench. Enthusiasm was rare in his classes. 'Some of the others—' He stopped and turned back to the rest of the pupils. 'You've seen this earlier, I know, and we're well into the computation of Easter, but—' He seemed stuck for a moment.

'We don't mean to interrupt, Brother,' Will said. 'If you've got it written down, we'll take it outside and study it in the daylight, while you get on with what you're doing. We'll have our own turn at the computation of Easter when you teach it next.'

'Yes. Very good.' Brother Byrhtferth decided he liked this new group of pupils, even if they'd brought their sacks and tools inside. They *wanted* to learn, and wanting to learn was the making of men who would pray and think and write, and not just turn the soil over or pick the apples. He would start them on reading lessons tomorrow.

The youngest two would be the quickest. They would begin with their letters and, with diligence, soon they would be reading the abbey's Bede. Bede himself had had a far bigger library to draw on for his *History*, but Ramsey had four books and Byrhtferth was determined to add more.

He waved the new arrivals over to the bench and opened the leather cover of a folder. On the top sheet of parchment were written the letters A B C D E F G H I K L M N O P Q R S T V X Y Z & 7 Ᵽ Þ Ð Æ. He straightened the sheet to cover his notes and calculations, which were on the other pages.

'Each symbol makes a sound,' he explained, touching the 'A' and then the 'B'. '"Ah", "buh". You'll learn those. Then you'll be able to work words out. When you've practised for a while, you'll be surprised how fluid it becomes. You'll see whole words at once, simply because you've seen them before.'

Al had never imagined a time when reading might need to be explained – when anyone might lead a life so empty of written words. It wasn't the same as not knowing how to read. If you couldn't read in the 21st century, you still saw words all the time and the idea of reading needed no explanation.

'The first 24 letters, from "A" to "and" are Latin, from the Romans.' Brother Byrhtferth ran his finger along the rows of writing.

'Not 26?' Lexi said, before she could stop herself.

'Not 26, no.' Brother Byrhtferth smiled. 'But don't be discouraged. The alphabet's on your mind already, and that's a good sign.'

Lexi checked the letters – how had the Romans got by without 'J', 'U' or 'W'? What did they call Julius Caesar, for a start?

'After the Romans,' Brother Byrhtferth went on, 'I have ordered the necessary English letters. "Ond"—' He indicated a letter that looked like a seven. 'It's another way of writing "and". Then there's "wynn", "thorn", "eth" and "ash".'

When his fingertip touched the 'thorn', it started to glow and change shape. The 'E', 'M', 'O', 'R' and '&' changed from black to gold and slid across the page. As the 'thorn' formed a circle, they fell into it and spelt out '& more'.

'We need these letters, not just the Latin ones,' he was saying. 'My own name ends with a "wynn" and the abbey land was the gift of Earl Aethelwine, whose name starts with an "ash".'

A corner of the room would do, Al thought. They had the portal now. They didn't have to go all the way outside – just far enough from Brother Byrhtferth and his pupils.

'Brother,' a voice said at the door. It was a monk they hadn't seen before. His hood was up. He smiled at Byrhtferth.

'Some new arrivals to start on your letters? At least this lot look interested.'

'Yes, we are,' Grandad Al told him. 'But we're interrupting Brother Byrhtferth—'

He was about to mention again the idea of taking the folder outside, when the monk said, 'Bring it out here, out into the light God's made for it. The letters are so much bolder in true light, and there are some illuminated pages in there that you really should see.'

He stepped back out of the doorway and pulled the door fully open.

'Yes, yes,' Byrhtferth said. 'Thank you, Brother.'

He closed the folder and handed it to Grandad Al, who tucked it under his arm as he picked up his sack. The word hunters followed the monk outside. The sun had broken through the cloud and the fenland almost glowed in the late afternoon light.

The monk shut the door behind them.

'There are some benches around the side of the building, where you can sit and look through it properly and catch a little sun at the same time.' He put his hands on Mursili and Lexi's backs to steer them in the right direction.

'We can probably just—' Will didn't need a bench. They had the portal. He just wanted them to step away from this monk so that they could activate the '& more' button.

'No, really, it's much nicer around there.' The monk took Grandad Al by the arm. 'I've noticed some other letters there – a "J" and an "H" marked on the bench.'

So the word hunter's mark was there, as well as the portal. And this monk would take them right to the spot. It was almost too good to be true.

Lexi decided it *was* too good to be true.

She stepped in behind the monk as he tried to lead Grandad Al away. She'd noticed a bulge under his robe. It was hiding something. With her next step she stuck her foot out and it hit the bulge with a *clunk*. The bulge was a sword.

She threw herself forward to tackle the man from behind and screamed out, 'It's a trap!'

The monk fell to his knees and kicked and kicked to free himself. Lexi tried to hold him, but his heels hit her chest and then her face and knocked her backwards. But she'd got the word hunters the time they needed.

As the grey-robe drew his sword, Will was ready. He swung at it and caught the blade between the tines of the fork. As he wrestled, Mursili lunged beneath their arms and drove the mason's trowel into the grey-robe's thigh.

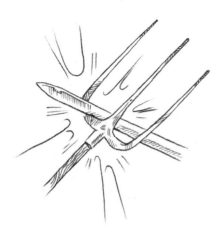

The man let out a scream and fell back against the wall.

'Go! Go!' Al shouted, dragging Lexi to her feet.

Five grey-robes had appeared at the corner of the building, running with swords in their hands.

As the word hunters turned to run too, Grandad Al took the alphabet sheet from the folder and dropped everything else. He pressed the button and it flared and began to open. Al swung his sack around and held it against his stomach with one arm as he ran. He reached inside for the peg.

'Close in!' Grandad Al shouted to the others, as Al brought the levers of the peg down and locked it in place.

The ground started to shake and fog rolled across the abbey buildings.

'We've got them!' one of the grey-robes called out. 'They're heading for the fen.'

In that instant, the portal opened as wide as a door and the word hunters threw themselves into it. The fog poured across the grey-robes and Will felt it push him from behind and drive him and the portal out over the marshy ground.

482

Northwic
East Angle Lands

Telescopium

𝒯HE WORD HUNTERS dropped through the safe, tight darkness, hit a smooth patch and passed through the other side of it. Their fall continued and Al tried to guess the centuries they were passing. Right on cue, the nausea hit.

'Dark Ages,' he called out, in case Mursili could hear him. Some kind of groan came in reply.

Then the sky seemed to split and they were in clear air and falling from a white cloud.

They were dropping towards forests and fields, with the bends of a river winding through, and a village on one bank.

Al recognised it first and laughed. 'Caractacus.'

The nausea was still there and the sweat, which felt cool on his forehead. He tried to focus on flight and getting his body shape right. Will rolled over to check for grey-robes, but the cloud the word hunters had fallen from was breaking up with no one else in sight.

'Arms,' Lexi called out to Mursili. 'Fly. Just a bit, or you'll hit the pig sty.'

Mursili's eyes were bulging. His arms flapped like broken windmills, his legs did a kind of mad breaststroke kick and, just as the other word hunters landed on their feet on dry ground, he hit the pig sty with a splat. And then he vomited. The nearest pig shuffled over and shoved its nose into his lost lunch. So Mursili vomited again.

'If it makes you feel any better, it's the Dark Ages,' Lexi said. 'Pretty much everyone smells the way you do now.'

'Sky's clear.' Will was still making sure. He'd looked away from it only to land. 'We weren't followed. They missed the portal.'

'What was that? I—' Mursili was still trying to process it.

'You're really one of the team now.' Lexi stood back as he climbed from the sty. 'You've just had the full word hunter experience. In the space of two minutes, people try to kill you, you stab them, you lose five centuries and fall out of the sky into poo. At least at this stop there'll be a drink from Caractacus.'

'I hope so.' Grandad Al hadn't seen or heard Caractacus yet. 'What year is it? I hope he's here.'

Instantly they were on their guard. They could fall from one trap to another, even if the second was in Northwic. Lexi had wanted to feel safe, and now she didn't. Will picked up a hoe that was leaning against a tree.

Al checked the peg. '482.'

'482?' It wasn't the year Grandad Al had expected. 'I've never been here that late. That'd make Caractacus 82, or thereabouts. Not a lot of Dark Ages people make it to 82. Will? 482?'

Will shook his head.

'And what about JH?' Mursili had stopped looking around for somewhere to wash off the mud and decided to accept that he was in the Dark Ages.

He still felt sick and his mind was buzzing from the fight at Ramsey Abbey, even if it had been only a minute long. He had lunged. He had got it right. It had been automatic. He couldn't recall a single thought that made him do it. He was trained now, and the lunge showed it. But the moment when the trowel stabbed into the grey-robe kept playing in his head, over and over.

'You did what you had to do.' Al was standing next to him. 'The guy had a sword. We didn't. They had six swords to our two garden tools. We were gone if you hadn't made that move. And gone if Lexi hadn't worked it out in time.'

'Al's right,' Will said. 'If they had JH anywhere, there was nothing we could do. Ramsey Abbey was the perfect place to trap us. You did well.'

The door of the mudbrick-and-timber cottage started to open. Slowly. Will lifted the hoe.

Then Caractacus's head appeared, bald and with a straggly white beard.

'Oh, you're here to do some gardening for me, Will?'
He stepped outside. His robes seemed to hang more loosely
on him and his arms were thinner. 'Good lad. Look at you.'
He studied each of them in turn. 'Look at you all. The gang's
all here.' He laughed. 'Can't quite place—'

Mursili stepped forward. 'Mursili Bogazkale.' He
extended his hand. 'Formerly chief librarian to King
Suppiluliuma II and the Empire of Hatti, now number two
at Cubberla Creek State School.'

'Goodness.' Caractacus shook his hand. 'I can't even
begin to guess what sort of selection process found you.
You're Hattusa? Bronze Age Collapse? Ugly time. Place
probably looked a lot like this afterwards. I was at a royal court
too. Four kings. Well, three and a—' He stopped himself.
'Librarian's good, though. Useful. Come inside. You'll need
some queasy water. And I'll need five cups.' He took a step
towards the door. 'Never needed five cups before.'

There was a scrabbling sound and Doug's head poked
out from the top of Al's sack. He had vomit in his whiskers.

Al groaned and felt a wave of nausea himself. 'Five
cups, a bowl and something to clean rat vomit out of my bag,
if that's okay.'

Caractacus took the vomit in his stride. 'Yes, of course,
Dark Ages. Sorry.'

However impossible it seemed, Caractacus's one-room
house looked bigger to Lexi and Al than it had before, and it
already looked improbably big inside. The shelves of scrolls
extended off beyond the firelight and into the dark.

'Ah, yes,' he said, when he saw Lexi and Al taking it all in. 'Learnt a useful trick from a word hunter a few years ago. I can bring much more back from the Alexandria library fire if I take a bag. Worth remembering.' He said it to them as if he was offering advice.

Lexi gave Al a look. This wasn't the time to point out that they were the word hunters who had said it in the first place, after Caractacus had almost got them stuck in the burning library.

Caractacus had a jug ready on the table, along with two cups and an urn. He brought three more cups from a nearby shelf, as well as a bowl for Doug and a rag that already looked pretty dirty.

'You're here for lost letters.' He set everything down. 'No hard work required this time. I've got the— Wait, it's your word, isn't it?' He pointed to Lexi and Al. 'Portal? Yes? I've been encouraging others to use it. Timeless, full of promise, very nice. I've got the portal.' He reached for the urn on the table and turned it around. It had a picture of a deer and some old writing on it. 'I've got it with me since it might as well be here rather than out there.' He waved his hand in the general direction of the door. 'Safer here. Out there the armies of Hengist and Horsa don't know when to stop. It's their alphabet on it. You'll call it the futhorc alphabet.' He paused, to make sure he had the right word hunters. He pointed to them individually. 'You're 20th century, 20th, 21st, 21st and—' He was still trying to get his head around Mursili. 'The bonus. Buy four, get one free. But

67

you're a librarian. You'll pick it up like *that*.' He clicked his fingers. 'The futhorc alphabet came with the Angles, but you arrive in 482 because it's only now that it's becoming properly established. Your name for it – a future name – comes from the first six letters. It's the same way "alphabet" comes from "alpha" and "beta".' He took a stick and scratched some marks into the dirt floor. '"Feoh", "ur", "thorn", "os", "rad", "cen".'

At 'thorn' there was a flash from the urn and a cluster of the letters started to glow. Caractacus had activated the portal. Al instinctively took a step towards the table.

'Don't worry. It always does that.' Caractacus seemed very matter-of-fact about it. 'Well, when I say "always" that's three times so far in, what, 1,500 years? We've got plenty of time for a chat, though. So don't all rush me poking at it.' He laughed.

'Could we please have the drink now?' Al was still feeling the Dark Ages nausea, and he knew Caractacus would find 15 distractions between now and pouring the drinks if he didn't speak up. 'This makes you feel better, Mursili.'

Mursili nodded and kept his hand on his stomach.

'Oh, yes, of course.' Caractacus picked up the jug and started pouring. 'The drink.' He handed the cups out one at a time. 'And take a seat, too.' He pointed to a stool, then realised it wasn't quite enough. 'A seat, literally. Um— Not quite used to these numbers. Perhaps for the librarian? Anyway, the alphabet. We've used a number of them on these islands, most recently the Roman. Which is disappearing now, but will come back with Christian missionaries in a few centuries. The futhorc is by the Angles and Saxons. It's adapted from an older version, from Germania. Not that that's necessarily where the letters originated, as you'll discover. You hardly use any of these in your time, but you need to know them. You need to know your language wasn't always written in your—' He thought about it. 'Twenty-six letters. That's right, isn't it?'

The others nodded, but Grandad Al raised a finger. 'I've got a question. We were attacked at Ramsey Abbey – Brother Byrhtferth and his alphabet. I've got a number of questions, actually. But first things first – did JH make it through? He was in Bruges before us.'

'Attacked? That's no good. And at an abbey, too.' Caractacus set the jug down. 'JH? Yes. John Hunter, early 1600s. Dark moustache and pointed beard?' He said it as if word hunters bumped into each other all the time. 'He was just here from Ramsey. Not a scratch on him.'

'Just here? But—' Mursili checked the room, as much as he could see of it.

'Yes, moments ago. Four hundred years before you. Plenty of time for trouble to develop at Ramsey, if it's going to. He was standing over there, taking a look through—' Caractacus pointed to a nearby shelf. 'Wait a minute. I think some scrolls have gone. I'm sure—' He moved quickly across to the shelf. He picked up a scroll and opened it, then checked several more. 'Yes, gone! Three of them. I don't— He mentioned hearing a noise outside and I went to investigate.

By the time I came back he'd gone and the portal was closing behind him.'

'A dark moustache and pointed beard?' The description was bothering Will. 'John Hunter? We were attacked at the Globe Theatre in 1606 by a pack of grey-robes, but one of them looked different from the rest. He looked like this John Hunter. But he said his name was John Johnson.'

'He didn't mention any—' Caractacus was holding a scroll in each hand. 'Grey-robes? Is that what you're calling them?' He pointed a scroll at Lexi and Al. 'You two have seen them before, haven't you? You mentioned them once.'

'And they had me prisoner for 30 years in Colchester in 1648,' Grandad Al said. 'We've also seen them at York in the 9th century. There are more of them as time goes by, and in more times and places. And they're trying to kill or capture us. Word hunters specifically.'

'Oh dear.' Caractacus set the scrolls on the table and sat down on the stool. 'Oh dear. I've been afraid of this and I think it's coming. I think it's upon us. Of course he called himself John Hunter when he was here. That's exactly what he'd call himself, if he knew what he was doing.'

'What do you mean?' Al had wanted Caractacus to say something reassuring, to have a simple explanation for what was going on.

'You know the problem's out there, the five of you. It's real with every step you take in the past.' Caractacus picked up the urn from the table and turned it around to look at the portal. 'The grey robe is the perfect disguise for the next thousand years. It doesn't change with fashion. It's the look of missionaries and then the look of monks. Eventually they'll seem like mendicant friars – set a Google onto that one when you get home – and that's when the disguise is particularly effective. They're too poor to rob as well as too godly – people must give them food if they have it – and they're expected to be able to read. They travel in an era when most people don't. Perfect. And all the time those robes could hide weapons, anything.'

'But our clothes change when we land somewhere new, and the grey robes are always the same.' Will set his cup down on the table. 'Do they change times and keep the same clothes, or do they stay in one time?' He remembered two of them falling, dropping from the closing exit portal above Bohemia in the hunt for 'dollar'. They'd kept their robes from one time to the next. 'And if they stay in one time, other than accidents like falling through the portal when they're trying to kill us, how do they know to be grey-robes? And is it really such a good disguise if we've worked it out? We're looking for them now.'

Caractacus looked at Will as if he needed to make an effort to bring him into focus. 'I think the sad truth is that they're not trying to disguise themselves with you in mind. Most word hunters who see them do so only once.'

Lexi was about to object, to say that she'd seen them four times already. Then she worked out what he meant. Most word hunters travelled alone and had their eyes on the history and their mind on the portal. They had no idea anyone might be after them. Their first encounter with the grey-robes would be their last, and the dictionary would lie where they had left it until it found another hunter.

'Why are they doing it?' She wondered if answering that might help. 'Why are they hunting us?'

Caractacus looked as if he was about to tell her, but stopped himself. 'I need to make you something. Will, would you please stoke the fire? I'll need more heat. Librarian, I'll need your help finding the right scrolls. Can any of you blow glass well?'

Lexi laughed. 'Grandad Al's warrior boot camp hasn't quite got to glass blowing yet.'

'Well, unless you were planning to make glass boots—' Caractacus was only half paying attention. His mind had already moved on to the minerals and powders he might need.

He wrote a list, guessing at the language that might be on each container – Egyptian, Greek, Angle runes – and he sent Lexi off to look for them. Al poured a bowl of Caractacus's drink for Doug and emptied his bag until he located the vomit. It took a few deep breaths, but he managed to clean up most of it. Meanwhile, their grandfather cleared benches and did his best to identify the tools Caractacus said he wanted.

Caractacus had four particular scrolls in mind, fortunately none of them stolen by John Hunter. As each was located, he reached up into the dark near the ceiling and drew down a hook to hang it on.

He checked the fire and, when he thought it was right, pushed a beaker of something that looked like sand into the glowing embers. He turned it and stirred it and, with a long spoon, scooped out some molten glass.

'Nearly there.' The glob of glass was starting to harden on the hearth as he prodded it. 'That one's just a test of the temperature.'

He went across to a bench, set out two bowls and squinted at one of the scrolls, which was slightly too far away for him to see easily. Lexi had placed all the ingredients he had asked for on the bench, but he realised he needed more and walked off into the near-darkness towards the far end of the room. He came back carrying a tray loaded with vials and jars of liquid, as well as more powders and seeds.

'Here's how it looks to me,' he said, as he went to work. 'Alastair, you might remember we saw someone in the flames when the Library of Alexandria burnt. Or you might not remember – you were a bit emotional at the time.'

'Because you made a dud peg key and we were all about to die horribly in ancient Egypt?' Al wasn't impressed with Caractacus's version of it. 'I'm pretty sure I can remember it.'

'I think that's our John Hunter. And our John Johnson.' Caractacus tipped a large scoop of something red and gritty into a mortar and started to grind it with the pestle. 'He might have started out as one of us, but he's not one now. He has our way of travelling, but his own way of using it. It doesn't need the dictionary. And he can get to the Library of Alexandria himself, which isn't supposed to happen. He was taking scrolls from there, just as he took them from me. We have an enemy. We who would not be seen have been seen, or are in the sights of someone who was once one of our own.'

He walked around the bench and ran his finger down a list on one of the scrolls, checking the ingredients. He took two bottles of liquid and measured small amounts of each into a mixing bowl.

'He wants powers greater than mine.' He whisked the two liquids together, added some of the red powder and kept whisking. 'I know what he's taken from here. I can guess what he's taken from Alexandria. I don't know what else he's got, though.' He set the whisk down and looked up. 'I think he plans to make his own book. He plans to destroy the book you know as the *Curious Dictionary* and the language you'll come to call English, and to use the disarray – as the Angles and Saxons did – to take over the country, and perhaps much more. Depending on when he strikes, he might take the Angles and the Saxons, too. Across time, he is building an army. There are cells of them where they might trap word hunters. I think that's just the start, though. I think there's more to it. Which is why you'll need this.'

He picked up the bowl, which had become hot to touch. The red liquid in it had foamed, but was now settling.

Al wondered if any of the others would ask what the liquid was. Or maybe, like him, they figured Caractacus wouldn't give a straight answer anyway. They would, as usual, be told what Caractacus thought they needed to know, and be told when he thought they needed to know it.

Lexi just stared at it, wishing Al hadn't picked up the dictionary during the library renovations – wishing it was up to someone else to save the future of the English-speaking world. Then she thought through her friends at school, all of them at home, finishing homework or watching TV or sending each other photos of shoes they'd just bought.

The foam in the bowl had cleared and the still surface of the liquid reflected the light of a candle at the far end of the bench. It had to be her. And Al and this team.

She would be going into battle so that her friends could have those phones, buy the shoes, send the photos. So that they could exist and their parents could exist, and their language too. And none of them would ever know, or ever be grateful, but that was the job. To make history behind the scenes. To stop it falling apart, or being torn apart.

Caractacus kept working and the word hunters helped when they could. He mixed other liquids in the second bowl, then took crystals the colour of red wine, crushed them and mixed them in. He placed the mixture in a crucible and burnt it in the hottest part of the fire until it was a perfectly white dust. When the dust had cooled, he mixed it with a colourless oil.

He took more sand, turned it into glass, then rolled the molten glass into eight balls, each about the size of a blueberry. He drew the red liquid from its bowl – exactly the right amount – into a pipette he held in his mouth, then he slipped the tip of the pipette into the middle of one glass ball and blew the liquid down it. The glass ball turned into a small red egg. He made four red eggs and four white eggs and left them to cool.

From a drawer, he took a set of peg levers. He checked one of the scrolls – one that had diagrams on it – and he heated the levers in the fire until they glowed. With a small hammer and other fine tools, he reshaped them to match two metal pieces in the diagram.

As Caractacus went to check the diagram to work out what was next, Will asked if there was anything the word hunters could do.

Caractacus looked surprised, and blinked. 'Actually, there is. I have some eggs and some fresh goats' milk. Over there.' He nodded towards another corner of the room. 'Would you beat a dozen of the eggs, mix them with all of the milk and a cup of oil, then whisk the mixture until it's fluffy?'

'All right—' It hadn't been the answer Will had expected. 'And that's for—'

'*Ova spongia ex lacte.*' Caractacus smiled, but no one knew what he was on about. 'The 20th century and 21st. Hmmm. Pancakes? An omelette, but sweet? It's a Roman treat. There's no direct translation. I thought we might have a snack. I realise what I'm doing is taking a while. I haven't made one of these devices before and it's turning out to be a bit fiddly.'

Will went to beat the eggs, while Lexi and Al put more wood on the fire. Grandad Al joined Caractacus at his workbench, shaping and cutting the pieces of metal Caractacus needed. Mursili seemed to be the only one without anything to do. He couldn't help himself. He started cataloguing and reorganising Caractacus's scrolls.

'This'll be much easier for you,' he said when he noticed that Caractacus was looking at him. 'Dewey Decimal System.'

'Very good,' Caractacus said warily. 'Thank you.'

He brought his magnifying lens back to his eye, picked up a small tool and focused again on the metal plate in front of him. He shaped the spaces for the two glass eggs it would hold, one red and one white. He fitted the back and front together and made sure they would rotate and click into place. He attached the locking levers. The finished object fitted in the palm of his hand. Several times he checked the mechanism, rotating and locking.

When he was satisfied he checked it against the final diagram, then picked up his eight glass eggs, brought them to the bench and fitted two into place.

'Right,' he said. 'Time for that snack.'

He set a pan onto the embers of the fire and, once it was hot, he poured some of the *ova spongia ex lacte* mixture into it, tilting the pan to make the mixture spread evenly. After a few minutes he folded the pancake, slid it onto a board and poured honey across it. He cut it into strips with a knife and offered it around.

Al was happy to eat it – it was food, after all – but he hadn't come here for a snack. The fire had kept him busy, sort of, but there were two pegs in his bag and, wherever they would soon be going, John Hunter or John Johnson had been there first. Word hunting hadn't been easy to start with, but now anywhere they went might be a trap.

Caractacus licked the honey from his fingers, went to the workbench and brought back the device he had made.

'With this in your possession you won't be alone.' He set it down next to the board, where they could all see it. 'You are five, which is better than one. And you're more ready now, some of you. Lexi and Al, think of the first time you

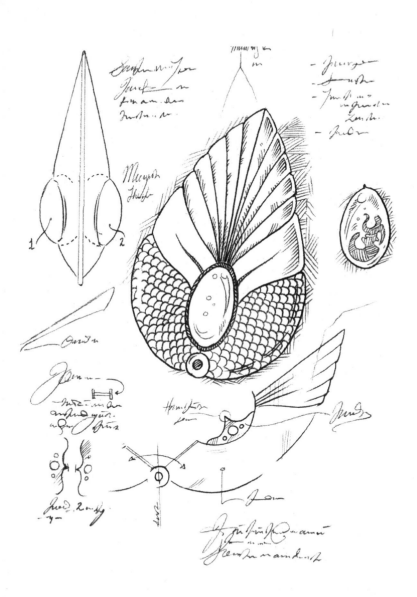

came here. Your grandfather's trained you well. But there will be times when you need support.' He touched the device. 'This will bring it to you. You'll want to know its name. It doesn't have one. Some might call it a talisman or an amulet. The Greeks long ago might have called it a *phylacterion*. But it's a machine, not a jewel to rub for luck. When you are attacked beyond your capacity to defend, you turn it—' He picked it up and mimed the act, but didn't go through with it. 'That mixes the liquids. There will be pressure and heat, so you must lock it into place.' He moved the levers in and out. 'Support will come. Think of it like your portable telephones, but with an app your time has yet to even dream of.'

He brought the levers into the side, but didn't lock them. He handed the device to Lexi. It felt solid and strong in her palm.

'It's your job, I think,' he said to her. 'I've made you as many of the capsules as I can. Four sets. I used every bit of rutile in the place, so that's all I can make for you now.'

Lexi tested the levers and eased the capsules in and out. She practised loading them and tested the mechanisms with the device empty. She could do it. If she travelled with a set of capsules in place, all she would need to do was twist and lock when the time came.

She looked up at the others. 'I'll just need a couple of seconds of fancy sword work from you four and I should be okay to use it.'

'Oh, yeah.' She'd reminded Will of something. He looked at Caractacus. 'Weapons. Do you have any we can take that'll go through the portals with us? Or is there something we can do to take weapons? They just seem to vanish between time periods.'

'Yes, that's the ancients trying to stop—' Caractacus paused and shook his head. 'Well, the kind of thing we're facing now. If people could take weapons through portals, imagine how much power they'd have then? It's too dangerous, so anything like a weapon doesn't make it through. There seems to be no way around that. It's probably why John Hunter didn't simply raise an army in his own time and bring them straight here. Not that the portals last long enough to fit an army anyway.'

The thought of a grey-robe army descending on Northwic had Lexi listening for landings outside, the rogue word hunter and his men setting down near the pig sty.

'What if he did?' she said. 'What if he could, and did, even if they didn't come with weapons? What if he just had ten strong men and they came for you?'

'Me?' Caractacus smiled, as if he wasn't bothered at all. 'Well, he was here a moment ago and he didn't harm me. He stole from me, yes, but he's wise enough not to try to harm me here. This room is better defended than it looks. He's going to have to bring quite an army if he wants to get the better of me here. Don't worry about me.'

'I'm worried about us all.'

Even that didn't go far enough. Lexi was worried about *everything*. But not in a pathetic way. Everything was at stake, and everything needed to be worried about. But one word at a time, one fight at a time. And she'd been training for that.

Caractacus picked up the urn with its flashing '& more' button. 'There's damage being done somewhere while we talk here. Alastair, I believe you have the pegs.'

It was time to go. Lexi put the talisman in the top of her sack and pulled the drawstring tight. Will activated the portal and Caractacus stepped back.

The floor shook and the smoke from the fire was sucked back into the coals.

The door blew open, fog tumbled in and Lexi called out, 'See you next time,' as the word hunters fell.

The last thing she saw was Caractacus lifting his hand to wave.

93

Bauzanum
Raetia
Roman Empire

Telescopium

$\mathcal{T}$HE NAUSEA CAME in again and then lifted. The air was thinner, faster. Mursili felt his lungs being pushed down into his stomach and his stomach pushed somewhere lower.

Al breathed out, one long breath. He guessed two centuries had passed, then three, then there was daylight.

The word hunters dropped from a vanishing cloud into bright sunshine over a mountainous landscape, with snow on the peaks and densely forested slopes. As they flew they could make out some fields beside a blue-green river in a valley, and then a single road leading through a town directly below them. At the edge of it were two buildings larger than the others, with rectangular roofs, and rows of small square tents extending along the hillside.

Lexi checked the others to see if any of them had ideas about where to land, or where not to.

Grandad Al caught her eye and called out, 'Play safe. Uphill, trees, other side from the tents.'

He steered to the right and the others followed.

'Glide, Mursili,' Al shouted. 'Don't flap.'

Mursili did his best, but he was still correcting his arm position all the way down. He landed with a clang, just downhill from the others and at the foot of an apple tree.

There was no doubt about what they were wearing this time. They were Roman soldiers, with shields and short swords and satchels on sticks over their shoulders. Or, in Mursili's case, emptied out on the ground. Grandad Al had some kind of plume on his helmet and Al wondered if he was more senior, perhaps even a centurion.

'You'll get there,' Lexi told Mursili as he repacked his satchel. 'You should have seen Al when he started. He'd fly worse than that and then vomit when he landed.'

'I didn't—' Al wanted to argue. 'The vomiting was only sometimes, on ships and things. But, hey – weapons. How good is that?'

He drew his sword and felt the weight of it in his hand. He swung it from side to side. He'd last used a Roman sword to fight someone dressed just as he was now, and then Lexi and Al had shoved the man into the mud. Battle of Teutoburg Forest, 9AD. When they made their escape, they got attacked by grey-robes. The sword saved them. That was the last time a Roman sword had been in Al's hand and it had done its job.

'Much better than garden tools.' Will checked his own sword. 'If the grey-robes are here, we're ready.'

'And if there's 50 of them, we've got our lucky charm.' Lexi patted the flap of her satchel. 'What do you think it'll do?'

Grandad Al smiled. 'It's from Caractacus, so who could guess? It's supposed to give us support. It'll be better than stockings, but not as good as an aircraft carrier. Where it lies between those two is a total mystery until we have to use it.'

Al slid his sword back into its scabbard and tried not to think about using it. All the practice in the world felt nothing like actually sticking a sword into someone. 'Wouldn't you like for him, just once, to tell us something directly?'

'He didn't sugar-coat the trouble we're in.'

Al swung his satchel around and opened it. He could see the writing on the peg glowing inside. Doug pushed his way to the top, blinking at the daylight and sniffing at the new air – goat poo, wet ground, snow. No food yet, and he was hungry. Al reached past him and lifted the peg out to show to the others.

'Bauzanum? Raetia?' He was guessing at the pronunciation. 'Anyone been here before? Or know where we are? I'm pretty sure all those tents are a Roman army camp.'

Grandad Al looked around. 'From the landscape and the buildings, I'd guess somewhere in the Alps. And I think the year means that the emperor's Domitian.' The others waited for more. 'That's it. He's not one I know much about. We're not in Rome, obviously.'

'We were dropping towards the— What is that? A palace with a temple next to it?' Will's sword was still in his hand and he used it as a pointer. 'I guess that's where the action will be. And the trouble, if there is any.'

Lexi tried to picture John Johnson, or John Hunter, with his moustache and goatee, dressed like a Roman and somewhere ahead of them, waiting. Or gone centuries before, with his own soldiers left behind, watching the hills and the sky, or whatever door the word hunters were likely to come through.

'Well, we're not here to farm apples,' Grandad Al said. 'Someone somewhere is about to do something with an alphabet, and that's where we need to be.'

He opened his satchel and took out his binoculars.

'The smaller of the two big buildings might be a temple.' It was built of pale stone and stood on a platform, with four pillars holding up its roof at the front. '"*Divus Augusto Caesari*".' The bronze letters that ran in a line above the pillars were clear through the binoculars.

'Divine Augustus Caesar?' Al guessed. 'Augustus was made a god after he died, wasn't he?'

'I think he was.' Grandad Al didn't shift the binoculars from his eyes. 'I'm sure you're right. Roman alphabet, too. Nothing extra going on there.'

He checked the other building, which was of the same style. People were coming and going from a number of entrances. Two carried baskets of food, but most had documents, sometimes several rolled scrolls under their arms. There were sentries with spears on each door, but they didn't seem to be stopping anyone.

He adjusted the focus to look at the camp that lay beyond the temple. There was no doubt this was a legion of the Roman army, but not one in any hurry or expecting to fight a battle. The only other sign of life nearby was a group of people in rough cloaks herding goats on a bare stretch of hillside over to the word hunters' left.

'Anything?' Will said, as Grandad Al watched the goatherds picking their way through the rocks.

'No. Nothing that looks like a threat. There's business being done in the palace. It might be where the regional administration is. A good place to check for a portal connected to an alphabet, I'd say.'

It made sense, Lexi thought, and, while every entrance seemed to be guarded by an armed soldier, the word hunters were soldiers, too, this time. It was 84 years since the Battle of Teutoburg Forest, the last time she'd seen a Roman army. And fought them. And the first time she and Al had been attacked by grey-robes.

She stayed with her grandfather at the front of the

group, as they made their way out of the orchard and down the slope.

Just before Grandad Al put his foot on the palace steps, Lexi grabbed his arm and quietly said, 'Stop. Over to the left, near the corner.'

Scratched onto the bottom step as if with a sharp rock were the initials 'JH'. Will's hand went to his sword.

'Good,' Grandad Al said, though it seemed to Lexi like the worst thing to have found. He took his blue pen and wrote 'BEWARE' in front of 'JH' before adding his own initials. 'If he's here, we sort this out now. If we get him, the grey-robes have no reason to come after us in future. There won't be grey-robes in future. And if the building's packed with them, we just have to deal with that. And hope Caractacus's new device is something special. Be ready. Lexi, we need you in the middle.'

'But I can fight just as—'

'That's not the point. You've got the device. We need you to be able to use it.' He glanced up at the doorways. One of the sentries looked his way and nodded.

Two men came outside, one rolling a scroll and the other – the older one – complaining about their chances of fixing the local road with cuts to their quarrying budget. But that was like Byrhtferth and his Easter maths. Ancient lives could be distracting with their weirdness and their ordinariness, sometimes both at the same time. Meanwhile, the eyes of enemies could be in the nearest shadows.

The word hunters listened for every sound, watched for every movement. Al imagined an army of grey-robes packed inside and waiting. His hand was ready for his sword as he went up the steps.

The sentry stood straighter and stared directly ahead as they approached him. They reached the top of the steps, the door opened and Grandad Al led the way in.

Lexi could see past him into a room with a tiled floor and a mural on the opposite wall. There were more guards, no grey-robes, and two men in togas sat on turned wooden chairs eating figs and cheese and drinking wine. Both had a purple stripe on their chest, and one had a helmet next to him far grander than Grandad Al's. A woman was massaging his bare feet with oil.

The man without the helmet glanced in their direction. The word hunters stopped and bowed, and he looked away as if they weren't there. He reached for a fig.

'I'm glad to be away from Rome, Lucius,' he said, sounding bored. 'If I'm to be honest. Not that I'd want to be prefect here permanently, but it's peaceful enough. Halfway between the emperor and the barbarians.'

'You're well placed, then.' Lucius cut himself some cheese.

'I'm sure you'll be all right. He might have called you back to Rome to do some dirty work, but that'll be as bad as it gets. He's put enough senators in prison already.' The prefect smiled, but it wasn't what Lucius wanted to hear. 'You're the emperor's own legion, First Minervan. He even put it in the legion's name after you crushed the Germania Superior revolt – "loyal and faithful to Domitian".'

Lucius still looked gloomy. He turned the cheese over in his hand. 'Before my time.'

Lexi counted six guards in the room, along with two servants and the woman massaging Lucius's feet. There were doors to two other rooms, both of them shut. There were no signs of danger, but she wondered if they were in the wrong place. There had been writing on the outside of the other building – perhaps there was more inside. These two Romans didn't seem likely to talk about someone else's alphabet. But she didn't know how the word hunters could leave. She was pretty sure it wouldn't go down well to walk out on a prefect.

Lucius ate his piece of cheese. He looked around the room and out through the open doorway at the hillside. 'What do you do here?' He seemed unimpressed. 'Besides lie low while the emperor sees enemies all around him and does away with them?'

'I'm writing,' the prefect said. 'Or reading and making notes. Planning to write. Before you leave for Rome I'll need you to tell me about the Germanii around Bonna, and wherever else you've been. I'm thinking of doing a book on Germania. I've read Pliny and others, and I make a point of talking to anyone notable who passes through this way.'

'You're writing about Germania without ever planning to go there?'

'That's exactly what I'm aiming to do.' The prefect split the fig he'd been holding and took a bite of it. 'I hear they're lazy barbarians for the most part.' He stopped to swallow. 'Why would I want to go there?'

Lucius laughed. 'They're brave in battle and faithful in marriage. You can put that down in your book. It's something you can't say about half the senators in Rome.'

'And not necessarily the half the emperor's put in prison.' The prefect dipped his hands in a water bowl and held them up for a servant to wipe with a cloth. 'But you need to tell me these things when I have a scribe in the room. I want details, and I want them in the morning. Right now I have some entertainment for you.' He looked directly at Grandad Al and the word hunters. 'Bring in the holy man and his bag of tricks.'

Grandad Al nodded, said, 'Yes, Prefect,' and turned to march towards the nearest door.

As Al followed the others outside he heard the prefect say to Lucius, 'The Raetians sing like trapped cats and they dance as if someone's stabbing them. I think you'll prefer this. And even if you don't, at least there's decent wine and passable cheese.'

On the steps, villagers waited with petitions and other business. A wagon moved slowly past on the road, pulled by four oxen and carrying logs. Behind it a goatherd was moving his goats along. Away from the petitioners an older man sat with a staff leaning against his shoulder and a leather bag at his feet.

'The holy man and his bag of tricks,' Mursili said quietly.

Will stepped forward. 'Holy man, the prefect is ready to see you.'

The priest stood slowly, pulling himself up with the aid of his staff. He clutched his bag to his chest and the contents rattled. Al reached out to help him and his satchel swung forward. The flap had come undone. He checked inside. The peg was still there, but he couldn't see Doug. He looked around at the ground nearby, but there was no sign of him. Perhaps Doug was asleep deeper in the bag.

The priest had no shoes, and his feet were silent as he followed the word hunters up the steps.

He stopped in the doorway to give a small bow, barely more than a nod, to the prefect, who waved him in and said, 'Good, good. Holy man, I'm sure the legate here has a question for your gods.'

The priest nodded to Lucius, who said, 'Oh, I didn't know there'd be questions.'

'Yes, he tells the future. Or his gods do. He's got bits of stick—' The prefect stopped himself. 'I don't want to spoil it. Please.' He waved his hand in the priest's direction. It was clearly a signal to get started.

The priest lowered himself to the floor, first to a kneeling position and then sitting. So far he hadn't said a thing. He drew a white cloth from his bag and spread it out in front of him. All of his moves looked long-practised, even automatic, but without any hint that he wanted to be doing them here, putting on a show.

Al caught movement out of the corner of his eye, at the prefect's table. Doug was sitting in the middle of the silver food platter with his face shoved into a fig. For now at least, the two Romans were giving all their attention to the priest. But they weren't so focused that Al could step between them and pick up a rat without them noticing. He wanted to move, or create some distraction, but he couldn't think how to do it.

The priest looked up at the ceiling, raised a hand above his head and appeared to sprinkle something while chanting. At first Lexi couldn't believe what she was hearing, and then she realised it was the peg that allowed it to happen. She and the other word hunters could understand every word, while the Romans heard an old and foreign language and a ritual appeal to the gods.

But what the priest actually said was, 'May your mocking of my faith make your bowels block with boulders and your wives develop snouts.'

He shook his bag, opened it and tipped it over the white cloth. Wooden discs fell out, cut from tree branches. Each one had a sign carved into it. Some of them looked like Byrhtferth's extra letters or the writing on Caractacus's urn.

The priest scooped them up and put them back into the bag. He lifted his head to look at Lucius. 'Your question, Legate?'

Lucius leant forward in his seat and cleared his throat. 'There's only one question. That's what my friend the prefect would say. What awaits me in Rome?'

Doug's nose appeared. He had eaten his way right through the fig.

The priest nodded, reached into the bag, drew out a rune and placed it on the white cloth in front of him. He added two more and set them out in a row. He gazed down at them and rocked backwards and forwards.

'They mean nothing, because this process is a game for you.' He placed his left hand over the runes, raised his right and again seemed to sprinkle something that wasn't there. He chanted something that the word hunters heard as, 'Blah, blah, blah,' and then clapped his hands. He stared at the legate and looked troubled. 'My Lord, they say something of blood.'

'What?' Lucius stood up. He glanced back at the prefect, then strode over to the priest. 'What do they say? What exactly?'

'The god of wisdom is leaving the emperor.' The priest touched the first rune and then the second. 'The third means "blood".'

'The god of wisdom?' Lucius raised his hands to his head. 'Minerva? She's the emperor's protector and the god of my legion. Blood? What—'

'Lucius.' The prefect left his seat. 'You might find him on a good day.' He smiled. 'It might just mean he's lost his mind and wants you to marry his sister. That could be

the "blood" bit.' He put his hand on the legate's shoulder.
'This is just a game we play. I can't spend all my time here
reading Pliny and counting taxes.' He bent down and picked
up a rune. 'They have an alphabet, you know. The Raetians.
It's based on the Greek, but some new letters are coming in
from the symbols the northern barbarians use when they
want to hear from their gods. You'd see them in Germania.'
He studied the rune in his hand. '"Thorn", yes?' He looked
down at the priest, who nodded.

Instantly the cuts that marked the letter started to glow. He tossed the disc back to the holy man, who caught it and put it back in the bag. Al could tell the other word hunters had seen the portal, but no one else seemed to have noticed Doug.

'Have you seen the emperor's sister? Do you know what she—' Lucius couldn't have cared less about the alphabet. 'That's not going to be it, anyway. Domitian and blood? What does that mean to anyone in Rome?'

'Oh, come on.' The prefect put his hand on Lucius's arm and tried to turn him back towards his seat. 'Have some more wine. This was just a game.'

'No.' Lucius pulled away from the prefect. 'What do you know?' He checked the sentries and stared at the word hunters. He reached for his belt before remembering he was unarmed. 'Do you have orders from the emperor? Tell me it's not here, not now. Where are my men, my own men?'

'Lucius, don't be—' The prefect tried to calm him down, but Lucius backed away. 'It was a game. Stop jumping at shadows.'

'I'm not. I—' Behind the prefect, he noticed something. Doug, standing on his back legs and gnawing a piece of cheese.

Al's hand went to his sword. Lexi bumped him. The last thing they needed was to bring on a fight. But Doug was on one side of the room, the portal was on the other and a lot of edgy Romans were hovering nearby. From the open bag of runes, the yellow glow pulsed across the white cloth.

'A rat,' Lucius said. 'A white rat. Mostly white.' He smiled and his shoulders dropped. The tension left his body. 'Could there be a better omen than that?'

'No, there couldn't.' The prefect put his hand on Lucius's shoulder and steered him back towards his seat. 'The holy man was for your entertainment, but a rat is a sign not to be ignored. A white rat – whitish rat – out of nowhere. Minerva sent you that. All will be well.'

Lucius reached out his hand and Doug ran over to be patted. The legate scratched behind his ears and Doug nuzzled into his thumb. Lucius picked up a fig, tossed it in the air, caught it and took a bite.

Doug jumped from the table and scampered over to the word hunters.

'My Lord,' Grandad Al said to the prefect. 'Allow us to escort the holy man from the building.'

'Yes, yes.' The prefect waved dismissively in his direction. He was already looking around for his wine bearer. He hadn't realised how edgy Lucius was. The game with the holy man had been a stupid idea. At least the rat had come along at the right moment.

The priest stood and allowed the word hunters to pass him, before following them outside and down the steps. They glanced to their left and right on the way out – sentries, locals, two priests going into the temple, still no grey-robes.

Once they were back on the bare ground, Al knelt down, took off his satchel and let Doug climb in.

'Omen,' he said to him quietly. 'Greedy, more like.'

As Doug, full of figs and cheese and ready to sleep, curled up in his nest of Flemish wool, Al reached for the peg.

'So,' Mursili said to the priest, 'does the bowel blockage start right away, or when they least expect it?'

The priest took a step back and his eyes opened wide. 'So you speak— I was just— You must have misheard—'

'Your secret's safe with us,' Will told him. 'You just have to lend us "thorn" for a moment.'

'Of course.' He pulled the bag open. 'Take whichever ones you want. But please don't—' He sounded panicky.

Al realised the priest was looking at him, and thinking that the golden peg in his hand was some kind of dagger. 'We won't.' He changed his grip on the peg and dropped his arm to his side. 'All we want is "thorn".'

The priest offered the open bag and Will picked out the glowing rune. He lifted it by its edges and turned it to see the portal. The lines carved into it had broken up and now spelt 'home'.

He stepped away, up the hillside in the direction they'd come from. The other word hunters followed as the priest watched them, the open bag still in his hands, as if any of them might come back for another letter.

'No John Hunter here, then,' Grandad Al said, as Will opened the portal. 'We're safely on our way, but the job's not done.'

It made Lexi turn around, as though John Hunter might be nearby. He was out there, somewhere. Not in Raetia in 93, not anymore. But somewhere, sometime, raising an army and getting ready for battle.

The letter 'o' in 'home' widened until the rune was no more than a gold ring. Al slid the peg in, brought the side levers down and turned the key.

The ground shook and a fog blew from the river and across the road and the temple and the prefect's palace.

The fog caught them like wind in a sail or a kite, and it lifted them far above the empire, high enough to see the curve of the spinning earth beneath them, but low enough to see the Romans retreat home and new kings, gods and alphabets come and go. Words spun by, carved in stone and wood, written on parchment and vellum, printed on fine Flemish paper in Middle English, Modern English.

And then they were falling, into early evening and towards a lit city, streets with lines of electric lights, the dark shape of the park, Grandad Al's car with the *Curious Dictionary* on the grass beside it.

This time Mursili got the landing almost right, though he overshot at the last second and tripped into the gutter.

Grandad Al looked up at the lights of his son's house. 'We'll talk tomorrow. There's a bit to make sense of.' He opened the passenger door of his car, lifted out a Tupperware container with an apple pie in it and gave it to Lexi.

Al opened the lid. 'It looks like it was bought from a shop. Not like the pies Grandma Noela makes at all.'

'Of course it's from a shop.' Grandad Al set the lid back on top, but didn't press it down. 'I can't just whip up a home-made pie on cue. Just say she's trying a new way of doing it, or something. You're resourceful. You can cover it. It's warmed up a bit. I got the shop to take it out of the foil tray and microwave it. That'll make it seem as if it was baked this afternoon. And take it in with the lid off. Your grandma wouldn't seal the lid on a freshly baked pie, because it'd go soft.'

'It's not *that* warm,' Lexi said. 'I'll tell them we're supposed to reheat it after dinner.' She couldn't believe that, with people all through history wanting to attack them, they were standing in the street arguing about a pie.

'All sorted, then.' Al stepped away from Lexi to make sure she didn't hand him the pie. 'You can do that and I'll have a shower.' He always sweated when they landed in the Dark Ages, and the attack at Ramsey Abbey hadn't helped.

'I'm sure we'd all be grateful for that,' she said, 'but you used up the hot water five minutes ago.'

Back in his room, Al emptied his pack to clean it properly. There was still a whiff of rat vomit in there and a smear of something brown and even more disgusting on the list of questions they'd agreed to ask Caractacus.

How long did portals last? Did portals come up once or more than once, for example, when a newspaper article was written and again when it was published? Al scanned the remaining questions to see if they'd remembered to ask any of them. How was it that people seemed to be expecting twins when they'd arrived in New York in 1839 hunting 'okay'? Was there a way to send Will home separately?

There was also the question about weapons not passing through portals – at least that one had come up. The rest hardly seemed to matter now, though they'd have to get Will home one day.

The job had changed again. At the start, it had been about staying alive, getting home and keeping words in the language. Then it had been about finding Grandad Al. Now they had an enemy and the job was about tracking down John Hunter. They'd trained for other people's ancient battles – trained to be on the edge of them and to fight for survival, without changing who won or lost – but having their own foe and needing to find him and defeat him was a different issue. Will was determined not to go back to 1918 until that was done.

Who was John Hunter and how could they stop him? The list of questions they truly needed answers to didn't have to go any further than that.

Al got online, but there were John Hunters everywhere – a governor of New South Wales, a surgeon, a hospital. Close to two million hits. And there were twice as many for John Johnson.

He found himself flicking through sites related to where he'd just been, in case there was some kind of clue there.

Caxton made it back to England within three years and printed his edition of *The Canterbury Tales*. There was a 19th-century painting of him showing the first pages to the king, though the man in the picture supposed to be Caxton might have been anyone. He printed over a hundred books and the man who followed him – who had the excellent name of Wynkyn de Worde – printed more than 400 and set up London's first bookshop.

There was less to find on Brother Byrhtferth, though some of his work had survived. There was a simpler version of his diagram in a manuscript in Oxford. It had a diamond within a diamond within an oval, with months, star signs, elements and winds marked and commented on. There were no clouds or cherubs, though.

Al also found Byrhtferth's alphabet. The letter 'wynn' lasted until around 1300, when it was replaced by 'uu', which became 'w'. Double 'u'. 'Eth' left English around the same time, but survived in Icelandic. The 'ond' symbol turned out to be Roman shorthand for 'and', and only Byrhtferth appeared to include it in an alphabet. Ash was a runic name for a Latin structure, a ligature, that bound 'a' and 'e' together. It dropped out of alphabets after Old English, but stayed around in words like 'encyclopædia' and 'archæology' until well into the 20th century. 'Thorn' outlasted the rest and Caxton seemed to get some credit for that, but Al could find no mention of the duchess's role.

Other letters came and went – 'yogh' and 'ethel', which was nothing to do with 'eth'. The alphabet could have become anything, but it came out almost Roman again, with three extra letters to bring it to 26. Al couldn't imagine anyone writing a different alphabet now, inventing new letters and throwing them in.

Since 1011 Ramsey Abbey had been extended, then mostly destroyed, then reclaimed by the church and rebuilt, then dissolved in 1539. The abbey gatehouse on Wikipedia was built hundreds of years after Byrhtferth, but Al still found himself enlarging the picture to look for signs of grey-robes.

'Germania' turned out to be written by Tacitus around the year 98. Al had heard of him, but only the name. He checked to see where Tacitus was in 93 and all he could find was that he'd served in the provinces in a variety of roles while Domitian's reign of terror went on in Rome. Perhaps, for some part of 93, he'd been acting prefect in Raetia.

Domitian was assassinated in 96, days after a dream in which his protecting god Minerva appeared and told him she was leaving him.

Al jumped in his seat and bumped his knees on the underside of his desk, when his mother knocked on the door.

'Dinner's ready,' she called without coming in. 'I hope you've still got an appetite.'

When their grandfather arrived to pick them up the next day, Al was full of things he needed to talk about.

'But don't you see, Lex?' he said as they got into the car. 'The priest said Minerva would—'

'Al, it doesn't matter!' Lexi didn't mean to snap at him, but that was how it came out. 'So the priest fluked something. And then they saw your pet rat, so that meant the legate was going to be okay?'

'He probably was okay, actually.' Al fastened his seatbelt. 'I looked up the legion—'

'How can you so not get it?' She turned round from the front seat to face him. 'There I am, dumped into trying to fool Mum and Dad into believing Grandma made a factory pie, and I'm figuring you're in your room doing something useful that might save our lives – but it turns out you're chasing factoids around. What help is that going to be with John Hunter or John Johnson, or whatever his name is? Him and his army?'

Al stared out the window. Now he definitely wasn't going to get her the First Minervan Legion T-shirt for their birthday. He'd found them online as well. They had 'SPQR Legio I Minervia Pia Fidelis' on the front – 'First Minervan Legion Loyal and Faithful' – but with Domitian's name dropped from the end since the T-shirt wording came from after his death. By then they were loyal and faithful to someone else.

Will and Mursili were waiting for them at the Simpson's Falls picnic area. Will had a soccer ball and he was trying to show Mursili how to kick it, when Mursili noticed the others coming over and waved.

'The air-filled ball,' he said when they arrived. 'Genius, really. Wish we'd thought of it when I was a kid.'

Will rolled the ball around under his foot. 'Just thought we might need to blend in a bit.' He flicked it up, then kicked it higher and bounced it twice on his knee before it hit at the wrong angle and bounced away.

Al ran after it, put his foot out to stop it and accidentally slid over the top of it. He almost fell over, then tried to make it look like a deliberate move.

'Dork,' Lexi said. 'Leave it to people with coordination.'

Al kicked the ball at her, but missed. It rolled away and stopped in some leaves.

'Like I said.' Lexi laughed. 'He was nerding it up big-time online last night, checking out the people we met. Flaccidus, whatever.'

'Tacitus.' Al corrected her before he could stop himself. She'd just been baiting him. 'I think it was Tacitus. The prefect in Raetia. And you seem to forget how often the things that I happen to know have got us to a portal or out of trouble.'

'Mursili's got something too,' Will said.

'I *might* have something.' Mursili didn't want to oversell it. 'John Johnson. It was the alias used by Guy Fawkes in 1605, when he was caught near the gunpowder the night before he planned to blow up the Houses of Parliament in London.'

'So, you're telling us—' Al was annoyed with himself for not looking harder.

'I don't know what I'm telling you.'

'It'd be quite a coincidence, though,' Grandad Al said. 'Not that "John" and "Johnson" are uncommon names.'

'No, but I've thought about it.' Mursili had the advantage of discovering it the night before. 'Guy Fawkes died in January 1606, and you've seen John Johnson at the Globe Theatre that year, but in warmer weather. So, later. So he's not Guy Fawkes. Or at least not the man who was killed as Guy Fawkes in January. He meets Caractacus as "John Hunter", because he knows he should. He knows he needs the name "Hunter". But I don't think he's one of us – one of you – because that would mean he'd got his hands on the dictionary, and I don't think he'd have given it up. He looks quite like the Guy Fawkes we see in pictures, but it's a common look at that time. And the alias would have been known then, and I suspect not as easy to find for centuries after, until the internet. It's only now you can punch in a name and hope to find anything. I think it means he's from the early 17th century, whoever he is.'

'And he can get back to the Library of Alexandria by himself,' Grandad Al added. 'He might be starting to work out how to move into the future, as well, though not far yet. 1648 and no further, as far as we know.'

'As far as we know.' Will picked the ball up and bounced it.

Al wished he'd stuck with it and looked past John Johnson the composer, the congressman, the basketballer, the Mohawk chief, the liver-eating frontier woodsman. It seemed that sometime somewhere a John Johnson had done everything it was humanly possible to do, including some things that had never crossed Al's mind. But Mursili had found the one John Johnson reference that might mean something. In comparison, Tacitus might as well have been Flaccidus for all the use they'd get from any of Al's new factoids.

'In the early 17th century, something went wrong,' Grandad Al said. 'Someone worked us out. The wrong kind of person worked us out. And he worked out how to travel.'

'And however long he's been working on it in his own time, he's been going in and out of the past repeatedly to places we go.' Will tucked the ball under his arm. 'He's been doing our word hunting, as if he has the dictionary, and he's been setting traps for us.'

'When I was captured they wanted those details from me,' Grandad Al said. 'Places, dates, words. I gave them some. They forced me to drink something. After that things aren't clear – but, yes, I can remember it now. That's some of what they were after.'

He shook his head and looked down at the ground. He tried to block the hazy pictures of it, the hooded heads. And he tried to block the thought that he had done harm, put word hunters in danger, put his grandchildren in danger and their enemy closer to his goal.

Lexi lifted her hand to his arm and tried to think of the right thing to say.

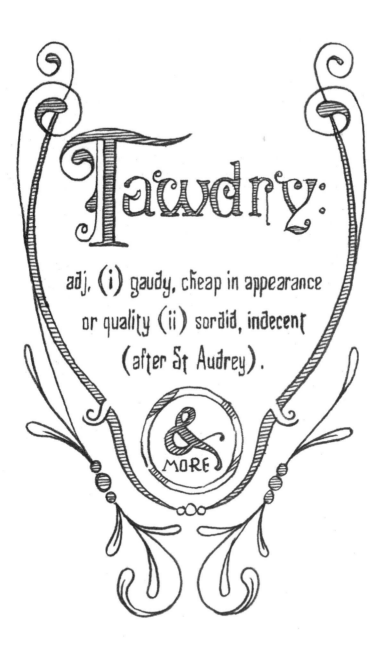

Tawdry:

adj. (i) gaudy, cheap in appearance
or quality (ii) sordid, indecent
(after St Audrey).

& MORE

I<small>T WAS A</small> Tuesday two weeks later when Al opened his bedroom door and saw the glow. The dictionary was buried under the usual mess, but, with the curtains drawn, the golden light blinking out from its closed pages was clear enough.

He put his schoolbag down and shut the door. He wanted it to go away, to stop. He wanted the language to be safe and stable, and not something that could take his grandfather for 30 years and put his own life at risk. And Lexi and the others.

He had googled John Johnson and Guy Fawkes in the hope of finding out more, but time after time all he found was the same information. Guy Fawkes had given the name when captured, and said he was the servant of Thomas Percy, one of the other conspirators. Al had chased that down, too, but there was no sign of a real Percy servant called John Johnson.

Whatever his name, there was a man with an army scattered throughout the past, hiding, waiting for word hunters. Waiting for the next word to light up and for the word hunters to appear in pursuit of it.

And here it was.

Al lifted two books off the dictionary, then scrunched up a burger wrapper from a couple of days before and threw it in the bin. The word looked like it was a long way in. He turned the pages carefully.

His first thought was that it wasn't the kind of word he'd expected. His second was that he should know better, and know not to expect anything in particular.

He took out his phone and texted the others. 'Go time. The word's "tawdry".'

How could the word have two such different meanings? And what did Saint Audrey have to do with it?

He flicked to Wikipedia and put in her name. She wasn't Audrey at all. She was from the 7th century and she had a name Byrhtferth would have loved. Æðelþryð. 'Ash, eth, e, l, thorn, r, y, eth'. Aethelthryth. It sounded like a name a speech therapist could help you with.

He was scrolling down to read more, when there was a knock at his door. 'Hey!' It was Lexi's voice.

He opened the door. Lexi had her phone in her hand.

'I'm across the hall.' She held it up. His text was on screen.

'Yeah, but there's five of us.'

'I know, but—' She could see the glow from the open page behind him. She glanced down the corridor. Their father was in the study with the door shut. 'Are you ready for this?'

'I practise fight moves in my sleep.' He stood back to let her into the room. 'And, no, I'm not ready.'

She nodded. 'Yeah. I don't even know what to be ready for. We had tunnel ball today and Maddie Bond fell over and cut her knee. Well – didn't cut it. Grazed it. She got carried down to sick bay and got a big bandage on it. She nearly got to go home. And we have to chuck ourselves into the past, find weapons when we get there and then maybe fight off people who are trying to kill us.'

'Yeah. Most days I feel like I've got a whole different life inside my head.'

'You always did.' She smirked. 'But this one's real.' She leant over the dictionary. 'Saint Audrey? What's that about?'

They met the others at the park.

'Seventh century,' Mursili said. 'Probably a few twists and turns before then, though I don't know exactly when they'll be. No one's done it before?'

He looked at Will and Grandad Al. They shook their heads.

'It puts us right in the zone.' Lexi had her backpack at her feet. 'A bunch of stops in grey-robe central. It won't be like "okay" when you can get it pretty much all out of the way in the 19th century.'

'No, it won't.' Grandad Al looked around at each of them. 'It may well be dangerous, but if it takes us where we need to go, it's the word we want.'

'Well,' Mursili shrugged. 'I pressed it last time, so it's not my turn.'

As Al opened the dictionary, Lexi lifted her pack and put it on her back.

'I'll take this one,' she said. 'Let's go.'

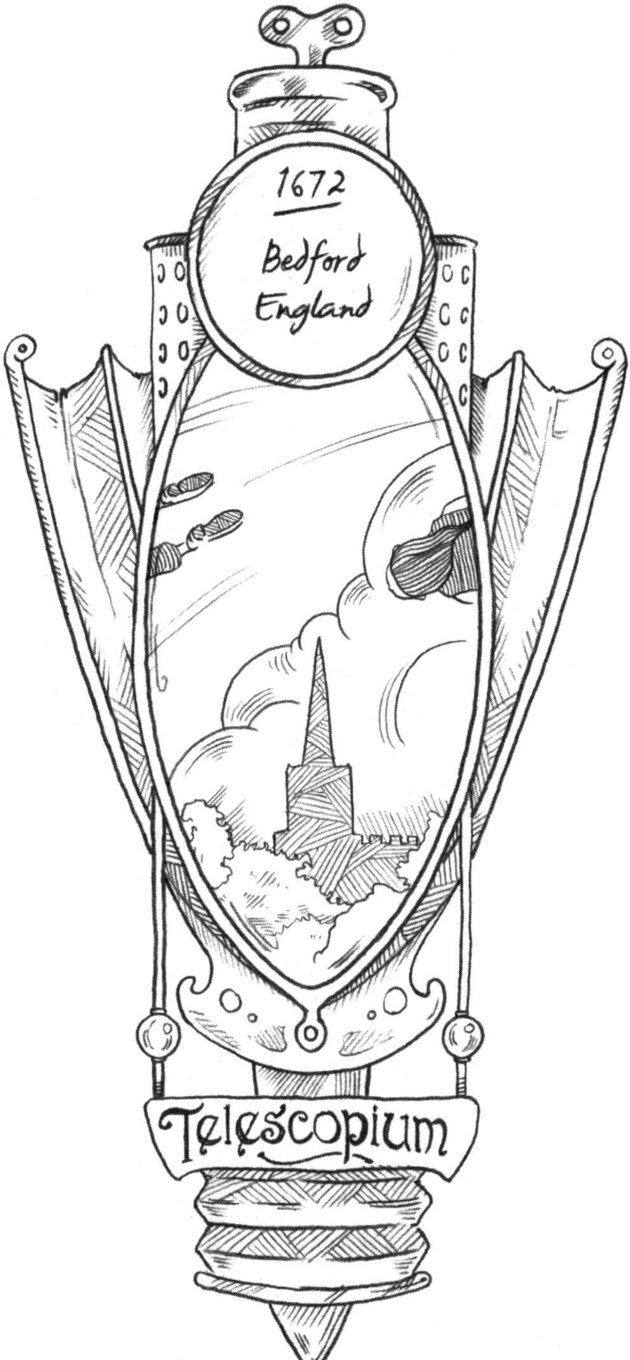
1672
Bedford
England
Telescopium

*T*HEY SHUDDERED AND thumped through the dark and then the bumps eased. Al guessed they had another century of falling through clear air before he felt pressure from below and their drop slowed a little. They'd just passed Doctor Johnson's dictionary, 1755. Al had most of the timeline in his head by now.

Light came in and the cloud gave way over farmland. There was no sign of a coastline and they were falling towards a village or a town next to a narrow river. No factories, no great castle, no sign of armies massed for battle.

This time, Mursili pulled off something like a normal landing. He'd been practising flight position on one of the swivel chairs in his office, with the door shut.

They were on a street, with stone and half-timbered houses on either side. There was no one nearby. No one immediately nearby, at least. Further down the street people were gathering outside a building.

'We're all looking rather serious,' Will said, lifting the hat from his head to take a look at it.

It was black, with a broad brim and a top like a tapered chimney. He had a stiff white collar, a black waistcoat with many buttons, black breeches, rough black wool stockings and worn black boots with wooden buckles. Al, his grandfather and Mursili looked just like Will. Lexi had a plain white bonnet, a long black dress with long sleeves and a pair of red shoes, which looked brighter and redder because of the lack of colour everywhere else.

'What did I do to get these?' She stuck one foot out from under her skirts. 'I mean, they're pretty cool, but with this bonnet?'

Doug was wriggling and groaning in Al's duffel bag. Al slid the bag from his shoulder and, as he set it on the ground, he noticed the corner of a book – a book bound in black leather – poking through the hole at the top. He crouched down and opened the bag. The book was a Bible. With it and four pegs, Doug had been feeling pretty squished in his wool nest. Now he could breathe – wet soil, sheep poo, oily wool and something malty, yeasty. A new smell, but a good one.

'A Bible and—' Al took the activated peg out, too. 'This. Bedford, 1672. So, Charles II is the king and the Commonwealth is over—'

'Are we Puritans?' Grandad Al looked down at his waistcoat. 'Or nonconformists?'

'But we're all totally conforming,' Lexi said. 'Except for my shoes.'

'I can't explain the shoes.' When Grandad Al looked at them, all he could think of was the *Wizard of Oz*. 'The nonconformists didn't conform to the official views on religion. Maybe we're here in connection with that. 1672. There was a law passed around now allowing greater

tolerance. Not that it lasts. It has to be something to do with religion, or there wouldn't be a Bible in Al's bag.'

'So we look for a church?' It seemed to Will like the obvious next step. 'We arm ourselves and we look for a church. There's a steeple over there.' It was in the distance, beyond the roofs of the row of houses and in another street.

'And a small church down there, just across the street from those people.' Al pointed to an old stone building no bigger than a house. 'At least I think it's a church. It's got a stumpy thing at one end that looks like a bell tower.'

They agreed to check there first. As they got closer to the crowd, each one of them studied the people more closely, looking for any sign of threat.

'I've just thought of something,' Grandad Al said. 'Henry VIII shut the monasteries last century. This won't be like Bruges in 1473. It doesn't mean there are no priests or monks around, but anyone in a grey robe is much more likely to be our enemy.'

They kept to the far side of the street and, as much as possible, to the shadows, as they tried to move past the crowd. The people were clustered at the door to a long stone building, trying to hear what was being said inside. The word hunters could just make out the voice of a man.

'Weapons – look!' Will said. He nodded in the direction of the side of the building.

There were straw bales, empty sacks and wooden stools and buckets all piled up against the wall. Leaning next to them were two pitchforks.

The word hunters crossed the street, waiting for someone to turn and see them, waiting for a threat to emerge. Will took one pitchfork and gave the other to Grandad Al. Mursili found a hook on a long pole.

'So what does that leave for us?' Al pushed a hay bale aside, looking for anything that would do.

'Well, Lexi has to be ready to use the device Caractacus made,' Grandad Al said. 'And you – we need your eyes to look out for trouble.'

'Right.' Al could tell when he was getting the brush-off. All that training and now that they had three pseudo-weapons, it was clear he wasn't going to get one. 'I'll wave a bucket at them or something. I'll just have to hope their swords aren't too big.'

'Someone needs to be looking out for initials.' Grandad Al thought – hoped – that sounded more like a real job. 'You're far more likely to see them than I am.'

It was still a partial brush-off, but Al could convince himself it was also true.

From a small window above their heads, they could make out what the man inside was saying.

'I was a sinner in my youth,' he proclaimed. 'I used bad language and danced and rang bells.'

'What?' Lexi wasn't sure she'd heard him right. Danced? Rang bells? That's all he had to own up to?

'This is it,' Grandad Al said, trying to keep his voice down. 'The Bible, where we need to be. It's not a church – it's here. They're nonconformists. Bedford, 1672. It's John Bunyan and he's just been allowed to preach again. He's going to say it. It'll be in there.' He tapped his pitchfork on the ground. 'Try to look like we've just come from a farm. Somehow we've got to get inside with these when he says it.'

For now, though, it would be enough to join the crowd near the door, to watch and listen and wait. 'Tawdry' – he seemed bound to say it sometime.

'I married a girl whose inheritance was two books.' John Bunyan said it forcefully, passionately. At the same time, it sounded as if he had said it before. He was standing

on something that put him well above the crowd. He had an untidy moustache and greying hair that fell to his shoulders. 'We had not a dish or spoon between us, but we had her two books – *The Plain Man's Pathway to Heaven* and *The Practice of Piety*. I read them whenever I had light to do it and still I struggled before coming to the Lord.' In the congregation heads nodded. 'But he kept his door open for me and let me come to it in my own sorry time. The women of Saint John's church – those women of God, rather than of means – were there to welcome me. In time I found I had a voice as well as a welcome, and God called on me to use it. So I preached. Some heard the Truth. Some called me a highwayman.' The congregation murmured and John Bunyan smiled. 'Some called me a witch.' This time they gasped. 'Some even called me a Jesuit.' There was a louder gasp. He held his hands out, as if asking for calm. He was still smiling, as if people could call him anything and he wouldn't care.

Lexi leant in towards Al. 'Isn't that just a kind of priest? How is it scarier than a witch? Witches freak these people.'

'I know. But religion gets to people more than anything. It doesn't have the same effect at home. Most of the time.' He wanted to say more, but this wasn't the place for it. He'd do it when they got back to Fig Tree Pocket. She'd thank him for his factoids one day. No, not his factoids; his grasp of history. The things he understood. It amounted to more than isolated bits and pieces, however great those were.

He checked the steps, the door and the stones in the wall – still no word hunter initials. Since it was his job, he wanted to be the one to find them.

John Bunyan was talking about the king and his restoration to the throne. Al knew that one. 1660.

'And the Lord saw fit to offer me greater tests and greater opportunities,' John Bunyan said. 'For preaching our faith in private houses, I was jailed by magistrates not of a mind to jail me, and who offered me the door if I would not do God's work. But God's work is our obligation and I could tell them only, "If you release me today, I will preach tomorrow". Each time they went to set me free, I told them the same. And any rare time they did set me free, I lived up to my word. My three-month sentence took 11 years to finish.'

There was more murmuring in the congregation, but again he settled it by lifting his hands. He didn't look at all unhappy about his time in prison.

He went on with his story. 'I had two books – the Lord's, and *Foxe's Book of Martyrs*. From tin I made a violin and from a chair leg a flute. And I had pens and paper and 60 men who would listen when I preached. God's work is everywhere, even in the county prison. And now the king has a new law and his magistrates can give me one of his licences to preach, so I may preach in more fragrant parts.' This time the audience laughed. Even outside the door, there was no disguising the smell of cow poo in the building. 'But Christ was born in a barn, so we can worship in one. And the smell the cattle have left us is at least as pleasing as the odour of five dozen unwashed men. Besides, it keeps away the stink of brewer's hops that we've grown too used to on the streets of Bedford.'

He quoted a verse from the Bible that had meant a lot to him in prison and talked about what it meant now in his life outside, with a preacher's licence. The audience listened intently. The word hunters waited for the word 'tawdry' and kept checking the crowd and the street.

But then John Bunyan finished and people started to move.

'Did he—' Al said, as his grandfather took his arm to steer him clear of the crowd that was starting to push through the door.

'Maybe I was wrong.'

It had made such sense, though. As they came out dressed in black and navy, Grandad Al was sure they were exactly the kind of people to welcome the word 'tawdry' in a sermon.

Lexi stepped back to get out of the way of an older woman, but the woman stopped to look her up and down. She poked at Lexi's shoes with her walking stick.

'You should examine yourself, child, and others should have examined you more strenuously before now.' She looked up and glared sternly at Grandad Al before jabbing at Lexi's toes again. 'Red shoes! Tawdry, tawdry, tawdry.'

The glow of a portal flared from under Lexi's right heel.

'Thank you.' Lexi couldn't help smiling.

The woman looked shocked and started to overbalance.

A younger man reached out to take her arm and said, 'Come, Mother. She'll have to answer for herself soon enough.' He couldn't even manage to make eye contact with Lexi.

'Al.' Lexi poked her brother in the ribs. 'Stop looking around. It's one of my tawdry shoes. The portal. I'd text you, but—'

Will led the way around the corner of the building with his pitchfork ready, but no one was there.

They stood behind the pile of hay and stools and barn rubbish, and Lexi took off her shoe and pressed the '& more' button. It fell back into the heel and left a shimmering gold ring behind. Al had the peg in his hand and he slid it in and brought the levers down.

The portal flared and widened. The cobbles they were standing on started to hum and shake, then drop away. In a single gust, the alley beside the barn filled with fog and the word hunters fell.

1590

London
England

Telescopium

LEXI'S LAST THOUGHT on the way out of Bedford was that she would like to keep the red shoes. As the word hunters dropped, she reached down for them – maybe she could put them in her bag – but they were already gone.

There was a bump, a rush of cool air and daylight. The fall was already over.

They were above a city clustered around a bend in a river, most of it on the north bank. There was one bridge, west of something that looked like a fortress and east of a cathedral or palace.

'London,' Al called out. 'No sign of the Globe, though.'

He guessed 16th century. The fall had been a short one, but the Globe had been on the south bank near the bridge from 1599 to the 1640s. They'd hit the Shakespeare bump, just, and come out the other side of it.

This time they were falling north of the river, towards the web of narrow streets leading down to the bank.

'Stick together!' Grandad Al shouted, as he brought his arms out from his sides.

The others followed him down and they landed in a laneway. Mursili had been so focused on not hitting the overhanging roofs of houses that his foot slipped on the rough wet ground and he fell over.

The bad smell hit him right away. 'Oh, dear, I think the street's a toilet.'

He stood up quickly and tried not to think about the dark stain on his breeches.

Under a nearby awning a man was cutting glass. Two doors down a blacksmith beat a glowing iron rod on his forge. The buildings were made mostly of rough pieces of timber with some stone and brick, and crammed in together as if they were holding each other up.

'This might be his time,' Al said, as he reached into his bag. 'John Johnson.' He pulled the peg out and showed the others. '1590. He's probably here, in this city, but he might not be onto us yet. In his own time, at least. His regular life.'

It wouldn't stop him having grey-robes here, or travelling. He could be in one part of the city as himself and another having travelled back. It didn't seem impossible.

The glazier looked up at them and then got back to his work.

Lexi checked her feet. She had red shoes again, but they were velvet this time, tied with ribbons and tucked into a bigger pair of shoes that looked like wooden sandals.

'Pattens,' Grandad Al said when he saw her wondering what they were. 'So the muck from the street doesn't get all over your nice shoes. We're richer this time.'

He had a black slashed doublet with red showing through, black breeches and white stockings. The others were in similar outfits, with flashes and stockings of different colours. Lexi had a full skirt and a patterned bodice.

'I don't like the look of this street, and I don't mean the muck.' Will didn't want to get distracted by a discussion of ways of keeping shoes clean. 'There could be anything behind these doors and we've got no weapons or room to move. 1590. We should expect trouble.'

Further down the street a boy threw a stone at a bird. A dog limped into a house and someone the word hunters couldn't see chased it out. The air smelt foul. The blacksmith's hammer clanged and sparks showered onto his bare floor.

'If he's here – John Johnson, John Hunter – should we try to get him now?' Al wanted to bring it on, if it had to happen. 'Get him before he starts doing what he's doing, before he finds out about us. We've got maybe two days to do it once we've found the portal.'

'If he doesn't know about us yet, he probably won't be John Johnson or John Hunter.' As soon as Will said it, Al knew he was right. 'Even if he does, it's not a name he answers to here. If we can track him down using something other than his name—'

'He's not at the Globe 'cause there is no Globe yet.' Al was thinking it through. 'And the way he looks isn't going to help much, since it seems to be pretty common.' Both the men nearby had John Johnson's moustache and goatee, but the glazier was shorter than him and the blacksmith broader.

Al felt something wriggling in his bag. Doug was making his way to the top again. Before Al could see what was going on, money started falling from under the flap, one coin at a time. Elizabethan shillings. He'd seen one before, left in the

New Forest in 1100 by a word hunter as a sign. Perhaps the word hunter from 1590, who might be in London now, getting on with his 1590 life, his head crammed with secrets from the past.

Mursili bent down to pick up the coins. 'Must be a sign, like the book in Bedford. What would we do with money?'

'Spend it,' Lexi said. 'There was nothing subtle about having that Bible. We had to find somewhere religious. This'll be a bank or a shop—'

'Or a mint. They probably made those shillings somewhere near here.' Al reached over and took two of them from Mursili. He studied the markings carefully. 'Different mints, I think. So, yeah, maybe a bank or a shop.'

He wanted to do something right. Actually, he wanted to do something great. He wanted to have an idea no one else had thought of, and for it to be right. He didn't want to be the person who got a weapon fourth or fifth, and who missed out when only three could be found.

To their left the street narrowed. To their right it ended at a wider road. A carriage went past, drawn by two white horses with mud spattered up their legs. There were pedestrians too, some of them looking well dressed, like the word hunters.

Grandad Al nodded in their direction. 'If we're after a shop, that might be the place to start.'

On the way they passed a house that had collapsed long before. Much of the better timber and stones had already gone, but something caught Will's eye. He stepped inside

and pulled a rusty knife blade from the rubble. He found a pocket in his breeches just big enough to fit it and slipped it in.

'Better than nothing.' He shifted it around so that it was comfortable.

One rusty blade. It would be close enough to nothing if a pack of armed grey-robes surprised them. Al couldn't think of any other options. It wasn't as if the blacksmith would sell them his hammer, or make a few quick swords for them.

They stopped at the corner to check the new street. It was wider, with shops on it, often with upper storeys leaning out as if they'd fall over in a stiff wind. A man was roasting nuts over a fire. He scooped some into a paper cone, gave it a twist to seal it and handed it to a customer.

Then Al noticed something.

'LH'. He pointed to it, scratched on the cornerstone of the first house in the street. So he'd missed the initials in 1672, unless LH came from before then and there had been none. Not one of the others mentioned it, but he wondered how many of them had thought it. It had been his one job in Bedford.

Will put his hand in his pocket and turned to check behind him. There was no one there.

'You're right,' Grandad Al said to him. 'If it's a rallying point for word hunters, it's a rallying point for grey-robes, too.' Nothing was the way it had once been, when the past itself was a big enough challenge.

Mursili moved to make sure Lexi was in the middle. They might have only one rusty knife, but she had Caractacus's device.

Further down the street someone tipped a pot from an upper window and its contents splattered onto the ground.

'None of us around that I can see,' Grandad Al said. 'And none of them either. So, shops. What are we looking for? Something to buy that's connected with "tawdry".'

The shop on the corner sold candles and oil lamps. Next to it was a milliner with a large painted wooden hat hanging from a hook above the door. The third shop along had a sign that read 'Fenwick & Sons – Purveyors of Niceties', with more writing on its open window shutters mentioning gloves, fans and hand mirrors.

'"Tawdry lace".' Lexi pointed to it. It was on the third open shutter.

'Well done!' Grandad Al put his hand on her shoulder. 'That must be us. "Tawdry lace" – the meaning must have changed or they wouldn't be advertising it.'

He led the way to the door, stopping only to look in the first window. There were shelves and benches piled with clothing accessories and a cupboard behind the counter with many small drawers. A grey-haired man – presumably Mr Fenwick – stood between the cupboard and the counter in a white shirt and faded waistcoat, while his only two customers, a mother and daughter, tried on scarves. There was one other door, and it was behind Mr Fenwick and shut.

'Looks clear.' Grandad Al glanced at Mursili, who was at the next window.

Mursili nodded.

Will and Mursili stayed on the street to cover their exit while Lexi and Al went inside with their grandfather. It was hard not to imagine grey-robes lying in wait behind the trunks piled with ruffs and gloves.

Al took a step to the right. Behind the trunks there was only bare wooden floor. He felt his heart slow down.

Mr Fenwick's customers bought their scarf and on their way to the door passed Grandad Al and Lexi.

'Anything I can help you with, sir?' Mr Fenwick said, catching Grandad Al's eye. He smiled as he leant on his counter.

'I'm sure you can.' Grandad Al turned the two shillings over in his hand. 'I'd like to buy something for my grandchildren. A keepsake to mark our lovely day together.'

Lexi smirked. What a lovely day together it had been, tumbling through history, fearing for their lives and ending up in streets that doubled as toilets. She could think of lovelier.

Mr Fenwick suggested a silver belt buckle for Al and a pair of gloves for her. He reached into a drawer and placed several pairs on the counter. They were made of soft leather with embroidered cuffs. She thought she could smell perfume coming from them.

'They're beautiful,' she said, because they were. They'd be embarrassing to wear at home, but she'd ended up in plenty of eras dressed in rags or in a soldier's uniform. Since the past often served up terrible clothes, the gloves definitely counted as niceties. 'But I have gloves and it would be—' she tried to find a fancy word that would work '—immodest to own too many pairs. And to allow grandfather to spend so much. Do you have anything small, but delicate?' Surely that would do it. 'Small but delicate' should make him mention lace.

'I have some folding paper fans from the Orient, and some brooches you might like to see.' Normally Lexi would be a sucker for a brooch, but this time she tried to look as though she wasn't entirely happy. 'Small, but delicate? What about some tawdry lace? I have some in the storeroom. A fine lace necktie?'

'That's exactly what I wanted to hear,' she said, though a tie was the last thing she'd expected. Somewhere nearby, perhaps in the storeroom, the portal had surely been activated.

Mr Fenwick was about to speak again when something behind Lexi distracted him. She spun around, faster than she should have, but it was only Will at the open shop door.

'Mr Hunter,' he said to Grandad Al. 'Some news. If we might interrupt for a minute? It's news for you all.'

'Certainly.' Grandad Al closed his hand around the shillings. 'Excuse us for a moment, Mr Fenwick. This way, children.'

'I'll just pop into the storeroom.' Mr Fenwick took a step towards the door. 'I have some new lace off the boat from Flanders this morning.'

Al looked out at the street through the open windows. No grey-robes. Mursili was standing calmly near the door.

They followed Will out and his news was immediately apparent. The 'a' in 'tawdry' written on the shutter had changed into an '&', with the word 'more' below it in glowing gold.

'Allow me, Master Hunter,' Will said, opening the flap to Al's bag.

'Certainly, Mr Hunter.'

'So not fair,' Mursili said. 'There's not one Bogazkale in this city, I bet.'

'Then please do the honours for us, Mr Bogazkale.' Will stepped aside to let Mursili touch the button.

It flared and the '& more' became a glowing peg-sized hole. Will pushed the peg in, locked the levers and turned the key.

The shutter flapped against the stone wall and the road started to shake. Through the window Al saw Mr Fenwick step through the storeroom door with a box of lace in his hand. Then the fog rolled in.

1545
Ely
Liberty of Ely
England

Telescopium

The WORD HUNTERS shuddered throughout the short drop, then burst into sunshine over a cluster of farms surrounded by lush wild land. In the middle of the farms was a town and, next to it, a large building in the shape of a cross, with a rectangular building at the end of its right arm.

Al concentrated on the cross-shaped building. They were dropping towards it – towards the base of the cross. It would be a cathedral, with the bishop's house or a chapel on the side and the town grown up around them.

As they fell, they saw crowds on the lawns in front of the buildings, and tents in irregular rows.

'Beyond the trees,' Lexi called out, twisting so that she veered off to the right. 'Too many people down there.'

The others followed and landed on a patch of grass behind a large oak.

The lawn in front of the cathedral had been converted into a fairground. Through the trees they could hear music and shouting, people laughing.

'Not quite so well off this time.' Grandad Al looked down at his drab belted tunic and leggings, which had worn through at the right knee. 'At least you got some colour, Al.'

Everyone else's leggings were one colour, but Al's had red-and-white vertical stripes.

'Winner.' Lexi laughed. 'Rocking the leggings, as always.' She had a straw hat and a brown short-sleeved dress over a long-sleeved off-white shirt. Nothing for Al to work with there.

'I bet those taste of mint.' Will couldn't believe how skinny the pattern made Al's legs look. 'Candy canes – that's what the American backpackers call them.'

'So, we're four beggars and 50 cents worth of lollies, then.' Al slipped one arm from its leather strap and started to take off his pack. 'How about we get on with the job, just in case someone's about to attack us?'

This time their packs were made of stiff woven wicker, like baskets, with wooden lids on top.

Mursili scanned through the trees as Al looked for the peg. 'Good place to land. I think it's just us here. What do you think the fuss is about over there?'

'It's a fair.' Will took a step to the left to look through the trees. 'A fair for a saint's day. Looks like it's on cathedral land.'

'Ah, religious celebration.' Mursili nodded, as if it now made sense. 'Slay the serpent, burn the incense, drink a cup of pig's blood. I know the score.'

Lexi started to say something, then thought better of it.

Doug climbed onto Al's arm and his nose twitched. Apples, grass, sweat. There was always sweat.

'1545.' Al held up the peg. 'So that'll be Ely Cathedral.'

'It'll be Saint Audrey, won't it?' Grandad Al was piecing it together. 'We know this gets back to her, so my guess is it's her fair. We've got one more peg after this one?' He waited for Al to check. '1545. Hmmm.'

'Henry VIII's dissolved the monasteries, but not long ago.' Al wanted to be first with at least some of the history. 'He's still king, but not for much longer.'

'Does that mean no monks if there are no monasteries? Will that make any grey-robes stand out more?' Lexi couldn't imagine it here, the final showdown with John Johnson at a fair. But it could happen anywhere, and grey-robes might be at any step along the way.

'I think the monks got a pension.' Grandad Al had read about it once. 'If they agreed to go quietly. But this place is a cathedral, so we'll see people dressed like them. Don't go whacking the first person you see in a grey robe.'

'All right. Weapons. We've still got to be ready to whack, even if we have to be careful who we do it to.' Will picked up a fallen tree branch and snapped it into the right length with his foot. 'We're poor people who've just wandered in for the fair. We've walked miles with these annoying baskets on our backs. So we can each carry a good strong stick and no one'll look twice at us.'

Since their fall looked like it might have ended at the cathedral door, they circled around through the trees to reach the side of the building. It was made of a yellowish stone and had rows of arched windows and more steepled towers and turrets than Al could count.

The first fair stalls were clearly visible. A man was throwing wooden balls at an unseen target to try to win a prize. If she could've edited the prospect of grey-robes from 'tawdry', Lexi realised she might actually have had fun on this trip. No wars so far, no danger, and it seemed to be about shoes and accessories and shopping.

Then, at the tower at the end of the cathedral wall, she noticed a man in grey robes leaning back against the stonework and gazing up at the sky.

She reached out to Grandad Al's arm and stopped him. They all stopped. After a few seconds the man stepped away from the wall, lifted his hood over his head and walked into the crowd.

Al looked up at the sky. It was clear. There was nothing to see. Had the man been watching for word hunters? Was that even possible? In all their landings, no one had noticed them until they were on the ground.

They kept the cathedral wall on their right as they reached the corner. The fair spread out in front of them across a wide lawn. At the nearest stall two men were wrestling on a greasy pole with an audience cheering them on. Many of the crowd, rich and poor, wore simple lace chokers tied around their necks.

The word hunters followed a family into the cathedral, but stopped inside the entrance for their eyes to adjust. There were candles clustered at some shrines but no lamps, though all the rows of windows allowed enough daylight in for them to see. Three tiers of archways ran on either side of the long nave towards the distant altar.

Most people seemed to be heading in one direction, talking quietly and with their heads bowed. Further down the nave towards the altar, Al could make out a group of robed men walking from one side to the other. Two of them had things that looked like shawls around their shoulders, with the fabric draped down over their arms to hold a tall embroidered hat and a crook with a golden top.

Will saw the men too and ducked into an archway.

'It's the bishop,' Al told him. 'The guy in the middle, the one with the beard and the black cap. The others are holding his mitre and his—' He couldn't remember the word for it.

Grandad Al stepped in. 'Crozier. Well done. Well spotted. That staff with the curved part at the top is a crozier. It's supposed to look like a shepherd's crook. The mitre and the crozier mean he's the bishop. No one else can actually touch them, which is why they've got that—' He indicated

on himself where the shawl would go. 'Garment. Not grey-robes, then. Good work, Al. Never a good idea to whack a bishop in a cathedral.'

He gave Al a knowing look, and Al smiled. Thomas Becket, Canterbury, 1170 – the only time a British king might have had a bishop whacked in a cathedral. It took Henry II years to deal with the fallout, whether or not he'd actually ordered it.

'Hey, did I just miss a history joke?' Lexi knew there was more to it. 'No, don't tell me. Seriously. Don't even tell me at home.'

They rejoined the worshippers, who were moving along a side aisle and soon they came to a shrine. Or a place that had been a shrine, but had recently been wrecked. Where it had been, people were leaving small strips of lace, candles and pictures of a woman in simple clothes, with a lace choker around her neck and a halo.

By the light of the candles, Al noticed something else, something darker. Among the white pieces of lace was a tobacco leaf.

JH had left a tobacco leaf in Bruges in 1473. John Hunter. John Johnson.

'Tobacco,' he whispered to his grandfather. 'He's been here.'

Mursili and Will stiffened and were instantly ready for attack. No one around them looked likely to be an enemy, but the archways threw up shadows all the way along the building.

Al leant forward and picked up the tobacco leaf. Scratched on the broken stone beneath were initials. 'LH'. Not 'JH'.

'False alarm.' He stood up again.

'Odd, though,' his grandfather said. 'Same clue, different hunter?'

For some time they waited in the hope that they'd found the portal, but the worshippers were hardly speaking at all. They were whispering prayers or silent and praying in their heads.

Lexi noticed Will put his hand up to Grandad Al's ear to say something. Her grandfather nodded. He signalled for them to step back and he led the way to the door.

'Will thinks it's the lace,' he said, once they were outside. 'We know that's what became "tawdry". People are wearing it and leaving it as an offering where the shrine used to be.'

'So we need to find a stall selling lace.' Will decided to step in, since it was his theory. 'Or a display to do with Saint Audrey and the lace, in a place where people can actually speak. We need to get someone to say whatever's next, and it wasn't going to happen in there.'

'Well done finding the initials, though,' Mursili said to Al. 'I would never have noticed that tobacco leaf.'

'Yes, sure, yes.' Will hurried to reassure him, too. 'That was great. I just think—'

'It's okay.' Al straightened his pack and tried to make it sit more comfortably. 'I stopped you mugging a bishop. That would have been a lot worse than standing near a shrine for 15 minutes while nothing happened. Let's check the fair out.'

They passed a stall selling pancakes and honey and a table where children stuck their faces into wooden tubs filled with water, trying to trap apples against the side and bite into them. Next came a fenced ring in which wolves were roaming around a chained bear. They were growling and darting in and out, as the bear roared and swiped at them with its paws.

'That's disgusting.' Lexi put her hand up to her face so she couldn't see it.

Beyond the bear-baiting, a thin man dressed like a monk stood at a table with a tent behind him. He had strips of lace of different lengths laid out, and hand-coloured cards with pictures of the saint. He smiled and beckoned them over.

He touched his neck as they came up to the table. 'Not properly dressed yet? You must have just arrived. Are you – you're a group? The five of you?' He looked at each of them in turn. 'I'm the man you need to see for your Saint Audrey's lace.'

'I think you're exactly the person we need to see.' Will tried not to be obvious as he glanced down at the lace chokers on the table to see if a portal had been activated. Tawdry –

Saint Audrey. They had landed in a time before 'tawdry' became a word.

'I have more in here, if you'd like to see it.' The monk took a step towards the tent and put his hand to the flap. It opened just a crack, but that was enough to show the golden pulse of the portal in the dark. 'You'd be welcome to come in and take a look – all *five* of you – if you'd like.' He made a big point of there being five of them.

He pushed the flap open with his arm and ushered them into the tent. They could make out the shapes of boxes, and curtains hanging from rods. As they stepped inside, Doug screeched from the top of Al's pack. Al jumped and grabbed Lexi's arm as the curtains were flung aside.

He heard Will groan and turned to see him falling to his knees with a sword in his side. As he fell, the hilt of the sword twisted from the hand of the grey-robe who had held it and Al instinctively grabbed it, pulled it out and stood over Will, ready to fight.

He couldn't see how many of them there were. The man who had lost the sword had backed away into the dark, but there were others. Six, ten, maybe more.

Grandad Al blocked one blow with his stick, but the sword sliced halfway through it and stuck there. Al crouched and lunged. He drove the sword into the grey-robe, below his ribs, and the man dropped to the ground.

Mursili grabbed the grey-robe's sword and twisted it free of the stick. Another blade swung towards him and the two swords clashed. Grandad Al lunged with his stick and thumped the grey-robe in the stomach, winding him. Mursili cut his arm and his sword fell. Mursili dragged it back with his foot and Grandad Al picked it up. They had three swords now, but too many enemies and Will was on the ground, silent.

'This way.' Al grabbed Lexi's arm.

She needed light to find the device and use it. He slashed at the tent. Two strokes and a triangle of fabric flopped down. He pushed Lexi out into the daylight and turned to fight.

She tore her pack off, grabbed the device and twisted and locked it in the way Caractacus had shown her. The red and white liquids swirled together like marble and the metal turned hot. Behind her in the dark she could hear swords crashing against swords. They hadn't trained to fight in half-darkness, in tents with curtains.

Support, Caractacus had said. Talisman, amulet, something else.

She needed it now, whatever it was going to be.

Through the cut flap she could see Will, on his side, looking out at the daylight and blinking. He pushed himself up and started to crawl towards her.

The device rumbled. It was almost too hot to hold.

And then it happened.

In the bear-baiting ring, the wolves all turned, as if they'd heard a signal that human ears couldn't pick up. They crouched and leapt, over the barriers and through the scattering crowd. The device roared like a firework, spitting red and white smoke and sparks and, as they passed through the smoke, the wolves became warriors. Men in wolf skins, tall and strong and straight out of the Dark Ages, swinging axes and swords and heading for the tent.

One axe blow from the biggest of them took the side of the tent out. Lexi could see six grey-robes still fighting, and Al and their grandfather backed with Mursili into a corner, protecting Will, who had one hand on the side of the tent and was trying to stand.

Al looked around as a giant strode past him and swung his axe into two of the grey-robes with one stroke. They flailed backwards onto piles of lace and rolled onto the floor.

Another fighter stepped in next to him and together he and Al took on two grey-robes. As a grey-robe's sword thumped into the warrior's shield, Al ducked and lunged past it. He struck something and the grey-robe screamed.

'Go!' one of the grey-robes shouted. 'Get word to Grendlaw.'

The man who had met them at the table went to duck out through the flap, but Mursili blocked him. The grey-robes were falling back. The Dark Age warriors were winning. They were fearless and powerful and had come ready to fight.

In less than a minute, Al could lower his sword. The warriors were finishing the job and the fight had gone from the word hunters' part of the tent. As he went to check Will, he realised his sword was stuck in his hand. There was blood all over the hilt and turning sticky around his fingers. A grey-robe blade had sliced his forearm and blood was dripping from his knuckles onto the grass.

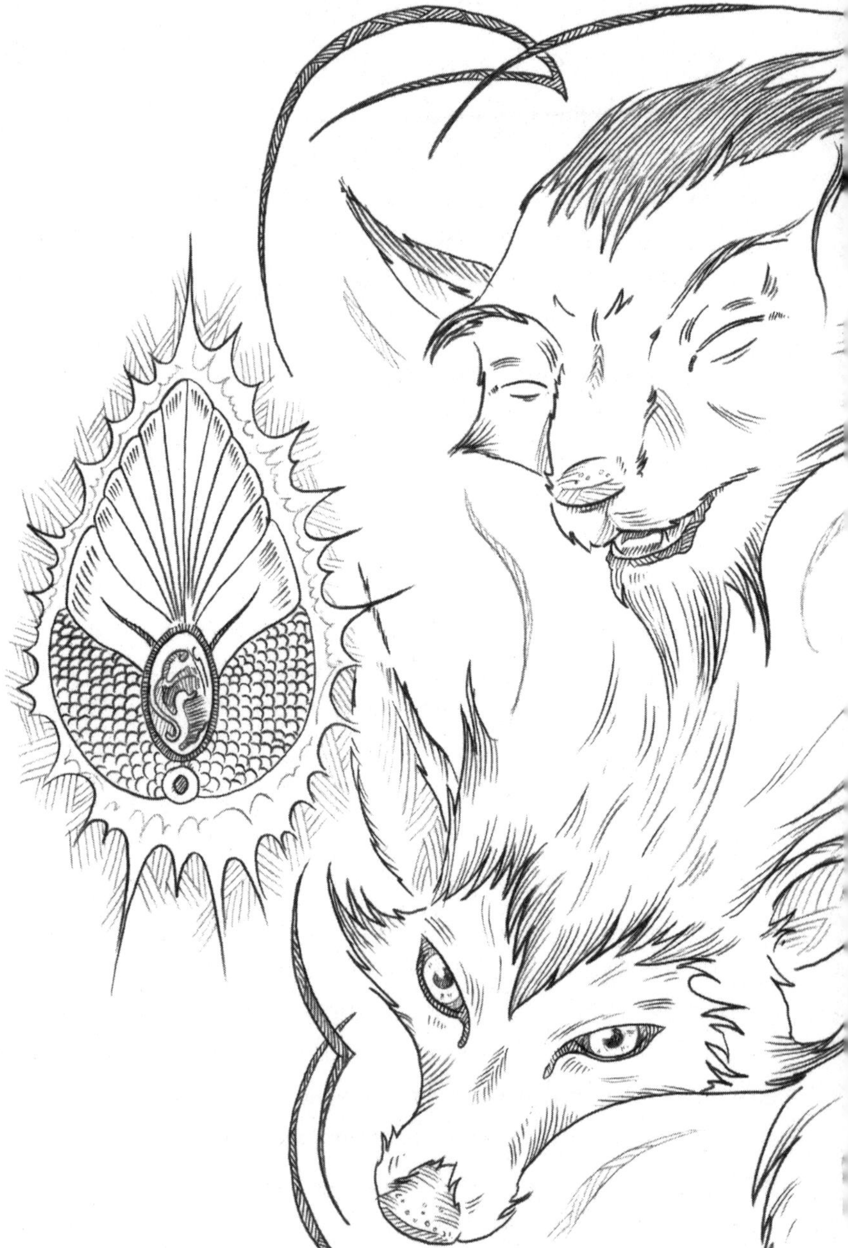

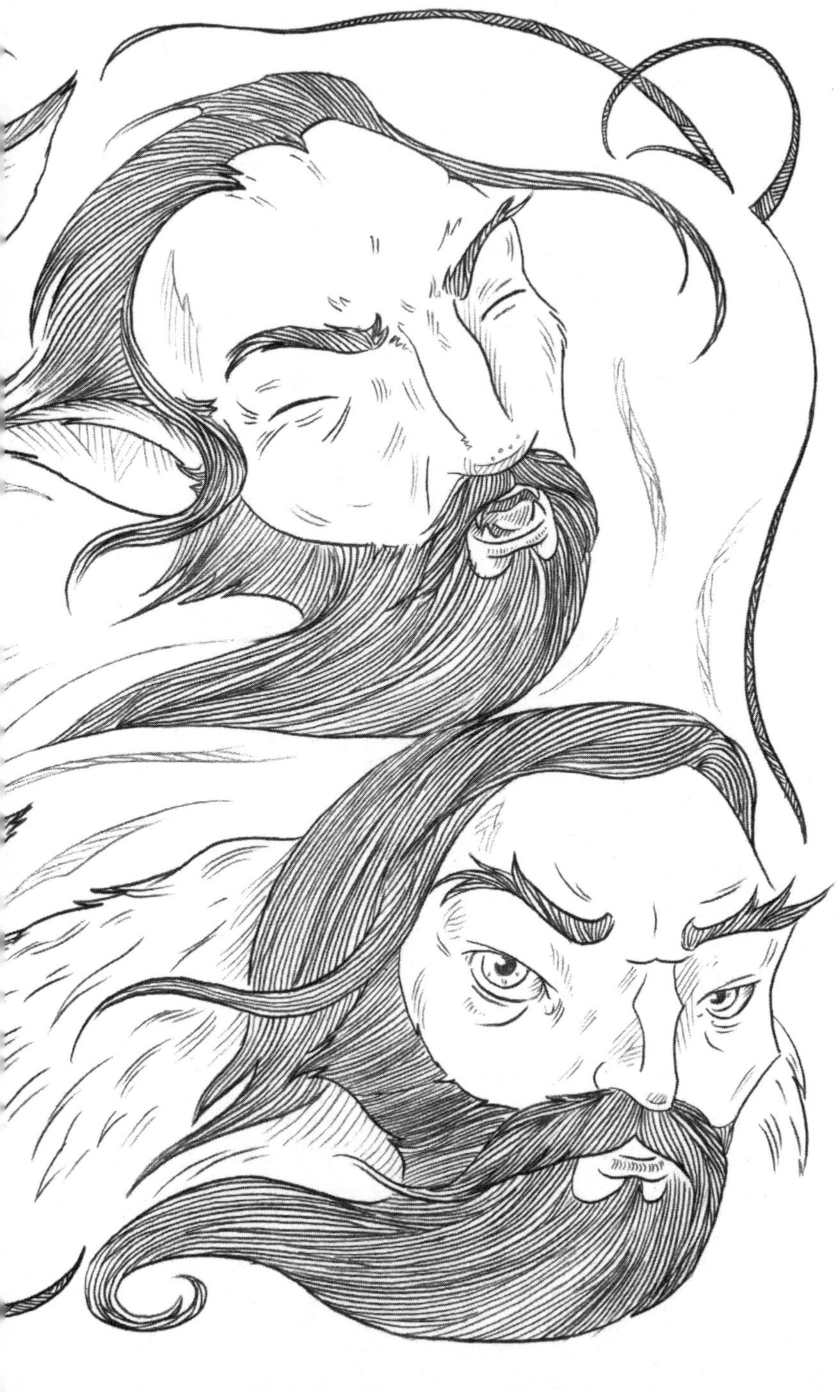

He went down on his knees and pushed the sword away. He reached out with his left arm to balance himself and gripped the grass so that he wouldn't fall over. The dizziness buzzed in his head.

He could hear Lexi talking to Will, checking how seriously he was injured.

'I think—' Will said, and then no more sound came out.

He was pale. He was clutching his side and there was blood on the grass. Lexi grabbed handfuls of lace and clamped them over the wound in his stomach. It was close to the left-hand side. The sword had passed right through him. She had no idea what it might have hit, how badly injured he might be.

She took Will's hand and pressed it down against the wad of lace, while she went through her pack to find her medical kit. There was nothing in it to fix this.

'Help!' she called out to the warriors. 'Did Caractacus send you with any medical supplies?'

'Um, no, we just fight,' one of them said. 'Aethelbert of Secgwic.' He noticed the giant axeman peering over his shoulder. 'This one's Osric Badaxe. He was born big and stayed that way.'

'Grandad!' Lexi needed help from someone. An axe-wielding giant was suddenly useless. She pulled out dressings and crepe bandages.

'We're at the portal,' Will managed to say. 'One more step, then I'm home. Twenty-first century. This'll be fine, then.'

Grandad Al knelt down next to Lexi. 'He's right. We can't fix this here. We have to do whatever we can and move as quickly as possible.'

He wiped antiseptic across the wounds and taped dressings over them, then he and Lexi wound a long crepe bandage around Will to hold the dressings in place and apply some pressure.

Mursili did the same for Al's arm. Al tested the movement in his fingers. Everything still worked. He was less dizzy now.

In the fighting everything in the tent had been knocked over. The portal was somewhere towards the back. Al and Mursili went scrambling for it and Mursili found it beneath a pile of fabric. It was a picture of a woman with a lace border around it and 'Saint Audrey' written along the bottom. The 'A' of Audrey was now a bright golden '& more' button.

They ran over to the others and knelt down beside Will.

'Do you—' Al looked up at the warriors. They were close enough to get swept into the portal.

'First time.' Aethelbert shrugged. 'No idea. The boss just said— Oh, wait. Is this that thing where you press something—'

'Travelling magic.' Osric's voice sounded nothing like it should have. It was as if his nose was blocked. 'We stand back for that, Aethel.'

As they stepped away, Mursili activated the portal and Al found his peg, passed it through the widening hole in the card and locked it.

As the ground shuddered and the fog rolled in, Grandad Al called out, 'Stick close to Will! We'll have to land him.'

679

Isle of Ely
Lands of the
South Gyrwas

Telescopium

$\mathcal{A}$L HAD GROWN used to the darkness of the fall, but now he had his good arm hooked around one of Will's and no sense of how Will was travelling. He felt the air leave his chest and the fall accelerate. Then they swerved. In the shudder at 1066, Will was almost pulled away from him, but he held on.

As the light came in, he could make out Will's face next to him in the cloud. Will saw him and forced himself to smile.

The cloud went from grey to white and then split open, spilling the word hunters into the sky above grassland and a patch of forest with a cluster of buildings in a clearing.

'Fens,' Grandad Al shouted. He was on Will's other side. 'It's Ely again. Much earlier. Land at the edge of the trees.'

He and Al each slid an arm around Will and together the three of them dropped like a giant clumsy bird. The ground came up at them in a rush and kept coming, swampy fenland they could sink in, drown in.

Al twisted to steer and they started to bank. He could feel his grandfather pulling on Will's other side. Slowly their fall shifted. At the treetops they slowed and dropped to the ground where the slope fell down towards the water.

Will lay on his back looking up at the sky. It came out in a whisper, but he managed to speak. 'Don't know why I've been doing all those landings myself till now.'

He undid the belt on his tunic and clenched his teeth as he tightened it over his wounds.

'Saint Audrey.' Mursili was already looking through the trees towards the buildings.

Al checked the peg. 'Yep – same place, but 679.'

Lexi was on her knees loading two fresh eggs into Caractacus's device: one red, one white. 'I'm going to keep this in my hands. We're going for help early this time if we need it. That was a trap. And they weren't trying to capture us, either.'

Al took Will's legs, his grandfather lifted him by the shoulders and together they carried him up the slope and through the willow trees towards the buildings. Mursili followed with all their sacks in his arms. Al felt Will's weight open the wound near his wrist and he saw blood seeping through the bandage and the sleeve of his tunic. He picked up his speed.

Ahead they could hear voices singing a hymn.

They came upon a garden with tools propped against a wall. Mursili took a hoe with an iron blade and a strong shaft and tucked it under one arm. Further along the path was a cart with bundles of cut grass in it. They lifted Will and their sacks into it and Al and his grandfather pulled them along.

'Why is nobody out here?' Lexi had both hands on the device, ready to twist it. 'This is weird.'

They passed a kiln that was still warm, with new pots in a row on the ground outside it.

The singing was louder now and coming from the next building, a stone church. As they reached the doorway, a nun came out to see who was there. She was thin and appeared tired.

'Abbess Aethelthryth,' Al said. He was out of breath and his arm was starting to throb.

The nun looked at Will sitting in the cart, his hand on his wounded side.

'You're too late,' she said. 'She's with the Lord now, and she won't be the last. I'm Seaxburh. Your friend needs the Lord, too. Bring him in. We'll wet his lips with water and add him to our prayers.'

Al and his grandfather lifted Will and their sacks from the cart and helped him over the single step into the church. The altar was lit by candles, and nuns were kneeling on the stone floor praying. On a raised platform, with her head near the altar, a woman in an unbleached linen robe lay with her hands folded across her chest. Around her neck was a strip of plain white lace, covering bulges caused by tumours.

'You're not from here,' Seaxburh whispered to Al, 'but you came to see the abbess?'

'That's right. We've come a long way.' He wanted the portal trigger, whatever it was. It would surely be about Aethelthryth, and Seaxburh seemed like their best chance. 'Please tell us about her.'

He thought he could see tears in Seaxburh's eyes as she went on. 'She was a princess and then a queen. She escaped the king with the aid of a miracle and gave her land and life to God. And now God has come for her. She gave her thoughts to finery in her youth. She had shoes of all colours, and always wore jewels around her neck. She put the tumours down to that.' Seaxburh touched her neck without knowing it. 'She said God was taking her through her vanity, and the envy she'd once stirred in others. But her life has long been virtuous and her presentation plain. I told her that's what God would know. So we've dressed her sickly neck plainly for her now.'

'Perhaps she could heal my friend.' Saints healed people – Al knew that. They sometimes became saints through miracles.

The portal had to show itself here, in this church, somewhere near the body of the abbess. He had to make Seaxburh say something, whatever it needed to be. Something above the murmur of quiet prayer. Perhaps it could be a call to healing.

'Yes, yes.' Her eyes brightened. 'You've come a long way to see her. This was meant to be. You'll be the first.' She looked across at Grandad Al. 'Go to her. Take him to her, all of you.'

Together, the word hunters helped Will forward across the uneven stone floor and through the kneeling nuns towards the body of the abbess.

'Sisters,' Seaxburh said behind them in a louder voice. 'These travellers come with wounds, asking for our sister Aethelthryth. Let us pray that God will heal them in her name.'

The murmur of individual prayers stopped the moment she asked for it and a louder group prayer began, all the nuns praying for God to act through Aethelthryth to save the wounded travellers.

Each time they spoke her name, the glow behind her head grew brighter.

Mursili tucked the hoe under his arm and treated it like a crutch as they moved forward. He scanned from side to side, checking every hooded figure.

They reached the altar safely. Behind the abbess were some of her effects – a white cross on a leather cord, a book of psalms, plans for a future, bigger abbey. On the plans, the first 'o' and first 'm' of the word 'dormitorium' had moved and fused together, with an 'h' and an 'e' joining them to make a bright button that read 'home'. Its light spilt across the Latin notes.

Mursili gave his hoe to Lexi and found the peg in Al's sack. He touched the button and the 'o' started to swell. He glanced around. The nuns' heads were all down in prayer. He slipped the peg into the 'o', locked it and removed the key.

The stones in the floor started to scrape and shake.

The word hunters pulled in close to each other as the glowing rim of the portal shivered and grew. From behind Seaxburh, fog blew into the church and they lifted from the cold stones and the abbess and the island in the fens, and they were gone.

Towers rose and roofs came down in fire. Kingdoms fell and new kings came, struck coins, built towers of their own and were lost in battle. Days, nights, centuries slipped past and Al and his grandfather fitted their arms around Will again and waited to fall back to earth.

Suddenly the air came past them in a rush. The fall had begun.

They could see the coastline below, and the bay islands with their sand dunes, and the red roofs of suburbs as far as the horizon. Then the river, streets, the patch of green that was the park. They slowed down as they drew level with the treetops and eased themselves down to the grass.

Will lowered himself to a sitting position and wrapped his arms around his stomach. He took in a breath and smelt the gum trees. He let the breath go.

'All right,' he said. 'Get me some help.' His whole stomach was sore now and starting to swell.

Grandad Al called an ambulance and, while they waited, they decided on the story. A ball had got stuck up a tree and Will had gone after it. He had fallen and hit the tip of a broken branch on the way down. It had gone right through him, but snapped off and come out as he fell. Mursili went to the nearest tree and broke off a branch to fit the story.

They could hear the sirens within two minutes. Grandad Al went to meet the ambulance at the road. By the time they came over with the stretcher, Will was Grandad Al's nephew and the bandages had been brought from home.

But the ambulance officers weren't too fussed about the details of the story anyway. They needed to know what they needed to know.

They talked it through as they cut off the bandages and checked the wound. One of them put his hand on Will's swollen stomach and then listened to it with a stethoscope.

They lifted him onto the stretcher and pushed it into the back of the ambulance. One of them put an IV line in while the other went to the cab.

Lexi heard him say, 'It's a through-and-through abdominal wound caused by a tree branch. Left flank. He's distended and his bowel sounds are way up. Systolic's one-ten, heart rate one-oh-eight. We're ready to go.'

Less than a minute later they were on their way, with the siren and lights on and Grandad Al travelling with them.

'I heard a lot of stuff then,' Lexi said. 'From one of the ambos. It didn't sound good.'

The ambulance turned the corner. The siren volume dropped, but then lifted to a louder *whoop whoop whoop* to pass through the next intersection.

'They'll be there in ten minutes.' Al was thinking the route through. 'Fifteen max. That'll be okay.'

'It'll be a lot better than being stuck at an abbey on the fens in 679,' Mursili said. 'How lucky that that was a quick one! Not just lucky. We did one or two things right.'

170

Al suddenly felt tired. He crouched down and then sat on the grass. The fingers on his right hand were going numb. The blood on his bandage was starting to dry and darken.

'Better get this fixed, too.' He took the clip off and peeled the bandage away, rolling it as he went.

He lifted the dressing off and, before blood seeped in and filled the wound, he was sure he could see his muscles and tendons in there.

Lexi bent down and put her hand on his shoulder to steady him. 'There were a bunch of us kicking a ball around. You fell on some glass.'

He nodded. It would work. It would do. He felt sick, but he held it in.

By the next afternoon Will was already much better.

Al had eight stitches and a clean dressing and the stiffness he felt in the muscles of his right forearm meant that he used his left hand to flick through sites on the iPad as he sat next to Will's bed. He and Lexi had come straight from school. Grandad Al had picked them up.

Will was sitting propped up in bed with a bag of fluids on a hook above him and a tube leading down to one arm. He was wearing a pair of Grandad Al's pyjamas and he'd put his string of peg keys back around his neck. A sign above his head had 'clear liquids' written on it in pen. There were four beds in the bay. Two were empty and the old man in the other was snoring behind a curtain.

Will had lost quite a lot of blood and the sword had sliced a loop of bowel, but it had missed his left kidney and a lot of other things that mattered. If he managed to avoid infection, he'd be out of hospital in two or three days and okay by normal standards in a week, but not ready for battle for a while. The regular rules didn't apply to word hunters.

'So, most websites run the same couple of paragraphs about Saint Audrey and the fair,' Al told him, 'but what they actually say is that "tawdry" came to mean what it does because everything there was cheap and trashy.'

'Whereas what we saw was that "tawdry" was fine until the Puritans got to it.' Will reached for a cup of water and sucked on the straw. His mouth kept feeling dry. 'First it had the direct link to the saint, then it was just that style of lace – the lace choker. Then people turned on most of Mr Fenwick's niceties, I suppose. All those moral judgements come in and "tawdry" means both trashy and something to do with dirty dealings.' He looked up at the bag of fluids above him and the orange labels stuck on the plastic. 'Hey, I've never had antibiotics before. Good, aren't they? And that anaesthetic was great, too. I didn't vomit at all. We always used to, last century.'

It was easy to forget that Will wasn't what he seemed, that he didn't know the 21st century like a local and that the 1990s birthday on his hospital wristband was a fake.

Al didn't want to think about travelling without him if another word triggered in the next few days. His own arm wasn't right, either. He wondered if they could let one word go, if it happened. Just one.

'Hey, good thing that rat of yours spoke up when he did,' Will said. 'I might not have been the only one to get it in Ely otherwise. He doesn't make a sound most of the time.'

'That's rats for you.' Al hadn't forgotten Doug's shriek in his ear at just the right time. 'Every horror movie has them screeching at anything, but they don't. It's got to be a big deal before they make a noise.'

It felt normal, talking about rats. A year ago that's what Al had been googling – rat details, to make a case for getting one as a pet. Now most of his time online was spent making sense of the past and working out how to survive it.

Lexi and Grandad Al appeared in the doorway.

'Clear liquids didn't give us a lot of choices.' Lexi had a bottle of apple juice in her hand.

'That's fine. Thanks for getting it.' Will took it from her and set it down next to his water. 'I still don't actually feel hungry yet, so it's not as if I'm missing the other options. Apparently that's normal. It sorts itself out once things start moving again in there.' He patted his stomach, which was still swollen.

Lexi shook her head. 'They could have got us all there in Ely. What's going to happen next time? What if a bunch of beefy guys from the Dark Ages isn't enough to save the day? Or what if I get stabbed before I get to turn the thing on? I mean, it's great that we've got our own berserkers, but it's no guarantee we'll be okay. This is us getting lucky – Will in hospital, Al with a cut arm.' She paused and took a breath. She had to say it. Someone had to. 'What if we stopped?'

'I want to stop.' Will moved his pillow. It was hard to get comfortable. 'But if we do, whoever comes along as the next hunter doesn't stand a chance. We're coming across grey-robes far more often and there are more of them. This is escalating. If we stop now, he wins.' They all knew who 'he' was. 'He wins and history changes.'

'Will's right.' Grandad Al couldn't look at Lexi when he said it. 'And if you think finding me changed things – the objects in your house, the books in your room, your grandmother, your father – that'll be nothing compared with what happens if John Hunter goes unchecked. We don't just have to go back and win this for every future word hunter; we need to win it for ourselves and everyone we know. Every one of us is the consequence of a million flukes of history – who met whom and where they went and what they did – and he'll undo thousands of them. From the moment he acts decisively, the history of English and Europe – and us – diverges from the path it had to take to end with us here in this spot.'

However much she'd wanted a different answer, Lexi knew he was right. And there was no point complaining about being chosen over all the other Hunters in Brisbane – or Australia, or the world – because there was no one to complain to and no process to complain about. Caractacus wasn't sitting in the past with a crystal ball, choosing word hunters. She could shout at the dictionary, but that wouldn't make it choose someone else.

Behind the curtain the other patient rolled over, snuffled and started snoring again.

Will looked across and shook his head. 'I'm not expecting a great night's sleep.' He straightened out the elasticised bandage protecting his drip site. 'The other reason we need to keep going and finish the job is we have to get me home. Don't think I don't love your century, but I do miss mine.'

Grandad Al checked his watch and glanced at Lexi and Al. 'Better get you two home as well, while there's time for some homework before dinner. Your mother already thinks it's odd enough that I've brought you along to drop in on some old friend she doesn't even know.'

'Come on,' Will said. 'It's good for them. Meet the old man and listen to his war stories.' He put on a shaky voice. 'I remember the time when I got stabbed in the 1540s. Seems like just yesterday.' He laughed, but his mind was back there without him wanting it to be. He'd had flashes of it ever since – the blade had felt hot and ice cold and like a punch. Then he'd been on his knees as the fight went on around him. 'Hey, what's Grendlaw? We hardly ever hear the grey-robes speak, but one of them in Ely said something about getting back to Grendlaw.'

'I don't—' Grandad Al was about to say he'd never heard of it. Then he realised that was wrong. 'One of them mentioned it in Colchester, too.' He tried to recall more, but he couldn't.

Al googled it on the iPad. 'G R E N D L A W?' It seemed as good a spelling as any. There were only a few hits – the sort of number you'd get if you put in random letters. It had been saved as a domain name and appeared once as the name of a character in a piece of Harry Potter fan fiction. 'I don't think it's a thing. Not now, anyway. And whatever it was there's no record of it.'

'One for Caractacus,' Grandad Al said. 'If we can get to Caractacus.' He turned, as if he was about to move towards the door, but then he stopped. 'Have you ever wondered why we go to London pretty often, but there's a few hundred years around the Dark Ages when we never do?' He wasn't looking for an answer, but none of them had one anyway. 'Caractacus said that too much damage had been done for him to save the British languages in England, so he had to start with the invaders' language and try to make something from it. Have you thought of what could happen if John Johnson smashes English? How much history would be rewritten and how much damage done? We all know the Dark Ages was the last time civilisation collapsed in England.' He pointed to the iPad. 'Al, look up "dark earth".'

Al entered the words. There was plenty of dark earth in the world. 'I'm guessing you don't mean the game or the zombie novel.' Then he found it. '"Dark earth". It's a soil layer in London. It's got charcoal and pulverised brick and tiles in it. It's between the Roman times and the 9th century.'

'That's right. The Roman times when we find pottery and mosaics and bath houses, and the time of King Alfred. And in between? Roman London had up to 60,000 people, but in the Dark Ages collapse London was abandoned. The Roman walls were still there, but in ruins. The city became farmland, with the ploughs sometimes digging deep enough to bring up and, over time, pulverise Roman bricks and tiles and burnt timber. And make dark earth. John Johnson could make that happen. I don't know if he could do it now, in the 21st century, but there are centuries when he could. And then the 21st century would be very different.'

Al minimised the page on the iPad.

Lexi wanted to know enough to argue, or at least put up some alternative. She wanted Al to do it, since he was the designated history nerd. But he just nodded.

⟶   ⟵

Al's stitches came out in a week.

'You and Lexi'll have matching scars on your arms now,' his mother said as she drove him home from the surgery. 'Is it your grandfather doing this? Making you into action heroes?'

Al faked a laugh. 'It's just two accidents. Lexi sleepwalked and I tripped in the park.'

'Yes, but there's all that climbing and bushwalking and whatever else you do. It adds up to quite a few bruises.' She reached out and changed the radio station.

'Yeah, I know. That's the big worry for this generation. We spend loads of time outside doing far too much physical activity, when really we should be inside getting obese and playing PS3 or going to the wrong kind of websites.'

His mother smiled. 'Okay, you've got me there.'

As they pulled up at home, it was the dictionary Al couldn't stop thinking about. It was always like that now. Anytime he was away from it, he wondered if another word had been triggered, if he'd open his bedroom door and see that glow.

He still had no memory of the arm wound, but he found it hard to stop thinking about fighting in the tent, about his eyes adjusting to the dark and the portal being right there, and then Will falling and grey-robes attacking from both sides.

He went straight to his room. Nothing. Life in the 21st century could go on a little longer. When he turned around, Lexi was standing in her doorway across the hall. He shook his head.

'Good,' she said. 'You were moving pretty quickly, so—'

'It's all dark in there. No sign of a word going off. I just wanted to rule it out.'

Weird:

adj, bizarre, strange, involving
the supernatural, concerned with
fate or the Fates
(OE, wyrd, destiny).

& MORE

I T STAYED RULED out for another ten days – just enough time for Lexi and Al to start fantasising that that might be it. Their turn might be over. The dictionary might have stabilised again.

It woke Al at 4.23 on a Saturday morning. Or at least something woke him and the light was there, not green and steady like the numbers on his clock, but golden and flaring and fading with the rhythm it had every time, like breathing. Enough light for him to see Doug's eyes blinking at him.

'Nice to see you're ready.' He propped himself up on his pillow. 'I don't think we'll go yet, though. Don't think the others'd appreciate a call right now. Try to get some sleep.'

Dumb advice. Rats were nocturnal. Al might not have been, but he lay awake for the next half-hour, trying to ignore the light and what was ahead of him. Then he gave up, opened the dictionary and looked at the word. 'Weird'.

He put his hand on his laptop, but talked himself out of opening it. 4.58. He went back to bed. He had soccer try-outs the next morning and Lexi had something planned with her friends.

'Weird'.

He wasn't sure that he slept at all, though there were times when his mind drifted off – to Colchester, where they'd found their grandfather; to the school library, where they'd found the book in the first place. But the drifting slipped into a dream, and the dream saw him lost behind drop sheets until grey-robes came through them and backed him against the wall.

6.10.

When he heard his father go outside for the paper, he got up and poured himself a bowl of cereal.

'Keen to get to soccer?' his father said as he came in the front door, pulling the plastic wrapping from the paper. 'Not usually your time of day. Have you finally worked out what you're missing?'

'If you mean dawn, no.' Al tipped milk onto the cereal. Too much milk. 'I'm just up, that's all.'

'I'm sure your grandparents'll be keen to hear how it all goes.'

'Yep.'

Al had played B grade last year and his father was psyched about him playing A grade. Al knew his grandfather was more interested in him saving life as they knew it, though, and today might be the day. It was impossible to care about soccer. And he couldn't tell his father his main concern was that his lack of sleep might slow down his reflexes in a sword fight.

'What's with all the noise?' It was Lexi. They heard her before they saw her. She appeared at the end of the hall with her hair in a mess. 'This is, like, Saturday, yeah?'

'Soccer try-outs,' their father said, sounding far too upbeat.

'Groan. Not for me. Sleep-in for me. Supposedly.' She folded her arms. 'Although I'm awake now.'

Al picked up the box of cereal and shook it. This time she actually groaned, rather than saying the word. She snatched the box from him, thumped it down onto the counter and sat on a stool.

Their father tipped water into the coffee machine.

'Got some news,' Al said to her quietly.

'Yeah?' She frowned. 'Couldn't it have waited?'

'Not indefinitely. A day or two. Maybe I should just include you in the text.'

Her expression changed. She glanced across at their father, who was carefully scooping coffee. Al nodded.

'If that thing's in your room,' she said, sounding annoyed, 'you should give it to me now.'

'Okay. If it's such a big deal.'

He put his spoon down in his bowl and stood up.

Before they had gone more than a couple of steps down the hall, Lexi whispered, 'What is it?'

'"Weird".'

'Sure, but what is it?'

It was Al's turn to groan. 'We're not doing *that* again.'

He opened his bedroom door and she followed him in. He lifted his schoolbag off the dictionary and found the page.

'Oh. "Weird". Right.' She read the definition. 'Can't say that has me feeling good. Fate, destiny, Old English.'

'Was anything going to make you feel good?'

'No. This dictionary going up in a puff of smoke would have. Waking up and discovering it was all a dream. I would have settled for either of those.'

Al reached for his phone. 'Or, alternatively, a completely unpredictable trip to the past, where one minute they're being rude about your shoes and the next they're trying to kill you.'

'I liked those shoes.' If only the past was just a great place to find interesting shoes. 'So, do we save the world *before* shopping and soccer, or after?'

After, as it turned out. Al sent the text to the others and their replies came in. Will couldn't make it before soccer, so they settled on meeting at Grandad Al and Grandma Noela's place before dinner. That way there would be no need for stories about apple pies or old sick friends. The dinner was already planned.

Lexi caught the bus to Indooroopilly. Her friends texted her most of the way there with ideas about which shops to go to, which movie they might see and the usual mixture of random complaints about their parents and school and annoying boys they possibly liked.

They bought donuts and stood looking cool and saying cool things near a group of boys. Sophie Heard bought a new skin for her phone and spent ages making the choice. Madison Bond said she was allergic to gluten now – well, not really allergic, but she had to be careful. They had an argument about gluten and donuts.

And all the time, deep in the *Curious Dictionary*, 'weird' was humming away. The horrible past lay in wait, but in the present there seemed to be such a waste of energy on things that didn't really count.

Al's soccer try-out didn't go well. He got through the skills part all right, but he didn't contribute a lot when they broke into teams. That was how the coach described it.

Al hovered around the edge of the action, not caring much about what was going on and at the same time knowing he had to come away without an injury. He could hear his father shouting from the sidelines.

The C team. That's where he ended up. A step down from last year.

'I don't know what went wrong,' his father said in the car on the way home. 'You just— I don't know. Maybe we could ask for a regrading. Say you had a virus. Something like that.'

'I'm okay with it.' Al really didn't want to talk about it, but figured they were going to, probably all the way home.

'Some of those boys are too big. Too old or too big. Does anyone check those things? It's not fair.' Mike Hunter thought his boy was A-grade material, that was clear.

'It's really okay.' Al tried to hide the smile. He didn't care about the grading. Any other year, his father's response would have been exactly what he wanted. 'Anyway, it's for the fun of it – right? It's not all about winning and losing and stuff.'

'Yes, but—' Mike Hunter wondered how many times he'd made that point. Now he had to live up to it. 'That's exactly right. It's for the fun. And you're good enough to have fun in A grade, but C'll be great, too. And A grade'll still be there next year.'

'It wasn't my day, Dad. That's all there is to it.'

His father took one hand from the steering wheel and put it on Al's forehead. 'A fever, maybe?'

'We'll check your gear now, before I fire up the barbecue,' Grandad Al said, as Mike put beer in the fridge.

Al and Lexi both had their backpacks slung over one shoulder. Al's had the added weight of the dictionary, but he was trying to pretend it wasn't there.

Their grandfather pointed to the stairs. 'Mine's down there in my study. Why don't you bring yours down and we'll check them all at the same time.' He had come up with a story about a backpack product recall, and a test you could do to see if the pack was faulty. 'There's a device they sent me.'

Mike was trying to twist the top off a beer. 'I think it's the kind that needs a bottle opener,' he said to no one in particular.

Grandma Noela had plastic salad servers in her hands and was tossing a potato salad, while their mother was shaking dressing in a jar.

As Lexi and Al followed their grandfather down the stairs, they heard her say, 'It's the wasabi. That's the secret. Not too much of it, but it gives the dressing a bit of zing.'

Lexi reached out for the cord and turned on the light. 'They don't really pay any attention at all, do they?'

'Practically none.' Grandad Al picked up his backpack from the floor. 'And yet we put all that effort into making up stories for them.'

He opened the door to the carport. Will and Mursili were standing there, waiting.

'Are you sure you're ready for this?' Grandad Al looked Will up and down.

'I'm ready. Go on, punch me.' Will lifted his arms out to his sides. 'Don't punch me. But I'm ready. I'll be an asset, not a liability.'

'Here's what I've got,' Mursili said, checking the notes on his phone. None of them had hunted 'weird' before, so he'd spent some time googling. 'The "destiny" meaning is Old English, and it changed more recently. The "odd" meaning is only a couple of hundred years ago, so I'm guessing that'll be our first stop. Then Old English. Beyond that it's "wurthis" in Proto-Germanic and that comes from a root "wert" in Proto-Indo-European.'

'Could be thousands of years, then?' Al was pretty sure Proto-Indo-European was as far back as European language had been traced.

'Could be.'

When Al opened the backpack, Doug slid off the dictionary and back into his nest. Somehow, despite lives being on the line, Doug had added some Saint Audrey's lace from Ely to the matted wool from Bruges.

Al opened the dictionary on the bonnet of his grandfather's car. 'Since it's "weird", maybe Lexi should press it.'

She pushed him towards it with her shoulder. 'Just do it.'

He touched the button and felt it give way under his finger. The golden light spread out as it crackled across the page.

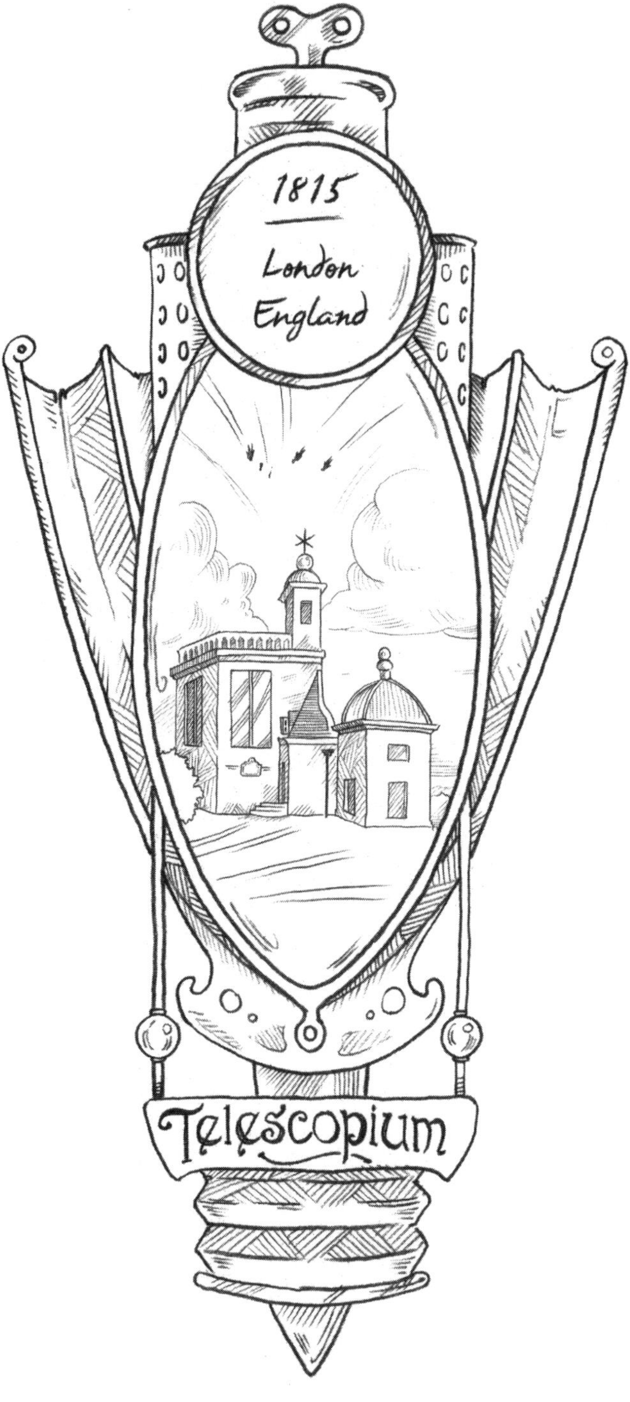
1815
London
England
Telescopium

*T*HE WORD HUNTERS dropped into blackness and over the rush of bumps that began each fall into the past. They hit clear air, but not for long.

The cloud brightened and parted, and dropped them out over a grey city divided by a grey river. There were a few factories trailing smoke and a haze drifting off on the breeze. It was London again and they were falling north of the Thames. Well north of the Thames.

There was no landmark in sight and no clear ground of any size. They dropped towards rows of houses, with no obvious place to land.

'Trees,' Grandad Al pointed just below where they were falling.

There was a patch of grass there, and it would at least bring them all down in the same spot. They banked as they dropped and, again at the height of the treetops, slowed for a steady landing.

They were in a churchyard, beside a brick church with two rows of arched windows and a white stone steeple with a clock.

'Christopher Wren.' Grandad Al looked up at the steeple. 'I bet that's his work. The architect who built lots of churches in London after the Great Fire.'

'Which was 1666, and the church isn't new.' Al wanted to get in on the history theorising. 'Plus there were signs of industrial activity.'

'Here's a brilliant idea, Sherlock,' Lexi said. 'There's a peg in that fancy bag of yours that'll tell you exactly when this is.'

Al's bag was a leather satchel on a strap. And, yes, it was fancier than usual and looked designed to complement his clothes. He wore a black hat, a white linen shirt with a stiff collar, a white waistcoat and a long black coat. Finally, his pant legs went all the way down to his boots, which came almost to his knees.

Lexi had a white dress with a high waistline and a ginger coloured cape. She wore a bonnet and her hair fell around her ears in tight ringlets.

'I'm going to get sick of carrying this pretty quickly.' She lifted up her wicker basket. 'I seriously hope grey-robes haven't made it to wherever we are.'

'You'd probably be okay if they had.' Finally, Al wasn't in disgraceful leggings and Lexi looked worse than he did. 'They probably wouldn't even think you were one of us. They'd just think you'd fallen off your tuffet while you were eating your curds and whey. Or that you were one of those plain but clever girls in books, who had a massive sad crush on some guy with mutton-chop whiskers.'

'Look, I—' She had practically no comeback, but she had to say something. 'You've never even read those books.'

'Watched the movies.' Al had suffered through more bonnet movies than he cared to count. 'Maybe we should get moving before the spider sits down beside you and frightens you away.' He had the peg in his hand. '1815. We're a long way from the Battle of Waterloo, so we should be okay. Not that we should make assumptions. There's also this.'

He lifted out a book. Doug stretched out and shook his head. He could deal with the sudden bag changes, but he really didn't like the times when something new and heavy ended up on top of him. He sniffed at the air. Smoke, badly managed toilets, thin soup.

The book had a plain black leather cover, with text on it in gold that read, '*St Leon* by William Godwin Vol I'.

'Maybe this is Saint Leon's?' Will looked around for a sign that had the church name on it. 'It's only a hundred years before my time. I can't think of a Saint Leon's in London. There's a Saint Leonard's in Shoreditch, but this isn't it. Let's try around the front.'

As they followed the path down the slope and past the side of the church, they noticed a newly planted tree. It had ropes leading from its trunk to iron pegs in the ground. Mursili pulled one up and it turned out to be as long as a Roman sword. He gave it to Will and took the other for himself. He couldn't imagine winning a fight with it, but he could imagine not losing one, buying time for Lexi to activate Caractacus's device and call up their berserkers.

The door to the church was well above ground level, and they crouched down and walked under the steps that led to it, then past the end of a low wall and out onto a street. There were no signs showing the church name and, when they looked up the steps, the door was shut. The only person in sight was a man sitting in the driver's seat of an empty carriage, holding the reins of the two stationary horses. His hat was on the seat beside him and he was gazing down the street and humming to himself.

'Well, there's a man not too busy to answer a question,' Grandad Al said. He strode over and called out, 'Excuse me.'

The driver sat up straight and accidentally pulled on the reins, making the horses take a step before he stopped them.

'Sorry, sir. Thought you were the guv'nor come out of doors without me noticing.' He took a good look at Grandad Al. 'I was away somewhere. What can I do for you?'

'We're wondering, is this church Saint Leon's, or is there anything connected with Saint Leon around here?'

'Saint Leon? No, I can't say I—' He picked up his hat and placed it in his lap, while he thought about the question. 'There's a Saint Leonard's at Shoreditch, but no one's ever called it Saint Leon's. Shoreditch church, they call it. This one here's Saint James's. Always has been. And I don't think they've got any bits of a Saint Leon in there or anything like that. Relics, or what have you.' He'd been frowning, but his expression suddenly changed. 'Tell you who might know. Mister Godwin. William Godwin. Didn't he write a book called *St Leon*? Haven't read it, but I've heard the name. His shop's five minutes from here, 41 Skinner Street.'

He gave them directions and pointed the way back past the church and down the street.

'So it's the author that's the thing, not the saint,' Lexi said when they were out of earshot. 'From the look of it. Any of you history nerds fill in any blanks with this one?'

When no one else spoke, Grandad Al said, 'I don't know *St Leon*, but I think William Godwin was known for more than his writing. He's connected to someone—' But the particular someone wouldn't come.

They made a right turn. Skinner Street was two blocks away and 41 was easy to find. It was in a terrace of brick houses with arched front doorways and white trim around their windows, and it had a sign next to its open door that read 'The Juvenile Library: Wm Godwin, prop'.

'No sign of trouble out here.' Will was checking the street. 'No one likely to block our escape if we need to get out in a hurry.'

The only people in sight were waiting with buckets for their turn at a water pump.

From the doorway, the word hunters could hear a conversation inside.

'But Father, we're simply living the life you believe in,' a girl's voice said. 'It's not enough to—'

'Mary. I won't have you telling me what is and isn't enough.' The father sounded far from happy. 'Nor what I believe in. You didn't come here for that, and you will not have my blessing today for it. Or for this—' He stopped himself. His voice had been rising and getting louder. 'Union.' It was clear he'd stopped to pick the word carefully. 'I agreed to see Percy to speak about his new poem, and that's what we will do.'

'You love it, don't you, Father?' Mary's voice said. 'It's Percy's own emotions, in their purest form. Tell me you think it's brilliant.'

Al stepped past his grandfather as quietly as he could. They might have been waiting for someone to say something about 'weird', but he wanted to see who was doing the talking. The shop was crammed with bookshelves and, if he stepped between two of them, he could just manage to look past another to see the shop counter.

An older man with a bald head and a red nose stood behind it in a faded coat holding several sheets of paper. A younger couple – who must have been Percy and Mary – had their backs to the door. Percy had a long sleek black coat and a turned-up white shirt collar and Mary was dressed quite like Lexi, but a few years older. Not many, though.

'It's not finished,' Percy said, when the older man hadn't spoken for a while.

'Really?' The older man looked up from the pages. 'It's long already for something not finished, though when I

first read it I did think it stopped rather than finished. Most people won't understand it, you know.'

Percy looked like he was about to take offence, but then he said, 'I don't write for most people, William.'

'No. Nor answer to them, Mr Shelley. That's right too, isn't it?' William Godwin said it sternly, but then he gave just a hint of a smile. 'Sometimes you need to let me be a father, and to accept that some of your qualities are more easily prized at a distance. There's a line I was searching for.' He turned the page towards Percy and ran his finger along the words. '"Mutable as shapes in the weird clouds."'

Every word hunter heard it. Somewhere nearby, the portal had surely been activated. Al glanced back at the others. His grandfather drew a sheet of paper in the air, as if he was about to read poetry aloud. He put his hand in the middle of the space he'd marked out and open and shut it. He was miming a portal. No, he was suggesting the portal was on the page William Godwin was showing Percy Shelley. Al sneaked a look back around the shelf. There was no sign of portal light coming from any of the pages. He shook his head.

'This "weird" isn't in common use, is it?' William Godwin was saying. 'I know of it as a word once used to refer to fate, and by the Scots in connection with witches, but I don't think you mean either of those.'

'No, it's a new use. It's come up in conversation and I think it's a workable fit for verse. It means odd or strange.'

'Really.' William Godwin seemed to want to make up his own mind about how workable it was. 'I suppose your friend Byron says it all the time?'

'Let's go,' Grandad Al whispered to the other word hunters. 'It has to be in here.'

He cleared his throat and stepped forward, with the heels of his boots clunking on the boards. William Godwin leant along the counter to look around the shelves.

'Come in, sir,' he called out, seeing three well-dressed men with a boy and girl in the last year of their childhood. His tone was different, warm and welcoming. It was as if the tension of his conversation with Percy had never existed. 'Come in, all of you. Books for the young folk, is it? Let me know if I can help you with anything in particular.'

'Thank you, Mr Godwin.' Grandad Al took off his hat. 'They seem sure they know their own minds, but we'll gladly call on your expertise if we need it.'

'Give it a few years.' William Godwin waved them into the shop. 'They'll be even surer of their own minds then.'

The word hunters spread out across the aisles, moving up and down them, looking for the telltale glow of the portal. Al wondered if it would be obvious, or somewhere inside a book. Grandad Al went towards the counter in case it was there after all. Al could hear him being drawn into the discussion about the poem.

'The working title's "The Spirit of Solitude",' he heard Percy say, 'but that's more of a description. I need something sharper.'

Two aisles away and towards the front of the shop, it was Lexi who found the portal. She saw the light pulsing from between two books and pulled them both out.

'I've got it,' she called out, because there was no reason not to. 'I've found the one I want.'

It was a book bound in navy-coloured leather, and the gold letters on the cover read, '*Tales from Shakespeare*, as told by Charles & Mary Lamb.' The '&' had lifted from the surface of the book and sat on a bright golden button with the word 'more' written neatly around it.

As the other word hunters came along the aisle from both directions, she pushed the button back into the book, and the hole it left widened around her finger. Al already had the peg in his hand.

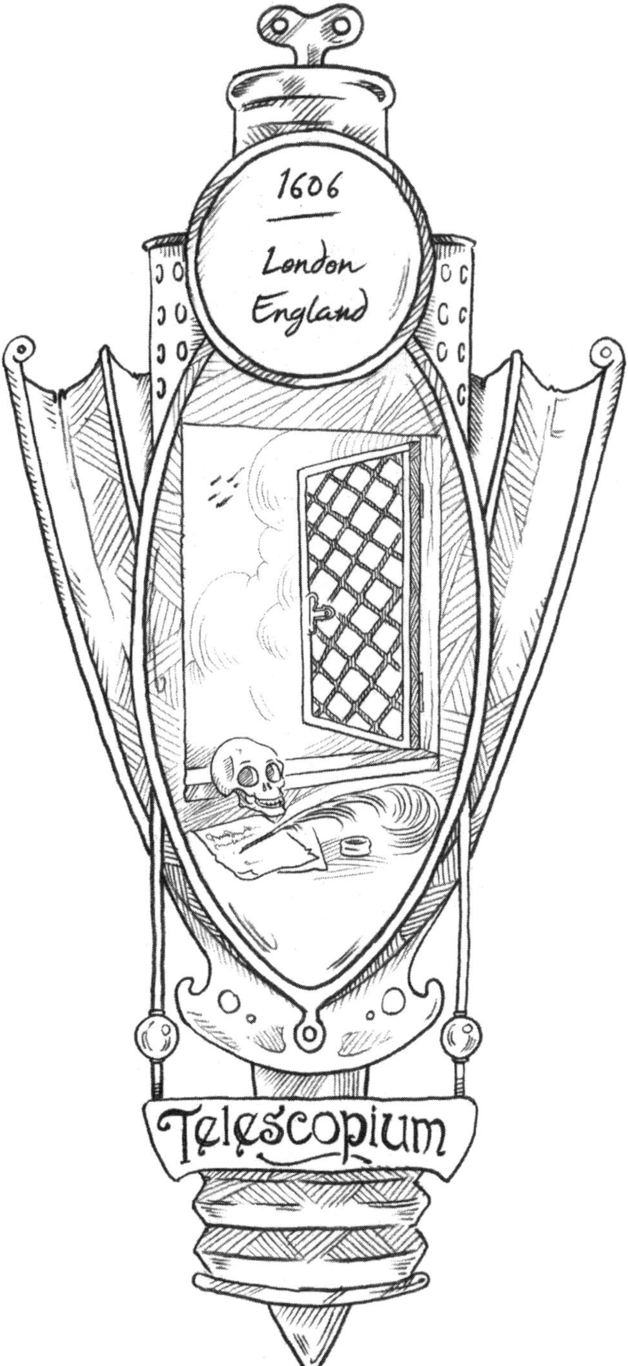
1606
London
England
Telescopium

$\mathcal{T}$HEY DROPPED BRISKLY and then more sluggishly, as if something had pulled them back. But they kept falling. Into the 1600s, Al thought. Into the danger zone.

There was a thump as the cloud split, and they were loose in the sky above a city. London again.

London, but south of the river, just, and falling towards a familiar thatched 'o' with a thatched square jutting out into the middle of it. The Globe Theatre.

'Outside! Outside!' Lexi shouted. Suddenly the shape of it felt suffocating. The grey-robes had been there last time and it looked like an easy place to be trapped.

She swerved and the others followed.

'What's wrong?' Grandad Al called out as he caught up with her.

'It's the Globe. Shakespeare's theatre.' She moved to correct her flight. She'd swerved too hard and was taking them off course. 'We got attacked when we were there with "dollar".'

He stuck beside her, and the others slid across so they'd land as close together as they could.

They came down next to the tall whitewashed walls of the theatre. On the other side of the street was a smaller theatre, the Rose, and a narrow lane leading down to the Thames. The tops of the half-timbered houses directly opposite jutted out over the street, but most of their shutters were closed. Not far away a woman was selling eels from buckets on a cart. She had a customer and there were other people on the street too, but none in grey robes.

Al opened his sack to find the peg. Doug ran up his arm and his whiskers twitched – toilets, salt, meat, sweat, not a clean smell in the air.

'Same year as last time.' Al showed the peg to the others.

Lexi groaned. 'This has to be trouble.'

'If it's trouble we'll be ready.' He wanted to have something better to say. 'We didn't see any initials on that last step. Maybe we're the first to do "weird". In which case, maybe the grey-robes don't know about it.'

'It's 1606 and we've landed at the Globe. It's Shakespeare. More than a thousand words go through Shakespeare.' He hadn't come close to convincing her. 'That's why there's the bump, remember? If you were a grey-robe in 1606 and you had no leads, this is where you'd hang out. You'd just pick the word hunters off, one by one.'

'Well, there's five of us this time,' Will said. 'Not one. And we're expecting them to be here. And it's where we met John Johnson last time. If he's here, we could finish this.'

Lexi took a deep breath. 'And we've got our berserkers.' She set her sack on the ground and undid the tie. 'Which means there's more than five of us.' She smiled. 'And one of us is an axe-wielding giant.'

'You can't tell me the grey-robes are ready for that,' Mursili said.

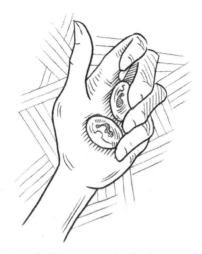

'No.' Lexi took Caractacus's device out and rubbed the two glass eggs with her thumb. 'Okay, meltdown over. What's our plan?'

They were dressed again in calf-length pants and rough coats with rope belts. They were the carpenter's men, there to do work on the stage. This time, though, they would arm themselves and look for the grey-robes first. The last thing the grey-robes would expect would be a pre-emptive strike.

They left the street for the narrow alley beside the building and circled around, past closed entrances for audiences and a low door set into the wall at the bottom of some steps. The alley branched and they followed the wall, checking every shadow, every doorway, every window open just a crack in the houses on the other side.

There was a bang as a shutter slapped against a wall above them. Lexi dropped her sack and gripped the device in both hands, ready to twist it.

'I'll give you a minute,' a woman's voice called out. She had a bucket on the windowsill.

Grandad Al thanked her and they kept moving. As soon as they were out of range, they heard the contents of the bucket splatter onto the ground.

The alley ended at an area of cleared land, with bushes growing against the theatre wall. Ahead another alley began. At the first building a man came out of a wide doorway pushing an empty wooden barrel. He rolled it along the bumpy ground past the theatre and away from the word hunters.

Doug nosed his way to the top of Al's sack. He could smell bread, yeasty beer, nuts, salted fish.

'Catering,' Grandad Al said when they reached the building and could see inside. There were more barrels, along with sacks of grain and a pile of wooden trays. 'This looks like

where they do the food and drink for the theatre. I'd never thought of that. It seems like a much more modern idea.'

The theatre wall had a double door facing the entrance to the catering building.

'So that's where they take it in,' Will said. He walked over to the door and tried the handle. It opened. 'It's probably the tradesmen's entrance, too, when there's not a show on. It could be a good way in. It might take us to some tools or other things we could use as weapons if we had to. There's nothing like that out here. No grey-robes either.'

Al could picture the way it would work. 'Yeah, and even if they see us coming in – the grey-robes, if they're in there – they'll see five workers coming in the door that workers use. What they're waiting for is one word hunter dropping from the sky into the middle.'

Carefully, Will pushed the door open. Al followed him in. They were at the side of the elevated stage, which had a group of actors on it, talking. Arguing. At the end of the stage, some steps led down to a door and the area underneath. The door was closed with a bolt and a padlock. To the left was the empty arena where they'd landed last time. To their right, some old pieces of set were leaning against the wall and beyond them was an open door. The room it led into was dark, but Al could see buckets and broad wooden-handled brushes caked with whitewash. There was no one around, other than the actors on stage.

Al moved towards the open door. He could picture grey-robes inside, crouching, waiting. He told himself not to be stupid. Word hunters were only here for the word, and therefore the stage. A workroom out the back couldn't possibly be a trap. There was no word to hunt in there.

He checked the others were with him and he pushed the door until it met the wall. There were buckets, rolls of twine, sacks of powder and a pile of straw, but also hammers, a saw, crowbars. They made their choice of weapons.

'Perfect,' Will said, as he tested the weight of the crowbar in his hands. 'We're ready and we're completely in disguise.' He pointed the crowbar in the general direction of the stage. 'Now, unless anyone can spot any grey-robes that need sorting out, the play's the thing. And it's about to get "weird".'

They moved back around to the side of the stage and then onto the straw, where the audience would sit.

The actors were on stage, three of them in ragged dresses and with fiendish make-up. One of them was having more purple added to his cheeks.

'Do we really need this, William?' He wasn't happy. 'We look ridiculous. This is just because we were too picky earlier, isn't it?'

'Don't blame me, Richard.' Shakespeare was holding the script in his hand and trying not to laugh. 'Blame the Scots. It's a Scottish play, and the consulting of the Fates was always part of the Macbeth story.

'But what about white robes, or something? The Fates could be—'

'We're always doing white robes. Boring. We need you to be far more interesting, far more witchy.' He laughed. 'Just

close your eyes and think of the takings. Aren't you on three-quarters of five-eighths of a third of everything we make? You'll do well enough out of this one, Mr Burbage.'

'I have a double share, because I put in more money at the start – simple as that. That's no reason to dress me like—' He waved his arms around, as if words couldn't do justice to his ridiculous appearance. 'And weird sisters?' He pointed to a line in the script. 'Why call us that?'

'Because it's a Scottish play and "weird" is Scots for witch.'

Al watched for the portal but there was no sign of it. He glanced around the entrances and the high rows of seating. There was no one in sight. No John Johnson, no grey-robes. Just the usual debate going on on stage.

'You really are very aware the king's from Scotland, aren't you?' Richard said.

Shakespeare decided not to bite. '"Weird" is also Chaucer's word for the Fates. See how it brings together England and Scotland? The king will like that.'

'Only once William's pointed it out to him,' one of the other witches said. The actors around him laughed.

'And will he thank us for dressing his Scottish witches up like this?' Richard wasn't going to be diverted. 'For putting Robert and Henry and me in these rag dresses and giving us this lurid make-up?' He held up his hand to signal to the man doing his make-up that enough was enough. 'Is this the look you call weird?'

Robert struck a witchy pose, sticking his bent arms out like the branches of a leafless tree. 'After this play, it's the look everyone'll call weird.'

He turned back to the script. Golden light glinted in his eyes. On the pages in his hand, the portal button had appeared.

'All right.' Shakespeare clapped his hands. 'Lines down. You're all looking lovely, so let's have a run through.'

'Sorry, gents, but we'll have to interrupt for a moment,' Will said, as he stepped forward. 'We're Mr Street's men, come to make some repairs.' He held up the crowbar as evidence.

The witches had all set their scripts down on the stage at their feet, and the portal was blinking in front of Robert as the word hunters climbed the stairs.

'Now?' Shakespeare didn't look pleased. 'Does it have to be now?'

'You'll hardly notice a thing, sir,' Will told him. 'We can work around you. Perhaps if the actors could just move a little further back—'

'And leave the scripts right where they are,' Shakespeare added quickly. 'Lines are supposed to be down so let's leave them down.'

The actors took a few steps back, with Richard Burbage dragging his script after him with his toe and staring at Shakespeare, daring him to say something.

Shakespeare couldn't resist. 'I suppose some of us have been so busy counting all our cash that we've only managed to learn three-quarters of five-eighths of a third of our lines so far.'

Will and Mursili moved each side of Lexi with their crowbars and she walked straight for the script that had the portal.

She was only three steps away when the floor fell out beneath her feet and she dropped through a trapdoor. Will

lunged at it, but it slammed shut. Through the floor he heard voices. Someone was down there.

'They've got her!' he called out to the others. 'They're under the stage.'

'Good thing you're here.' Richard Burbage stepped forward to look more closely at the trapdoor. 'That could have happened under any of us.'

Will and Mursili tried to stick their crowbars into the gap around the trapdoor, but it wasn't wide enough. Will lifted his crowbar over his head and smashed it down onto the trapdoor, but it barely dented it.

'The door at the side!' Al shouted. He was already running.

He jumped from the steps and the others followed.

'The door's locked,' Shakespeare called out. 'Padlocked. We think we had people breaking in from the outside that way. Burbage has a key at home. Street has one too.'

Will jammed his crowbar through the padlock and pulled till it broke into pieces. He yanked at the door, but someone inside was keeping it shut.

Above them all on stage, the actors were shouting. Something was happening up there, too.

Al ran forward, slid his saw under the door and thrusted it in and out. A man on the other side cried out as Will hit the door with his shoulder.

As the door gave way, smoke swirled out, white and red, and dogs of all kinds called from the neighbouring streets jumped past the word hunters and into the dark cellar.

They landed as warriors, and Osric Badaxe's blade brought up sparks as it crashed into the floor at the end of his first swing.

At the far end of the cellar, Al saw a rectangle of daylight, just for a second, and then it was gone. A grey-robe swung something at him and he fended it off with the saw. A warrior pushed his shield forward and went after the grey-robe as he backed away.

The grey-robes had knives, and they couldn't match the men from the Dark Ages with their swords and axes.

Al rushed over to where he could make out the shape of Lexi on the floor. She was sitting awkwardly with her sack tipped out around her, starting to drag herself back towards the wall.

'My ankle,' she said, when she saw him. 'That's all. I just landed badly. Have you got him?'

'Who?'

'John Johnson. He's here. I'm sure he is.' She peered into the dark.

The fight was ending. Grandad Al pushed the broken door fully open and more light came in. Everyone lying on the floor was in a grey robe. No John Johnson.

'I saw him,' Lexi said. 'He had a hat and a cape on. He tried to shove a cloth into my face. It had a chemical smell, like nail polish remover.'

'The other door.' Al remembered the rectangle of daylight. 'He left at the start of it.'

He ran over to the door and fumbled in the dark to open it. He found the handle and pulled it, but something had wedged the door shut.

'Mine, little man,' Osric Badaxe said behind him.

He swung his blade and the door splintered. He pushed the pieces into the alley and ducked through the doorway to step outside. Al followed him. The alley was empty. John

Johnson was gone, somewhere in the warren of laneways that he surely knew well and that the word hunters didn't know at all.

'No!' Lexi called out, as she watched Al standing there. 'We got so close. That could have been the end of it.'

Grandad Al put his arm around her and helped her up.

'I think I've found the cloth.' Will picked it up and sniffed it. 'Ether.' He turned his head quickly and held the cloth away from his face. 'They didn't have ether in the 1600s, did they?'

'I think it's mid-19th century before it's an anaesthetic.' Al tried to recall more, but he was at least certain of that.

'There was a Persian in the 8th century—' Grandad Al couldn't think of his name. 'I'm sure you're right about its anaesthetic use being 19th century, though, even if people were able to make it earlier.'

'Alexandria. The library.' Al could still picture the fleeting image of John Johnson there among the shelves as the library burnt in 48BC. 'I reckon that's where he got it from. Someone worked it out thousands of years ago and that's when we lost it.'

'And he tried to gas me with it.' Lexi stood up as straight as she could on her good leg. 'I think that's the real point. We have no idea what he's going to attack us with next. Caractacus isn't the only one pulling scrolls from back then.'

One of the warriors cleared his throat. He had the blade of his axe on the ground and he was leaning on the handle in the way a road worker might lean on a spade or a pick. 'I don't mean to interrupt, but I think our job's done. No more fighting called for here.'

'Yes, thank you.' Grandad Al took more of Lexi's weight as she leant his way again. 'Thank you, all of you. I'm sorry we didn't finish it.'

'Looks finished to me.' The axeman shrugged.

'Yes, you did everything we could have asked for.' The full story was too complicated. 'You saved my granddaughter.' John Johnson was gone, but the situation could have been far worse. He didn't want to think about it. 'Till next time, then.'

Will led the way up the stairs to ground level with a grey-robe's dagger in each hand.

Lexi's ankle hurt with each step. One grey-robe had grabbed at her when she'd fallen through, but she'd elbowed him in the stomach and then crunched Caractacus's device into his nose.

They'd had two candles lit and she'd seen the knives some of them carried. She'd twisted the device and the marbled light had glowed in an instant and the smoke had come out with a hiss.

'Zounds!' one of them had said as he stepped back. 'What devil stirs within her lamp?'

Even John Johnson had backed away, with the ether-soaked cloth held at arm's length and a hand over his mouth and nose.

The daylight in the Globe seemed almost too bright. Lexi had stopped walking and her grandfather was carrying her in his arms. She wanted to cry with the pain and the shock, but it was enough of a fight to get breath in, and then out again.

She had been away from the pegs in the cellar. She had heard the English of 1606, just as it was. She had looked into the face of their enemy. The device had saved her, bought her time until the door broke and the dogs came.

The actors were clustered at the far end of the stage with wooden prop swords in their hands.

Richard Burbage banged his against a pillar until he had silence from the others. 'All who refuse to keep working on this play until William agrees to stop messing around with witches say "Aye".'

'This is ridiculous,' Shakespeare said, though not with much hope of stopping it.

'It was havoc, William,' one of the others insisted. 'Your witches somehow let slip the dogs of Southwark and they came charging through here in the very moment Mr Street's men went mad and started smashing things. And here they are now, with knives.' He was pointing at Will.

Will shrugged, as if a knife in each hand didn't mean much. 'You were right, Mr Shakespeare. People had broken in. They were down there. All sorted out now though. Well, the robbers are. Bit of work to do on the doors. We'll be back later for that.'

Richard Burbage whacked his wooden sword against the pillar again and the other actors turned to face him. 'And there was that trapdoor. That needs fixing before we can safely work on the stage again.'

Will picked up the script that had the portal, which was glowing as if nothing had happened. Al pulled over the sacks they'd dropped and reached into his for the peg.

'One more after this,' he said as he pushed it into the glowing hole and brought the arms down.

One more step before they were home. One more chance to catch the man who had just escaped them. There were two ways of looking at it and, right now, Al wanted John Johnson to be there, wherever they were going, whatever weapons he had. They needed to stop him now, before he knew more.

The double doors they'd come in through blew open, fog poured in from the alley and the stage began to shudder.

492

Northwic
East Angle Lands

Telescopium

*T*HE WORD HUNTERS fell and kept falling, through the Renaissance turbulence, through the acceleration on the other side of Caxton and the swerve that came next. This time, it was a long, long way down. There was a clear drop of centuries, then a shudder. Al had braced himself for it. 1066 and Norman French.

They slid through the smooth air of King Alfred's time and shot through the centuries before. They'd clocked a thousand years in one fall, Al was sure of it. Then the nausea hit. The Dark Ages.

They dropped from cloud above a river village they now knew well. Northwic. Caractacus.

Lexi searched for signs of anything different as they fell, and she knew the others would be doing that too. Army camps, a trail of hoof prints, damage to Caractacus's house – though it always looked pretty wrecked from the outside anyway. The grey-robes hadn't been visible at the Globe or at Saint Audrey's fair, but it would be harder to hide near a shack on the outskirts of Northwic. She didn't know how many of them might fit inside Caractacus's place, since the inside was much bigger than it looked. Only with Caractacus and Doctor Who did that make any sense.

She swerved with the others and landed on her feet in

mud next to the pig sty. There was a flash of pain from her twisted ankle, but she managed to keep her balance. She checked the soft ground around her, but all she could see were occasional sandal prints and small circular dents.

Al and Mursili held onto the pig sty railing and tried not to be sick. Will turned in a slow circle, checking everything. Lexi reached into her sack and pulled out Caractacus's device. It was empty. She hadn't reloaded after the Globe. She got her grandfather to hold her sack out of the mud while she searched for the red and white eggs.

Doug's nose poked through the top of Al's sack. Pig poo, wet leaves, something savoury cooking.

'Welcome.' It was Caractacus's voice – thinner and scratchier – but his voice no doubt, coming from inside. There was a clunk and the door opened. 'Welcome to 492. I had a feeling you were on your way.'

He looked much older now. He was hunched over, his cheeks looked hollower and his beard wispy and thin. He was leaning on a stick. He smiled and waved them over.

'You've landed between showers. Not a great day for it.' He looked up at the sky and held out his hand, as if rain might fall on it. 'I've made soup. Good day for soup, I think. Come on in. I have a jug of queasy water ready.' He pushed the door fully open until the bottom of it hit mud and stopped. He noticed Lexi hobbling as the word hunters came towards him. 'Your foot—'

'My ankle.' She had the device in her left hand and her right arm around her grandfather. 'I sprained it. Fell through a trapdoor.'

'I'll make up a mixture—' His mind was already on a cure. 'I think just some strapping and some ice—'

Caractacus laughed. 'Ice? Where do you think we are? *When* do you think we are? I'll make up a mixture.'

He led them inside and set up a stool for Lexi's foot. As they drank the queasy water, he ground spices and leaves into a paste with a mortar and pestle. He spread it across her ankle and Grandad Al placed a dressing over it and wound a bandage around. Her ankle felt warm and started to tingle. She moved her foot up and down. The pain was going already.

Caractacus turned his attention to the spitting cauldron over the fire. 'You'll like this, I think. It's after Apicius, the Roman. I've got his book. Fancy stuff mostly – flamingos, milk-fed snails, truffles. Not easy to come across in the Dark

Ages. This recipe's all right, though. Barley, peas, a few vegetables from the garden. I can't recall exactly when you eat in your time. You're not nones eaters, are you?'

Lexi looked at Al, in case she'd missed something. She didn't always like trying new foods, but the name gave no clue about what 'nones' was.

'No,' Grandad Al said. 'Anyone else hunted "noon"?' No one had. 'Noon actually used not to be 12 o'clock at all. It was three in the afternoon – the ninth hour of daylight on a day with 12 hours of it. "Nones" comes from *non hora*, the Latin for "ninth hour". People didn't eat three meals a day then – they stopped work at nones to eat a big meal. It was also a time for particular prayers in monasteries. In the 12th century it all changed, and noon and lunch and the prayers shifted to a few hours earlier.'

'Nicely put.' Caractacus scooped soup into bowls and started handing them out.

'Smells great.' Al stirred it with his wooden spoon. It smelt pretty average, though he figured it was probably as good as food got in the Dark Ages. 'Where are the peas? There's nothing green in there.'

'We don't have green peas yet,' Caractacus told him. It sounded like a joke. 'Green peas are centuries away. I don't mind admitting I was quite taken aback when I heard of them. We have yellow peas.'

'Seriously?' Lexi stopped with a spoonful on its way to her mouth. 'Next you'll be telling us your pumpkins are purple.'

'We don't have pumpkins. Or tomatoes or potatoes.'
He pronounced 'potatoes' as if it rhymed with tomatoes.
'They're about a thousand years away here. They have to
come from America and we don't know about America.'
He watched as Doug scampered down Al's arm. 'Here.' He
stood and picked up a stale square of bread from a nearby
bench. 'Take a trencher for your companion.'

'Thanks.' Al took it before he'd processed what
Caractacus had said. 'A what?'

'Oh? Gone has it? Trencher? Pity. Old French. Probably
comes here with the Normans. Looks like it doesn't last.' That
seemed to be as close to an explanation as Caractacus was
planning to give. It still just looked like a slab of stale bread.
'I've got something else for you. I've just put it together.'

He leant on his stick as he made his way across to a different bench. He had a lamp burning there and he fitted his lenses to his forehead to check his handiwork. It was a silver peg. He oiled the levers and passed the key in and out of the lock.

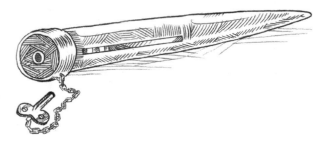

He brought it over and set it on the table next to the jug. The stone in the top was green and the key was connected to the shaft by a fine chain.

'You're here with "weird".' He put a hand on the table and sat down slowly. 'I've been waiting for "weird". I hoped it might be the five of you.'

'So we're going somewhere extra?' Lexi picked up the peg. 'But how do we get back? This is only one peg.'

'You'll only need one. The key stays in when you turn it, so you can take it out on the other side. Once you're finished you'll also use it to come back.'

'Other side of what?' It was making no sense to Lexi so far. 'And what are we finishing?'

'You need to cross the water. This isn't a time change, this one. It's just—' He waved his hand around as he searched for the word that would work best. 'Mechanical. You've a journey to make. Everything else you've done has been training for this – for tomorrow, across the water. This is the way it begins. Your boat is under the cliffs. With this device you will find unusual speed, and in the morning come to land. You must say you are hearth-companions of Hygelac and you must ask for Healfdene's son. His name is Hrothgar. He is king of a vanishing land. You will fight for him, and your battle will be with the army of Grendlaw – the land where Grendel's word rules.'

So there it was – Grendlaw. And this time it wasn't to be an ambush by a few grey-robes. This time it would be an army of them. Al put his spoon down in his bowl. He tried to tell himself he'd been in battles before and made it out intact, but they hadn't been *his* battles. He had only needed to survive them, not to win them. He wasn't sure how the five word hunters could make much difference to King Hrothgar's army.

Grandad Al started to speak. 'The only Grendel I know—'

Caractacus held up his hand. 'Don't believe everything you've read, Alan. But don't disbelieve it, either. It's another name of convenience. Grendel is our John Hunter, John Johnson. But you won't have to learn too many more names for him. This is the reckoning.'

So John Johnson was there, in the 5th century, in Scandinavia. Of all the centuries and all the places, that was his choice for his army. That was where and when he would fight to claim the language.

Al was trying to work it out. 'He's taking English out *now*? Before it's even properly started?' Then the scope of it sank in. 'He's taking down the Angles and Saxons, too – that's what he's doing. If he moves now, he gets much more than England. He gets northern Europe.'

'Yes. So eat up.' Caractacus sounded far too matter-of-fact about it.

'I really don't know that a bowl of soup'll make a difference.' Al couldn't help himself.

'I didn't say it would make a difference. It won't hurt.' Caractacus smiled. 'I've already done the things that'll make the difference. And then I noticed it was a gloomy old day and the hour coming up to nones and thought you might like some soup.'

He indicated that Al should keep eating and the others should too. Al looked down. His lap was full of crumbs and Doug had soup all over his whiskers.

Caractacus fetched a wooden box from a shelf. From it he gave them each their own device to call up the Dark Age

warriors. Each one was already loaded with two eggs.

'Is there a reason you're giving us all talismans?' Lexi had hers in her lap. 'Won't one do the job?'

'Perhaps not in Grendlaw.' For a moment it looked as though he was about to start into a long explanation, but then he just said, 'Work with your war dogs. Take their lead.'

He moistened his lips and put his fingers to them. He took a breath and appeared to whistle, though no sound came out.

Outside, somewhere far away, a dog howled. Another joined it. Caractacus stood and walked slowly to the door. The word hunters could hear the drumming of feet on soft ground, the splash of them kicking through puddles. As Caractacus eased the door open, the wolves burst in.

'All right, boys.' He patted the first one to come to him. '*Smyltnes mearcweardas.*'

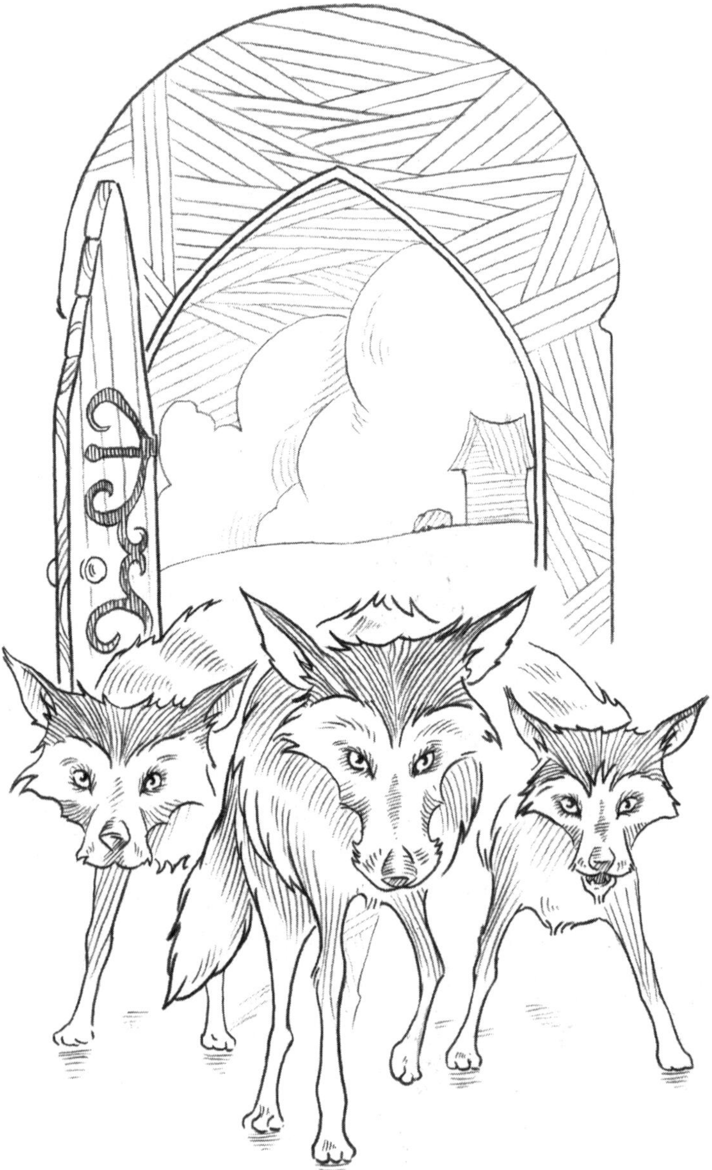

The largest of them loped over to Al. Al reached for Doug, but Doug jumped onto the wolf's shoulder, scrambled up to his head and sat between his ears. The wolf's massive tongue slurped from his mouth and cleaned Al's bowl of soup in one go.

'Osric Badaxe.' He patted the wolf's back. 'You started big and it's no surprise you stayed that way.'

Already, Al felt slightly better prepared to face an army.

'You realise he has some of your powers, though?' Lexi wasn't going to be as easily convinced by what Caractacus had to offer.' He tried to knock me out with ether just then, in 1066.'

'Ether?' Caractacus looked uncertain. 'Ah, yes. Ether. "Sweet oil of vitriol". It's had a number of names. You can't be surprised the ancients had it, even if the recipe was lost. The Sumerians had vitriol – which I think you'd know as sulphuric acid – and people long before them could ferment sugar. The rest of the manufacture of ether could be summed up on a piece of papyrus not much bigger than my hand. A small part of one scroll. That's all it would have taken him. Don't be too concerned about the ether. Let me show you what you can do with ten scrolls if you put them together the right way.' He nodded towards the door.

They followed him outside.

Five horses stood next to the pig sty, saddled and waiting. On each saddle sat a suit of armour. It wasn't exactly 5th-century armour. It wasn't really from any century.

'I think I've got the sizes right.' Caractacus picked up a helmet and placed it on Lexi's head. He tapped it with a knuckle. 'It feels light, but it should be very strong. There's a layer in there that does that. You burn grain husks with—' He stopped himself. 'Never mind.'

Lexi straightened the helmet and adjusted the chin strap. It was twice as heavy as a bike helmet, but nothing like the weight of steel. The jacket piled on her horse looked like it was padded fabric of the kind worn by people who couldn't afford chain mail, but when she picked it up she realised it wasn't that at all. There were hard plates inside it, linked together and overlapping.

Grandad Al took his from his horse and set it down on the ground, propping it against the wall of the house. He lifted the bow that had been hung from the saddle and drew an arrow from its quiver.

He lined up the shot at the slumped armoured jacket, then lowered the bow and turned to Caractacus. 'You don't mind if I—'

'Not at all.' Caractacus made a gesture towards the jacket, as if inviting Grandad Al to walk through a door before him.

Grandad Al raised the bow again, drew the arrow fully back and fired. It hit the jacket with a loud cracking sound and ricocheted off with a flash of sparks. The word hunters all moved in to take a look. The jacket had a small tear in its outer fabric and a white scratch on the grey armour plate beneath.

Will put his finger through the hole to see if there was more damage. 'No, that's it. An arrow at close range and it did nothing more than scratch it.'

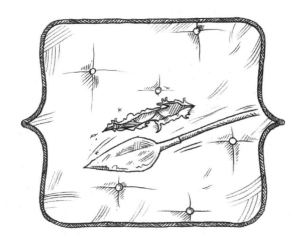

'It'd still feel like a punch, but—' Grandad Al rested the tip of the bow on the ground. 'That was a serious shot.'

Behind them, Caractacus cleared his throat. They turned and he held up the arrow for inspection. Its metal tip had been bent over and there was a split in the shaft just behind the head.

'I can't promise it'll stop everything,' he said, obviously pleased with himself, 'but it should do the job with blades and projectiles. If someone thumps you with a mace or an axe you'll still feel as though you've been thumped, even though it shouldn't cut you. So, you'll still need to be careful, but whoever you come up against should be surprised by what this can take.' He pointed to the horses and the weapons hanging from their saddles. 'The sword blades are tempered steel, which puts them 500 years ahead of their time. They're lighter, stronger and sharper than anything around in 492.

The shields are made of the same material as the jacket armour, and kite-shaped since the balance is good and it'll give you some protection lower down.' He stepped around a puddle and walked over to the nearest horse. He patted its neck, whispered something to it and then put his hand on its armoured breastplate. 'Same material here. We lost a lot in the library fire in Alexandria, you know. And this century. Like making ether, some of these techniques aren't new at all – just forgotten. Of course one or two are entirely due to people like yourselves bringing me the right kind of books from the future. Three thousand years of clever ideas here, and I hardly had to have any of them myself.'

Grandad Al set his sack down on the driest piece of ground he could find. He pushed a hand in and dug deep. When he pulled it out it was holding stirrups.

'Yes,' Lexi said. 'I'd forgotten we had those. You've been making us carry them around for centuries in backpacks and sacks and girlie baskets, and finally someone gives us horses.'

Caractacus couldn't quite work them out – two metal letter Ds on a long strap. Grandad Al didn't explain. He walked over to his horse, set them over the saddle and clipped them into place.

'Oh! It's where your feet go.' Caractacus was almost there. 'Don't tell me. Don't tell me. Stigraps? No, no. Stirrups. That's it, isn't it? Know the word, never seen them. Brilliant. Sometimes the best ideas are quite simple.'

He made his way over and tested the near stirrup in his hand. First he pulled down on it and saw how the saddle distributed the pressure. Then he lifted it to check its weight and was surprised by the lightness.

'Aluminium,' Grandad Al told him. 'They won't last forever, but they're easy to carry. And cheap, since we worked out how to refine bauxite in the 19th century.' He thought it was the 19th. He'd learnt that one at school.

'Brilliant,' Caractacus said again.

He opened the saddlebag and showed them the pickled vegetables and strips of salted meat he'd put in there. He lifted out a medical kit and unrolled it on the saddle.

He started rattling through instructions for its use before Will said, 'Hang on a moment,' and found a pen and paper in his sack.

Caractacus started again. 'This is for burns.' He held up some seaweed. 'This is for a clean wound.' Moss. 'This is for the bite of a dog or other animal.' A small bottle of dark liquid. 'And this is for an arrow that might be poisoned.' A tiny jar of off-white ointment.

Will wrote it all down and then checked the words Caractacus had used earlier – 'hearth-companion' and the Norse names.

Caractacus explained the food he'd packed as well, in case it wasn't clear.

They showed him the muesli bars they'd brought and he rubbed the packet between his thumb and finger and said, 'I'm not sure I like the texture.' Lexi told him it was the wrapping and he said, 'No I can see the—' He touched the picture of the bar that was next to the name. 'Oh, that's an image. Right. The real thing's inside, presumably. Do you mind if I—' Before she had the chance to answer, he'd torn it open and pushed the end of the muesli bar out. 'Compressed grains.' He sniffed it. 'Honey.' He took a bite and chewed it, making appreciative sounds. 'So you've come through here all those times with

these in your bags and never given me one? Grains, nuts, honey and little bits of dried fruit – why are we not making these now? We've got the ingredients. I know it's the Dark Ages and things are a bit rubbish, but, seriously, we're not completely useless. We should be able to stretch to a muesli bar. I'm going to work on that after you've gone.'

For just a moment, Lexi was reminded of home. Back in the 21st century, her mother and grandmother were making competing salads and her father was rattling through drawers for a bottle opener before getting the barbecue started.

But in the 5th, her brother was quietly trying on his armour and her grandfather was testing the tension in his new bow, while their war dogs padded around, ready to head off for battle.

It was best to focus on the job and get it done, not on her other life. She found her stirrups and fitted them to her saddle.

She patted her horse's neck and said, 'I'm Lexi. Nice to meet you. I don't know how to say that in your language.'

Her horse blinked its big dark eyes and nuzzled against her hand.

With his long armoured jacket on, Al felt like one of those reclusive billionaires in movies who turn out to be superheroes on the side. The suit made him bigger, but the weight was cleverly distributed, so it didn't feel heavy. When he twisted his body he could feel the plates sliding over each other. When he swung his right arm it moved freely.

'Some kings are lucky you didn't decide to have an army of your own,' he said, as he saw Caractacus looking at him.

'I did. I decided on the five of you.' Caractacus enjoyed watching the word hunters test out his handiwork. 'I've never liked big armies. You know me – I prefer to fly under the radio detecting and ranging device.'

'"Radar",' Grandad Al suggested. 'They decided to shorten it to "radar" in the 40s. 1940s.'

'Fly under the radar. Yes, that is better.' Caractacus nodded. 'I've seen kings close up. It's not a happy job and I wouldn't want it. I wouldn't want any job that had to be held by force. I just want a world that's a bit cleverer, a bit more decent. One that doesn't keep wrecking things and losing some of its best ideas and sending people back into hovels with poisoned water.' He leant on his stick and turned to see how the others were going. 'The more the dictionary remakes itself over time, the harder it becomes for me to know the workings of it, but it tends to find the hunters it needs. And for what we're facing now, one hunter or two would not be enough. It's chosen the five of you, as I thought it might.'

With his free hand he rummaged around in a pocket of his robe and pulled out the silver peg he'd shown them inside.

'"Weird" is one of the triggers that's built in to protect the book. It's set off by a particular threat pattern – the one Alastair identified earlier, involving action against the Angles and Saxons. It's not simply one word that's at stake here, but you know that. I think you're ready.'

He tucked his stick under his arm and asked the word hunters to gather around. He gave the key a quarter turn in the lock set into the green stone, and the peg started to hum. A red light like a laser appeared on its silver shaft, crossing it at an angle. He rotated the peg, but the line of the light didn't shift. When the peg pointed just to the left of the pig sty, the red light ran along its full length.

'There's your boat.' He followed the line with his finger. All the word hunters could see were trees. 'It's a three-hour ride, if you know what you're doing on a horse. This is your compass. It's under a cliff, remember. Once you've locked the peg into place, give the key another quarter turn and you'll be on your way. The boat will take you where you need to go and it will bring you back. I'll be waiting.'

He handed the peg to Grandad Al, who moved it around and watched the steady line shorten and lengthen.

The word hunters mounted their horses. The dogs knew the time had come and jogged around faster, panting.

Al flicked his reins and his horse started to canter. He could feel the added weight of the armour and weapons and supplies that hung from both sides of the back of his saddle, but riding still felt the way it did at the Franklins' place, when he'd had 21st-century horses and nothing on the saddle, and had been jousting at hay bales. He took the horse past the pig sty and back to the others.

He didn't know what tomorrow would bring, other than a battle. Caractacus had got them ready, though. As ready as they could be.

'"*Hie wyrd forsweop on Grendles gryre.*" That's how it will be written,' Caractacus told them. '"Fate sweeps them away into Grendel's clutches." Be brave, and this will be ours. And you'll get a good story.'

Swept into Grendel's clutches. It sounded dramatic – the bad kind of dramatic – to Al, but he told himself it was the kind of language old stories used, when wizards and witches and dragons were at work. Fate, or something, had brought them close to John Johnson's clutches several times already and they'd survived.

They were well into the trees and Northwic was out of view before Lexi realised what Caractacus had said. 'Hey, "weird". That was it, wasn't it? "Weird" meaning "fate". That'll be its first appearance.'

But Al was off in his own thoughts and didn't hear her, even though he was riding close by.

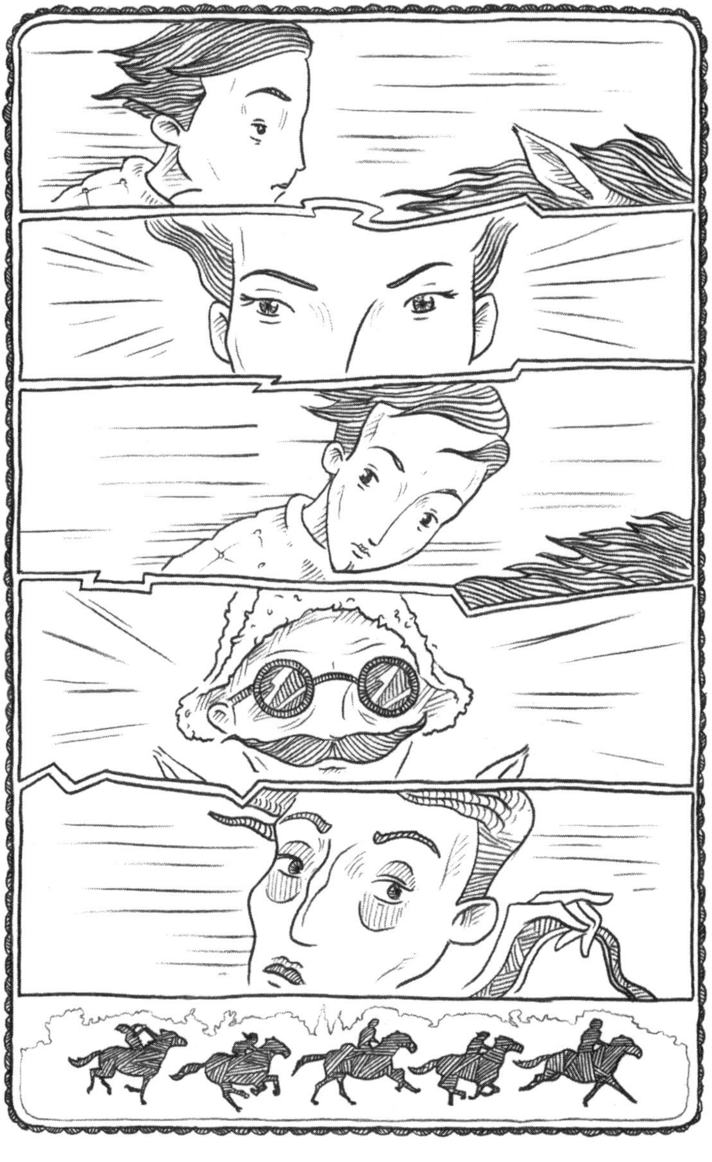

For the rest of the day they rode, breaking only for their horses and wolves to rest and drink, and to refill their water bottles where the water ran fast enough. The land was mostly flat and the riding easy, though none of the rough roads ran straight.

There were patches of cleared ground and some farms, but also houses that had been burnt down and not rebuilt, and land lying fallow.

Caractacus had told them not to wear their armour yet, and there were times when Al wondered if it was the right advice. With it on they would blend in less – actually, they would look totally out of place – but they'd be ready if an attack came.

But they hardly saw any people and the people they did see didn't stop to look at them. A line of men worked their way through a field of grain with scythes. A boy walked cows through a paddock.

When they stopped under a willow tree beside a stream, Lexi persuaded Will to swap some of his muesli bars for the pickles Caractacus had left in her saddlebag. She felt stiff from the riding and walked around to stretch her muscles. There were birds far above in the streaky sky, a V-line of them, flying east. The sun was lower now.

She ate one of her stash of muesli bars and wished the past could always be like this, with streams and horses on a cool afternoon and no sense of threat. No battle ahead or planned or foretold, or whatever it was. It'd be a story one day. Caractacus already knew the words. Now the word hunters just had to go and make them.

As the sun settled into the low hills behind them and the eastern horizon started to turn purple, they saw the sea. The road they were on led to a coastal village. Grandad Al took out his binoculars and counted eight houses. Some of the beach was visible beyond them, and two fishing boats had been pulled up on it.

But their compass wasn't pointing them there. It had been angling further and further to the left. It was time to take to the abandoned farmland.

They crossed a field with weeds that sent some stalks as high as their stirrups. In some places there were patches of grain, in others saplings that had sprouted in the time since the fields had been left. Perhaps this was the work of the army of Hengist and Horsa, burning and wrecking in the middle of the century. Al had googled them. The internet put them somewhere between myth and fact, but Caractacus had mentioned them at least once.

The damage had gone on, though, and the lawlessness. So much that the place now had no name that would be recorded, and would go years without a history. It had had one, in the time of the Romans and the Iceni, and it would have one again, but the word hunters were crossing it in its missing years, before its new Angle citizens established enough order to become the North Folk and then the people of Norfolk.

At the crest of the next rise was a ruined fort with most of its stonework gone. It had a clear view of the empty sea. It had been built on the clifftop and an overgrown path wound down the slope to a sheltered cove and a beached wooden boat. The red line pointed right at it.

Grandad Al led the way, pointing the peg in front of him, though he no longer needed to. They scanned the beach for hoof prints and footprints but there were none. Grandad Al, still on his horse, reached out and put his hand on the high stern of the boat where the timber curved up into a white dragon's head.

'This is it, then,' he said, gazing out to the flat blackening sea for any sign of what was to come.

The boat looked newly made and had no signs of being used. Its bow had a dragon-head prow that matched the stern, but in red. A sail was rigged to a yard on its single mast, but the yard was down and the sail lay bunched up.

In the last of the light the word hunters walked their horses on board and the wolves followed. With the armour and supplies unloaded, Grandad Al checked that the others were ready, pushed the peg into the hole at the base of the tiller and gave the key its second quarter turn. The green stone flashed and the hum they had heard at Caractacus's rose again.

There was a scraping sound as the yard slid up the mast and locked into place, lifting the square sail. With a gust from the west, the sail snapped taut and the boat pulled away from the sand and onto the water, gathering speed.

They sailed all night under a sky full of stars and took turns on watch, though there was nothing to watch for on the sea and they'd been told to trust the boat to find its own way. Lexi and Al had never seen so many stars. Not even on their weekends away hiking and climbing had there been so little light on the land and so little smoke and dust in the air.

Will wondered if there was any way to count the stars. The London sky of his time had had practically none at all.

For Mursili, it was the first clear night sky – truly clear – that he'd seen since he left Hattusa, though the skies for his last weeks there had been smudged with smoke. As the Kaskians advanced on the capital, they had lit the grain fields, sending fire through the wooden Hittite watchtowers. With this armour and these weapons, it might all have been different then. But there was no way to go back and fix Hattusa.

Here he was instead, fighting for a language he didn't really speak, but a language that had needed his or others like it in order to exist in the first place. He was the world's last Hittite, and a librarian, and his job was still to fight for words and knowledge in the best way he could.

They were travelling south when dawn came and the sun rose as a pale glow through the fog that sat on the still water. Despite the calm, the sail was full and the boat moving at a speed that sent a headwind whipping across the deck. It wasn't science operating in the usual way, but it was no surprise that Caractacus had access to better science than that.

Al opened a pouch of salted meat and passed a piece to Doug, who had slept the night tucked under Osric's jaw, with the wolf's huge white teeth interlocked just above him.

'We were heading northeast most of the night.' Grandad Al was standing at the bow trying to get his bearings. 'Why would we—' He marked it out with his hands on an imaginary map. 'Denmark? Have we gone far enough to make a turn around Denmark?'

The others assumed he wasn't actually looking for an answer. They were going where they needed to go, or where the boat was taking them.

Lexi drew her sword from its scabbard. She tested the feel of it in her hand, and on a clear area of deck practised cutting and thrusting. Will picked up his shield and sword and her shield, too, and together they worked through some moves.

Ahead of them the fog thinned out, breaking up and shredding on the waters of an inlet. They slipped between two headlands with watchtowers on them, and the guards lit signal fires as they passed.

'Whoever they are,' Grandad Al said, 'they now know we're coming.'

Will watched the smoke start to rise behind them. 'This should be the people we're fighting for, shouldn't it? I'll get the wording Caractacus gave us.'

The inlet widened and the watchtowers vanished behind them, their smoke signals trailing off into the clearing sky. The boat was skimming across the surface of a huge bay, or perhaps the headlands had been islands and they were still at sea. There was no way of telling.

When more land appeared in front of them and then to the port side, they put on their armour. The boat was heading for a channel or a river mouth and soon they had land close by on both sides. Much of it was forested, but there were cleared sections with crops almost ready for harvest and areas of pasture with goats grazing on them. Outside a shingle-roofed wooden hut a man with a spade stood still and watched them pass at a speed he'd never seen before.

The channel widened again, but the boat stayed close to land and then slowed down. With a watchtower just ahead of them, it turned towards a small beach and slid up onto the sand. The wind fell out of the sail and the air was still.

Grandad Al checked Caractacus's message. Mursili clicked the peg key back a half-turn, slid it out and put it in his saddle bag. The yard dropped down the mast and the sail folded.

A man appeared on the grass at the top of the beach. He had a helmet on and was carrying an axe and a shield.

Will and Al slid the gangplank over the side and onto the sand, and the word hunters led their horses from the boat. The wolves came after them and ran up and down, sniffing.

Grandad Al stuck the point of his shield into the sand and stood beside it, with his sword in its scabbard and his gloved hands clearly empty.

A second man appeared, mounted on a horse. He had broad shoulders and a long moustache, and was wearing fox furs and carrying a spear. He rode down onto the beach and stopped in front of the word hunters.

'Warriors,' he said to them as he eyed them off. 'Who are you in your strange mailcoats to bring your ship to such a speed and bring it here? And then to carry shields and arms so openly onto my lord's land with such noble bearing and yet no word ahead of you of your arrival?'

There was no doubt what had to happen next.

'We are hearth-companions of Hygelac,' Grandad Al told him. 'We are here to serve the son of Healfdene by doing battle with Grendel. There is damage being done to your lord's land and people, and damage to him and to you is damage to us as well.'

The guard seemed to relax a little in his saddle. 'Five's not many, but five who aren't afraid is more than we have now. And if you fight as well as your boat sails, you're as good as 50. Perhaps better. Where exactly are you from, that you speak just like me and yet look like—' he struggled to work out what they looked like '— you?'

'We've come from the new lands of the Angles and Saxons,' Grandad Al said. 'Across the water. The place the Romans once called Britannia.'

'Ah.' The warrior nodded. It seemed to make enough sense to him then. 'Mount your horses, cousins, bring your hunting dogs and follow me to the Hall of the Hart.'

He led them from the beach and past the watchtower to the start of a path that took them up a grassy slope and into forest.

He told them he was Wolfgar, thane of the area where they had landed and a distant cousin to the king. He reached out and touched Will's armour as they rode.

'Is this ready for dragons?' He tapped it with a knuckle. 'Are they a problem in the New Territories? I noticed one on the bow of your ship. Is that why you've been sent? You and your dogs know how to do battle with dragons?'

He wanted the answer to be yes.

Will hesitated before saying, 'One man well thought of in our country – George – was a soldier who slayed a dragon.'

It seemed to be enough. Saint George and the dragon.

As they rode, Wolfgar told them of Grendel, who had not been seen by a living human but who was thought to be some kind of fire-breathing monster. He attacked at night, with the noise of his destruction sounding across the land and a village gone the next morning, scorched by fire. Neither the sound nor the sight of the damage was like anything anyone had known.

'And you can hear him too,' Wolfgar said. 'Cursing us all. His voice has been heard through the banging and crashing. It's human, but not human. It travels a long, long way. That's what we're told by farmers who have fled to the forest. I think he's a dragon, with all that fire. Whatever he is, we've got no answer to him yet. He's taken half the country. Once he's burnt a place, no one dares go back.'

The forest gave way to fields and scattered houses and then a long wall appeared ahead of them. It was made of earth several metres high, with a fence running along the top. There were guards above the gate and at each of the two visible turrets. Outside the wall, men were digging post holes next to a pile of cut tree branches.

'Escapees from the burnt country,' Wolfgar explained. 'The attacks are getting closer. The wall's new and already there are too many people to fit inside it. King Hrothgar has allowed them to build there, but—' He shrugged. 'It's not the answer. We don't have one yet. If the hall falls, the country falls, and then it's all the monster's.'

He raised his hand to signal to the guards and the gate swung slowly open. The builders stopped to watch the foreigners in their bizarre armour as they rode by.

There were more huts crammed up against the defences on the inside. Most of them were no more than a few poles with woven dried grass for walls and rough thatch for roofs. The smoke of cooking fires was in the air, along with a smell that made it clear there were no toilets.

Space for passage had been left down the middle and Wolfgar led them along it, with huts crowded on both sides. There were children playing on the last clear scrap of ground, marking it with a stick and tossing a pebble onto the grid they'd drawn. A woman walked past with an empty bucket in each hand, going wherever she needed to for water. On both sides people sat doing nothing, staring, waving their hands at flies.

'The Hall of the Hart,' Wolfgar announced, indicating a solid and much older building at the end of the path.

Its doorposts were tree trunks and its walls broad timber planks and posts. Its roof was covered neatly in wooden shingles and looked like the hull of an upturned grey ship. The shape of a deer standing on its hind legs had been burnt into the door.

Wolfgar dismounted and handed his reins to a guard. 'Dragon hunters from the New Territories,' he said. 'Look after their animals.'

The guard stared at the word hunters in awe. 'What do you use to slay a dragon, sirs?'

'Your wits, mostly,' Grandad Al told him.

Wolfgar explained that their quarters would be inside, so they should bring anything they needed.

As Al followed him through the doorway into a dimly lit room, he had a flashback to the tent at Saint Audrey's fair and the grey-robes, and his heart raced. Instinctively he swung his sack to the side to defend himself, but there was no attack.

'Cousin King,' Wolfgar called out. 'I have good news.'

'Then you're more welcome than usual,' a voice replied in the distance.

The word hunters followed Wolfgar past areas partitioned off with animal hides and woven rugs hanging from the beams. There were families in there. Somewhere further along, a girl laughed. The smell was far better here. There was still smoke in the air, but nowhere near as much, and there was some kind of incense, too.

Beyond the final screens, the hall was open to its full width and the ceiling was at maximum height, with the long trunks of trees joined far above in the dark. The walls were covered with tapestries and decorative shields and antlers. A fire was smouldering in the middle of the floor, giving just enough light to see.

On the far side of it stood a man with a band of gold around his head and a white fur cloak closed by a jewelled clasp. He had guards near him and an old man sitting between him and the fire with runes laid out on a mat.

He took a step closer to the fire. His hair was gathered back in a plait and he had a droopy moustache that matched Wolfgar's.

The guards held their spears ready as the word hunters came into the light, still with swords hanging by their sides.

The king looked at them warily, and then at Wolfgar. 'Good news?'

'Yes, Cousin King,' Wolfgar said. 'These men have just arrived. They're dragon hunters sent from the New Territories.'

The king held out his arms as if he wanted to embrace the idea. 'We sent word. We didn't know it had got through.

I'm so glad to see you.' He glanced past them into the dark. 'Five of you? Are there more of you outside?'

'No, sir,' Will said, since King Hrothgar seemed to be looking right at him. 'There are only five of us anywhere in the world, and we're all here.'

The king nodded. He blinked and wiped smoke from his eyes. 'Grendel can turn a village into a hearth in one night. There's no life in it in the morning – only ash.'

Lexi told herself there were no dragons, but it was getting harder to believe it. She had spent months learning to fight humans, not huge fire-breathing creatures that could destroy whole villages. Caractacus might have given them swords 500 years ahead of their time, but she couldn't see what good they could do against a dragon.

She took a sideways glance at Al. His hands were clenched into fists by his sides. He too was waiting for someone – their grandfather, Will, the king – to say the thing that would make it better.

At first nothing made it better. They were given food, quarters in the hall to sleep in and blankets to put on top of the straw. They fed their dogs and horses. They talked to the people who had escaped Grendel, but no one could add anything useful. A strange booming voice, banging and crashing, fire. Villages burning in an unnatural way.

There was nothing there that they could plan for. The escapees were the wrong people to tell them anything. They were too afraid and, Al realised, simply also the wrong people. They had dragons and monsters in their heads already, so that was all they could report. They had 5th-century answers – answers from 5th-century stories. No one had actually *seen* a monster. That much was clear. But the noise and the damage meant some kind of monster to them.

As night came, the locals got edgier. Grendel had always attacked at night.

Al lay down with his sack for a pillow. The peg that could take them home was inside it and the portal was on the other side of the sea. Doug curled up next to him on the blanket.

When Mursili blew out the candle, Al gazed up into the darkness. A monster. A dragon. What could it be? How could it be?

It was shouting that woke them, from the guards on watch. Al's eyes opened to more total blackness. He rolled over and looked for his clock. Straw spiked his cheek. Fifth century. Monster nearby. He sat up.

Will and Lexi were already moving. Light came through the cracks between the screens as someone ran down the central hall with a burning torch. Al pulled his own 21st-century torch from his sack and turned it on.

'What are you doing?' Lexi's face was bright in the light, her hair a mess.

'They want us to be dragon hunters, Lex,' he said. 'We look like science fiction to them already. They want us to have special powers.'

'Someone else out there already has them.' It was Will's voice. There was a click and his torch went on. 'Soon we're going to need to convince hundreds of these people to join us in a battle against him. A few special powers on our side are only going to help.'

'Sounds good.' Mursili's torch went on as well.

'Suit up, then,' Grandad Al said. 'We need to be ready and we need to look ready. Let's go and see what the problem is.' It didn't sound like a battle, not yet.

They had left their armour waiting, ready to pull on. Al took the activated peg from his sack and slid it down inside his jacket. Doug climbed up onto his shoulder. Everything else could stay.

No one was asleep in the hall now. As they moved towards the door, they could hear a girl's voice say, 'The new soldiers – they brought stars in their hands.'

Wolfgar was already outside with the king and his guard. There was panic in the huts, people crying. Some were moving towards the gate, in case their chances were better in the forest.

'I told you,' Wolfgar said to the king. 'Dragon hunters. Look at the lightmakers they've brought. These are no normal soldiers.'

He led the word hunters to some steps and they climbed to the top of the wall.

There was a flash in the distance and a ball of fire rose into the sky and faded. On the ground, something burnt. Then they heard a faint cracking sound, no louder than a firework in another suburb.

They could just make out a voice, a long way away. 'I'll cook your village in my own breath and grind your bones to make my bread.'

'Grendel,' Wolfgar whispered. He looked terrified. He put his hands on his ears and crouched down. 'He's never been this close.'

The distant voice went on. 'Feed me. Feed me. I need every one of you.' It was odd and distorted, even metallic-sounding.

Grandad Al almost overbalanced, but grabbed hold of the fence. 'That's my loudhailer from sports day. I lost it in

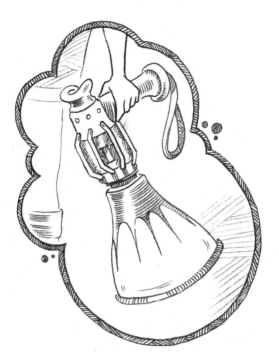

Colchester.' He reached down and put his hand on Wolfgar's shoulder. 'Nothing we haven't come across before.'

Al smiled at the absurdity of it – a megaphone from 1983 striking fear into a country, because they had no way of making sense of it – but then there was a whoosh of flame and the village being attacked was alight from end to end. John Johnson had more than a megaphone to fight this war with.

Al wanted to do something, to take the fight to John Johnson rather than hold back watching, but the village was already gone and there was no telling exactly what was out there in the dark.

Grendel came no closer that night. The flames dropped and the voice went quiet.

Soon after, the guards at one turret heard horses, but the riders passed without stopping. Through Wolfgar, the word hunters learnt they'd been escapees from the land around the village.

When dawn came, people on foot could be seen making their way through the trees, carrying whatever they'd grabbed when they left.

Grandad Al fetched his binoculars. There was still a trail of smoke drifting into the sky, and at the base of it he could see an earth wall mostly intact, and behind that the blackened embers of houses.

'That doesn't tell us much,' he said, as he lowered the binoculars. 'I think we have to go and take a look.'

The gates were open and more escapees streamed in.

'They're getting this all wrong, aren't they?' Will said as he watched them walk in, stop and just stand there, with no idea of what to do next. 'They'll be trapped in here.'

'If we're going to go out there, we should go now.' Lexi noticed that the building work had started up again outside the walls. 'They'll send soldiers with us if they know there's plenty of daylight ahead. Have you noticed how less freaked they all are now? Even though things are actually worse and Grendel's got closer?'

'They're just relieved it wasn't them.' Grandad Al's binoculars were on a strap around his neck and they rattled against the armoured plates in his jacket when he let them go. 'They were already afraid of the night. That's when wolves come. These people don't go out at night. John Johnson's playing right into their fears.'

'So we can't take him on at night, either, or it'd just be the five of us.'

They had to move now, with 14 hours or so before dark came.

King Hrothgar gave them 20 soldiers for support, with Wolfgar to lead.

A dirt road led straight to the ruined village and the word hunters checked the forest for grey-robes as they travelled, but there was no sign of them.

Caractacus had mentioned a 'reckoning', but Al couldn't guess what form it would take. The locals had put dragons and monsters in his head, but it couldn't be that.

After less than 20 minutes of riding, the trees ended abruptly and, across an area of pasture, the village stood silent. The gates were smouldering and fire had eaten away sections of the fence that ran along the walls.

'I don't really want to go in.' The sight of the outside made Lexi wonder what they might find inside. 'I wouldn't even watch this on TV.'

'Almost everyone in there got out, you know,' Mursili said. 'Wolfgar told me.'

Will turned around in his saddle. 'It's about creating terror, not as much about wiping out a village. It's at least as good for John Johnson if people hear the voice and run. He obliterates the houses and they spread the terror. I don't know where his plan goes from there exactly. I suppose he creates chaos, brings down the king and then—' He shrugged. 'Maybe he steps in to save the day. He's the only one who can make the chaos stop. Maybe he then signs the locals up for a more conventional army and keeps going.'

At the walls, two of Wolfgar's men dismounted to pull the damaged gates open, while others held arrows to their bows and watched for any sign of attack. One gate fell from its post and slammed onto the ground, bringing up dust and ash.

The soldiers hung back and let the word hunters ride in first.

Iron cooking pots and stumps of posts marked the sites of huts, and fine grey ash had drifted into piles against the fallen blackened timber. Among the wreckage were metal bands from a wooden trunk and pieces of smashed pottery.

Ahead of them, the timber longhouse had collapsed and parts of it were still burning. There was no one around.

'That smell,' Grandad Al said.

Al sniffed. 'Fireworks.'

'Gunpowder.'

Al took a moment to get it. 'Which they can't possibly have. It's not in Europe for hundreds of years. That's what's making the loud noises people hear. They've got gunpowder.'

'That's how you get around travelling without weapons. You bring the knowledge to make them.' Will dismounted and with his toe pulled a blade from the ash. It was a hunting knife with the handle burnt off. Not a sign of any fight. 'That wouldn't work with 21st-century technology – you can't build a fighter jet or a missile just because you know they exist – but you could do gunpowder. Sulphur, charcoal and saltpetre.'

'The gunpowder plot in 1605.' Mursili had been reading about it hours before they left. 'John Johnson was Guy Fawkes's alias. Maybe our John Johnson was actually something to do with that. Maybe he knows gunpowder well.'

Wolfgar's men took up positions on the walls as the word hunters started to search for more signs of how the attack had been conducted. The fire damage didn't make that easy. It wasn't like the work of an army, with arrowheads and discarded weapons left to be dug up centuries later. Al had read plenty about old battlefields.

He and Lexi were standing next to his grandfather when Wolfgar came up to them.

'We don't make this.' Wolfgar had a piece of pottery in his hand. 'It's all over the ground – or in quite a few spots at least. It's not our style, or the style of anyone we trade with.'

'Could I—' Lexi had noticed something. She took the pottery and turned it over in her hand. Then she sniffed it. The fumes from it made her blink. 'Weird smell.'

Al and her grandfather sniffed it, too. The smell was something chemical, but they couldn't pin it down. Grandad Al called Will and Mursili over.

'I know what it is.' Will went back to sniff it for a second time. 'Greek fire. I've seen it. The word was "tulip" and

there was a siege in Constantinople. It's pine resin mixed with some kind of petrol or oil. I can't remember everything that's in it. Not sure I knew, anyway. They blasted it from one ship to another. The flame could travel quite a way. They also made bombs out of it.' He took a step back from the others. 'That's how they did it here. That's why fire's the big feature. The pottery's everywhere.' He pointed out more of it. 'You fill the jar with the liquid, stick some kind of wick or fuse in the top, light it and send it in. It smashes when it lands and everything burns.'

They had solved the puzzle of the dragon – the voice that carried, the banging and crashing, the terrible fire. They could explain every part of it now.

And the tactics of King Hrothgar's people to prepare for attack couldn't have been more wrong. Pile up an earth wall and build a wooden fence. Build a wooden town inside. And wait. The Hall of the Hart and every shack crammed in around it was kindling, just waiting to burn.

King Hrothgar was fighting the wrong war.

'So how do we tell them all this?' Lexi whispered. Wolfgar was still close by. 'How do we tell the king?'

'We don't.' Mursili had no doubts. 'Trust me. I come from a suspicious people. Everyone in that town believed in dragons before this one came along. They didn't even need proof, but Grendel is it. We can't go in and say, actually, that's all wrong. Now here's a story about three pieces of technology from the future – one that makes sound louder, one that blows things up and another that burns. That would seem like crazy talk. Three crazy answers when they've already got one that makes complete sense.'

'But—' She decided not to argue. She came from a time when three pieces of technology would always make more sense than a dragon story, but she'd seen enough of the past to know that kind of thinking was a long way in the future.

Mursili was right. They would have to win this as dragon hunters.

They put their proposal to the king as soon as they got back. His mind was on defence rather than attack, but it was attack they talked about.

Wolfgar backed them up. 'The dragon spits pots of fire. We can't beat that by building our wall higher. And they're right to say we can't wait till nightfall. We'll be next. We'll hear that voice and then the fire will come. We asked for experts.' He indicated the word hunters. 'We have them.'

The king didn't like what he was hearing. 'It was one thing for a small group of you on horseback to go a short distance down the road, but it's another to put an army on the march and send them to this creature.'

'The only other choice you can make to save yourselves is to leave now and keep going,' Grandad Al said. 'We can win this in daylight. Let me talk to your people.'

King Hrothgar could picture himself giving up his country, field by field and village by village. He had no alternative.

Guards were sent to spread the word through the town. Building stopped, cooking cauldrons were moved away from fires, mending was left on the ground.

As they made their way to the town wall, Lexi asked her grandfather what he was going to say.

'I don't know yet,' he told her. 'But I'll get there by asking the question I always ask myself when the past gets a bit tough. What would Sean Connery do?'

'The Scottish movie star? He's, like, 80—'

'You'd be surprised how often it's got me through.' He gave her a wink, which she assumed was something Sean Connery did. Grandad Al had made them watch three of his films. She'd hardly understood a word Sean Connery said. And he wasn't even supposed to be Scottish in two of them.

The word hunters climbed the steps in full armour and stood with their helmets tucked under their arms. From his end of the row Al thought they looked like an Apollo mission. He'd seen the TV footage, men with bulging suits and helmets tucked just that way.

Below them in the alleys and any open spaces, a thousand or more people were standing waiting.

'People of King Hrothgar,' Grandad Al began, his hands held high. 'I know you are afraid. But I also know you cannot build walls high enough to protect you from this enemy.' It was Wolfgar's line, but he was happy to use it. 'Your enemy is most powerful at night, and the day is your time. Our time.'

He went on, trying to motivate them, but their faces were blank.

Below him at the base of the wall, the word hunters' wolves started barking. They stood as if they'd heard a signal and arched their backs and howled at the sky. He stopped mid-sentence. He looked towards the ruined village, but there was nothing to see.

'Grandad.' Lexi pulled on his arm. 'This is what Caractacus meant. "Work with your war dogs. Take their lead." That's now.'

Her sword clunked against each step as she ran down and back to the hall. She worked her way through it in the dim light until she got to their quarters. When she'd found all five of Caractacus's devices, she hurried back to the door.

As she stepped outside she could hear dogs in the forest, yowling and barking. From all around, across the fields and through the trees, dogs were coming.

The townspeople's fear was now in the open again. Grandad Al was talking but they'd stopped listening. Dogs were scrambling to climb the walls and get inside.

'They're setting wolves on us,' she heard a man say as she hurried back.

She twisted one of the devices and the red and white liquids flowed together, making a milky pink. As smoke spurted from the top, she rolled the device towards their war dogs.

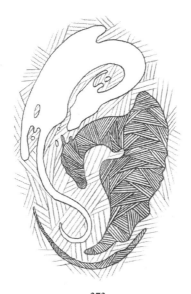

'Will! Mursili!' She threw the remaining four devices up to the word hunters on the wall, one after the other. 'Twist them and throw them over. Here's our army.'

One by one, the wolves leapt through the smoke at the base of the wall and turned into soldiers. The crowd gasped and then started to cheer. An army was appearing in front of their eyes. The dragon hunters had brought magic.

The other word hunters spread out along the battlements, activated their devices and threw them over. As the dogs below Al started to jump through the smoke and become warriors, he looked back at his sister and grandfather. Osric Badaxe was at the foot of the steps, towering over the people around him.

There were voices outside the walls, warriors shouting. The guards opened the gates and the people streamed out to meet their army.

'Al!' It was his grandfather, calling out to him. 'Back over here. We need to finish off and I've got to be near the peg or they won't understand me.'

Al made his way back along the fenceline, stepping around the guards. With dogs turning into humans directly below them, he could have climbed right over them and they wouldn't have noticed.

'People of Hrothgar!' his grandfather shouted once Al was close enough. He signalled for quiet, and paused for the noise below to settle. 'You are not alone. As three wolves can bring down an elk, so can an army of wolves bring down this monster. But we need you with us. This will be no ordinary

battle and there will be times when you will be afraid. But our powers, in the end, will prove stronger than Grendel's. You will not see a dragon today. You will see fire in the sky and on the earth, and the earth will shake, but once you start fighting instead of running, this monster will take the shape of an army of men. And together that's something we can beat.'

'Show us more!' Someone called out. 'Show us more magic.'

People started to cheer, but Grandad Al held out his hands to make them settle. 'You will see more when more is needed. For now I will give you an incantation to beat your enemy. You need to fight like wolves today, but there's another tongue to say it in. A future language. I need you all to say this.'

He caught Al's eye. 'Another tongue' – Al didn't know exactly what his grandfather was planning, but he knew what that meant. He moved away along the battlements, putting Grandad Al out of range of the peg.

Once the distance was great enough, Grandad Al raised his hands, thought of a certain ageing Scottish movie star and called out in his most dramatic voice, 'Be a wolf.'

He repeated it and repeated it and the people below took it up as a chant. 'Be a wolf, be a wolf, be a wolf.'

The town had changed. The word hunters had their army.

They travelled east down the road towards the ruined village.

If John Johnson had gunpowder, did he have guns too? There was no sign of any so far. A good gun would be hard to make, but a cannon full of stones or lead shot might not be.

Al could imagine blacksmiths working away to make them, but he could imagine anything if he let himself. Somewhere ahead, though, was the army, whatever shape it would take. Grandad Al had his binoculars out, but he'd reported nothing so far. And somewhere, sometime, perhaps from the cover of the forest, John Johnson's men would be watching them and realising that things had changed.

Lexi rode next to Al. She was eating a muesli bar. 'Do you think they're better with chocolate, or is that just wrong for the whole muesli bar concept?' she said before taking her next bite.

'Really? That's what's on your mind at the moment?'

'What am I supposed to be thinking about?' She held her hand up to her mouth while she chewed. 'The next 15 bad things that might happen to us? I figured I'd leave that to you.'

'Seriously, what kind of warrior are you? You're riding into battle in the 5th century with a sword, a bow and a bunch of arrows, and you cover your mouth if there's food in it when you talk?'

She laughed and tried not to choke. 'I'm a warrior with manners. Even if manners don't come along for hundreds of years.'

Al wondered when manners did come along. He could google that when they got home. He imagined his parents freeze-framed in the kitchen as he fitted in this bright day in the Dark Ages on the way to some kind of battle. In seconds, in home time and if the day went well, he could be on his way back up the stairs to grab his iPad and safely google whatever he wanted.

'Are you thinking Teutoburg Forest?' she said when she'd swallowed her mouthful of muesli bar.

'Trying not to.' The year 9, Germania, three legions of the Roman army wiped out in an ambush on a forest path. 'That track was really narrow and this is still a road. Plus, the Cheruscans all came at us down the hillside. It was steep; not like this. And they'd made the path all boggy first.'

Three reasons it was different – none of them convincing.

Judging by the height of the sun, it was late morning. Behind them they could hear more and more people saying 'be a wolf' over and over. At first there had been optimism, even excitement, with the transformation of the dogs into fighters, but the further east they travelled, the more the locals remembered to be afraid.

Then they saw the village. The chanting of 'Be a wolf!' lifted in volume. Beyond it they knew they were in Grendlaw.

It was Will's turn with the binoculars when something flashed in the sky ahead of them. There was a bang, and a ball of smoke smudged into a streak and disappeared. He was the only word hunter to miss it. He'd been watching the trees.

'We've been spotted,' Grandad Al said. 'Now we know how they're signalling. And that they'll be ready.'

The berserkers hadn't appeared to notice, but for the

townspeople it was a sign of the dragon, and a sign that daylight might not be so safe after all. A messenger from the king arrived, telling the word hunters to stop.

'We can't lose most of our army now,' Will said, while they waited. 'They can't stop just because one bomb goes off in the distance.'

Further back on the higher side of the track, King Hrothgar was lifted on his shield by four men. Everyone went quiet.

'We've all seen what we've seen in the sky,' he began. 'It may be a sign of what's to come. But we must go on. If we don't advance, all that's left for us is retreat. And if we keep retreating we'll be taking to our boats. Today we have the gift of an army and five dragon hunters, and we have daylight. Some of you have fought with me against the Heathobards and the Franks. All I can ask of you is that you fight the way you did on those days, whatever we have to do battle with. We cannot stay afraid of the dark in a country growing smaller and smaller. Let's win and sleep well. March on.'

He drew his sword and pointed it to the east. There was a murmur of approval and some cheering and the shield was lowered. The army was intact for now.

The march continued. Soon the road left the forest for a grassy plain that, well ahead of them, tapered into a valley where two ridges grew closer and then met.

'Hang on a second.' Lexi had the binoculars. She fiddled with the focus and tried to keep her hand steady. 'Below that tower thing, at the end of the valley—'

She passed the binoculars to her grandfather. For several seconds he peered through them without speaking and then he said, 'Yes, that's them.' He caught the attention of one of Wolfgar's men. 'Would you tell the king there's something for him to see?'

He gave Al the binoculars. Al zeroed in on the tower, which looked like it might be a ruin, and then dropped down. At the end of the valley, where the slope began but was still gradual, there were tents among the trees and across the grass. Square tents, too many to count, like the tents of a Roman army.

The view of the ground in front of them was blocked by a small rise in the valley floor, but even as Al watched, the first rank of grey-robes came into sight, moving forward. He lost count trying to work out how wide the formation was. They were too far away and he couldn't hold the binoculars still enough. He guessed 40 or 50. There was no way of telling how long the columns behind them were.

King Hrothgar and his guards arrived at a canter.

The king eyed the binoculars suspiciously when Grandad Al told him they made distant objects seem larger, but after two of the word hunters had put them to their eyes without being harmed, he agreed to try them.

Grandad Al focused them on a tree not too far away. 'Have a look at that,' he said.

The king gasped and jolted back in his saddle as the tree jumped closer. He shifted the binoculars and it fell back. He tested them again on a different tree, then a rock beside the road.

'Now look into the distance,' Grandad Al said. 'There's a tower on a hill.'

'A tower?' It didn't make sense to King Hrothgar. 'The Franks have towers. The Romans built them. We don't.' But he found it in his binoculars. 'There was a longhouse there in my grandfather's day. Its lower walls were stone.' He moved the binoculars, rubbed his eyes and looked again. 'Someone's built that from the ruins. I don't understand—'

'Now look below.'

The king lowered his view. He showed no surprise this time. He studied the details carefully. And smiled.

'It's an army of men.' He gave the binoculars back to Grandad Al. 'You told us it would be. There's a lot of them. But we can fight men.'

Grandad Al nodded. 'Be ready for the signs of the dragon, though. You'll only have to fight men, but be ready for those.'

The king gave him a look that suggested he wasn't quite making sense, and then he thanked him and moved his horse to the side of the road to let the berserkers pass so that he could rejoin his people.

They called a halt at the start of the valley to drink from one of the streams that ran across it and to rest their horses and their legs. The water was no more than ankle deep and easily forded, but the land around it was boggy. Al checked on either side, but there was no cover for an ambush. Wolfgar pointed to some small trees just ahead and told them the ground beyond was firm.

Once they'd passed the trees, they were high enough again for the grey-robe army to come back into view. It had stopped moving forward and was waiting. The front rank carried spears and round shields.

As Al tried to count them, using the binoculars, a voice crackled along the valley. 'Come, people of Hrothgar, into the jaws of the dragon.'

Something crunched into the ground and made a fizzing sound, then there was a loud bang just above them to their left. Stones and shards of pottery tore divots out of the grass nearby. Another bomb crunched into the ground and fire spilt across it.

'Two gunpowder, one Greek fire,' Will said, as he rode across to check the first to land. 'Yes. Should have gone off in the air.' There were pieces of smashed pot and stones everywhere, along with a dark grey streak of gunpowder. The fuse was a rag burning on the grass with the neck of the pot still around it.

Another shot burst in the air, spraying stones at the berserkers. Two of them fell, wounded. Someone among the townspeople started shouting. They stopped moving.

'Come forward.' It was Grendel's voice, echoing between the ridges. 'I can almost taste you.'

A fire bomb smashed into the ground to the right, spraying burning liquid across the front rank of berserkers. It stuck to their shields and their bearskins, setting them alight.

'Roll!' Lexi shouted out. 'Roll on the ground!' It was 21st century first aid, but it would work just as well now.

Al scanned the ridgelines through the binoculars. High on the ridge to the left, he saw a group of grey-robes among the trees. They'd built two wooden frames and made a fire. Behind each frame, a grey-robe was pulling back repeatedly on a long pole. Another appeared with a claypot bomb that he seemed to set down near the back of the machine. A burning torch was carried across from the fire.

Eoforwic – York – 866. Al had seen Vikings building their war machine Gunnhildr.

'Got it!' he called out. 'They're firing from that ridge.'

He pointed, without lowering the binoculars. The grey-robe with the torch had done his job and stepped aside. The man next to him went down on his knees, lifted a mallet and brought it down hard. A wooden arm swung up and slammed into a bag mounted at the front of the frame.

'There's another one on its way!'

They lifted their shields above their heads and the bomb burst in the air. Al felt something smack into his, and saw a stone drop onto the grass beside him.

Lexi's head whipped around, but he was still in his saddle.

'Just a mark.' She slipped a glove off and reached out to touch his shield. 'Just a dirty mark on the fabric. Everything's totally fine.'

There was a crunch over to the right, another fireball.

'We've got to knock them out,' Will said from under his shield. 'There'll be panic otherwise. We've got to get up there.'

'Wait!' Lexi held up her hand. '"The jaws of the dragon". Al, check the other ridge. There might be more of them.'

She was right. There was a second identical crew loading and about to fire.

'Um, hunters—' one of the berserkers said as he strode over, holding his round shield above his head as if it was no heavier than an umbrella. A wisp of smoke was still curling from his shoulder, but he didn't seem to care. 'Aethelbert. We met in that tent incident in Ely. Our lot's ready to go.' He indicated behind him with his thumb. 'Just say the word.'

Within a minute and before more bombs could land, the word hunters came up with the best plan they could.

Half the berserkers charged forward, while the local archers fired arrow after arrow over them and down on the grey-robes, whose shields went up.

Meanwhile, the word hunters and some of the local mounted warriors rode back through the middle of the foot soldiers and down the slope, where they couldn't be seen. They split into two groups, with Wolfgar leading one and the word hunters together in the second with ten other riders.

They rode hard away from the battle, out to the sides, where the ridgelines started to rise from the plain. In the distance they could hear the yelling of the berserkers and the first clash of axes and shields.

They slowed down to make the climb through the trees, but still managed good progress. They stuck to the side away from the valley and for several minutes the ridge blocked out the sound of the battle. Al pictured the plan coming unstuck without them – the berserkers hitting shields and not getting through, bombs dropping, the locals in disarray.

All the way along he wanted to climb to the top to check, but they held off until they guessed they were close to the bomb launchers.

As they reached the summit, they could see that the second wave of berserkers had gone in. The grey-robe defences were holding, but they'd suffered casualties. King Hrothgar's men were spread out, crouching with their shields over their heads.

There was a thump below and to the word hunters' right, and a bomb flew past – a shape and then a speck against the blue sky. It hit the ground with a spurt of flame across an empty patch of grass.

They lifted their bows from their saddles and drew arrows from their quivers.

'Is that blood I smell?' A voice buzzed down the valley. It was John Johnson as Grendel. 'Come closer. Cloooooser.' It was coming from the stone tower.

'Artillery first,' Grandad Al whispered. 'Then the tower. We'll finish this today.'

The horses picked their way carefully along the slope. Another bomb was launched just as the grey-robes came into view. There were a dozen of them, some working on the bomb throwers, others standing nearby with swords and axes, watching the battle.

As the word hunters spread out, Mursili's horse kicked a loose rock and sent it tumbling down the hill.

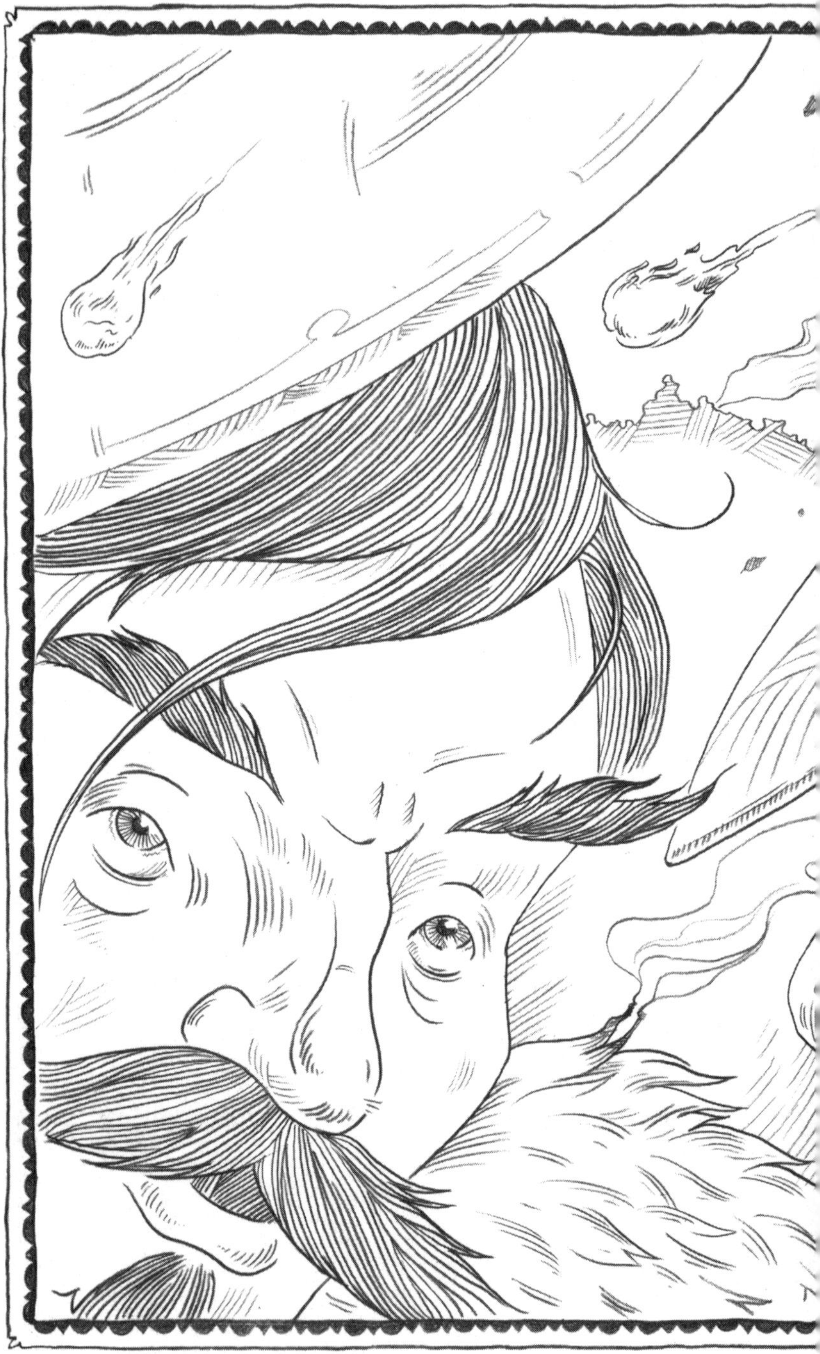

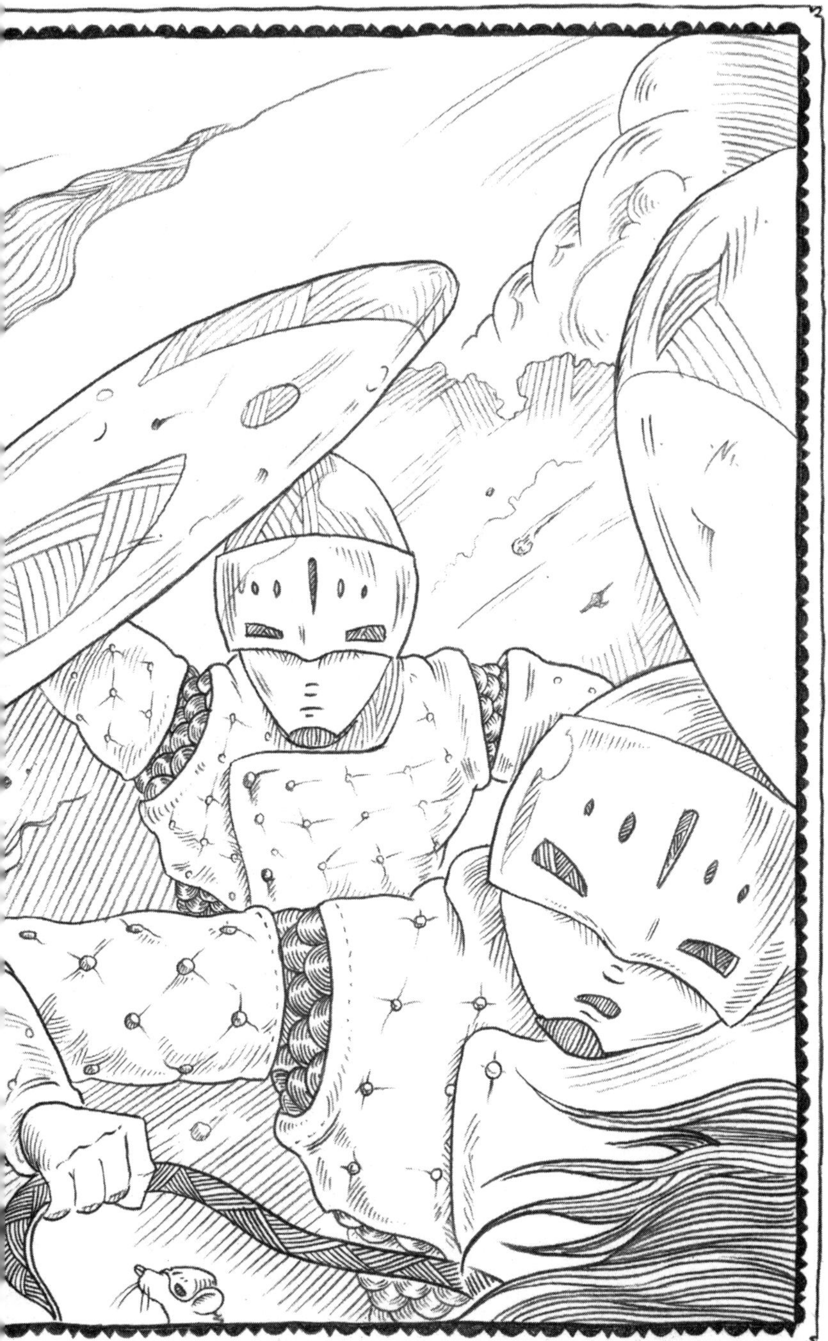

One of the grey-robes turned. 'Look out! We're being attacked!'

The others scrambled for their weapons, as the first arrows flew. Some of them hit trees, others fell short, but one hit a grey-robe in the arm. Wolfgar's men had their second arrows in the air in seconds. The grey-robe with the torch was hit in the chest and sagged to his knees. Another was hit in the thigh. The rest clustered together behind shields or around the solid frames of the bomb launchers.

As Wolfgar's men fired another shot, the word hunters hung their bows and dismounted. The horses would be no advantage on a slope with loose rocks and fallen branches. The locals, with their smaller shields and shorter swords, came down the hill faster, jumping over logs and shouting.

'We're not running now!' one of them bellowed as he knocked a grey-robe sword aside and slashed down between two shields.

The grey-robes around the pot-thrower frames scrambled to their feet and ran down the hill, stumbling through the trees.

Lexi stood with her sword in her hand, as the local warriors finished the fight in little over a minute.

'I think they're onagers,' Will said as he took a close look at the weapons. 'I did some reading about war machines after we were in York. They're a Roman design. Except their onagers used a sling.'

Each machine had a strut with a bowl on the end of it for the projectile and a rope that allowed it to be wound back tightly and held in place by a pin, before being shot. Ceramic pots with thick rag wicks in them were lined up in rows on one side of the two machines and a fire was burning in a cleared area on the other side.

Together the word hunters and the local warriors lifted the bases of the onagers and dragged them around so that they faced the grey-robe army. Through the binoculars, Al had seen them being fired, so he knew what to do next. He picked up a pole and started cranking one into position. As he ratcheted it back, the firing pin clicked and held it in place. With each pull he brought the bowl of the firing arm a little lower.

His grandfather was ready with a bomb once Al had taken the arm as far as it would go. He set it in the bowl with the wick facing up. Will had relit the fallen torch and brought it over.

'Just before I get it going,' he said, 'do you know how to fire this?'

Al picked up the mallet. 'This is for knocking the pin out. I think that's what I saw them do.'

'And if you're wrong—'

'Stand back. Seriously.' He waved at the others. 'All of you. Get out of range.'

'But—' Lexi started to argue.

'Someone's got to do this, and I'm the one who's seen it.' Once, at long distance and almost out of view. But someone did have to do it.

He took a breath and nodded to Will. Will touched the torch to the wick and backed away, as it started to burn.

Al steadied his hand and slammed the mallet down. He didn't hit the pin squarely but he hit it well enough. The firing arm leapt up and slammed into the chaff bag at the front of the machine and the bomb sailed up into the sky.

It flew high and long, out over the grey-robes, then past them, and it exploded above the first trees of the forest on the other side of the valley.

Al stood up, flipped the mallet in his hand and caught it by the handle. 'There's a bit of a range issue, but you get the idea. Obviously we don't have to crank it back quite as far.'

The local warriors stepped in and started working both machines. The second shot was closer. The third dropped a fireball right into the middle of the grey-robe army. The next shot hit close to the same spot, as did the one after. Gunpowder and then Greek fire.

From the other end of the valley, they heard cheering. King Hrothgar's men were up and on the move.

The chant began. 'Be a wolf … be a wolf …'

The word hunters were already on their way back to their horses. The onagers thumped again as they mounted.

From the crest of the ridge they were above the tower and could see signs of more building work – foundations laid for something much larger. There were armed grey-robes standing guard.

Lexi rode with her sword in her right hand and her left holding the reins. John Johnson was not far away. This was the reckoning. Everything depended on the next ten minutes.

As they broke from the trees the guards saw them and scrambled to form a defensive line. Other grey-robes ran from a lower building on the far side of the tower.

The ridge top narrowed and a cliff dropped away to the right, with water far below at the bottom of it. To the left the slope fell less steeply into forest and towards the valley and the battle.

Will led the charge, riding right at the defenders. His horse reared at the last second, taking the point of a spear in its breastplate. The spear snapped and its metal head dropped uselessly to the ground. The horse clattered into two shields and trampled the men holding them as Will hacked with his sword.

Lexi cut a spear in two as her horse crunched into the defenders.

Al brought his sword down on a shield as his horse kicked and kicked.

The grey-robes fell back, bunching together, but leaving three on the ground. One of the survivors jumped forward with an axe, but Al turned his horse's head just in time and the blade brought up dust as it hit the ground.

The horse staggered as it turned, and Al dropped his sword. Before the grey-robe could move, he stood in his stirrups, swung his leg over and dismounted. He grabbed his shield, slid his arm through the loops and ducked down to pick up his sword.

The man with the axe was already charging at him, and Al instinctively moved into position. His enemy swung mightily, Al took a half-step and, as the axe head smacked into his shield and skidded off, he lunged. He felt the point of the sword hit something soft and keep going.

The man breathed out and as he dropped to the ground, his axe clattered beside him. A red stain spread out under his hands and across his robes. It was as if he was trying to hold it there, stop it growing bigger.

The shock distracted Al for a second, but there was no time to lose. Another grey-robe was coming towards him. Their swords clashed. Al checked his balance and swayed to dodge the next strike. He took a swing, but the grey-robe got his shield up in time. He watched the man's face, anticipated the next strike, moved to block it and lunged. This time the edge of the grey-robe's shield caught the blade, pushing it down and wider, but still it cut his thigh.

Lexi's shield came in then – she was on her feet now, too. She shoved the man's sword arm and he overbalanced.

Soon it was over. The last few grey-robes ran and the word hunters were at the tower. There were scrape marks on every shield, but every one had done its job. Mursili had a torn sleeve with a wide white mark running down the exposed armour tiles.

'Big bruise coming.' He gave his arm a rub. 'That was an axe.'

Al felt something pulling at his leg. It was Doug, who had fallen out of the saddlebag he'd been travelling in. There wasn't time to put him back.

'Wait,' Al told him, as if rats took orders.

Will led the way through the open door and into the tower. There was no one on the ground floor – just a table with a bucket next to it, and picks and trowels against the wall.

It was like a building site, Lexi thought. It *was* a building site. Nothing special.

Will held his shield in front of him as he took to the stairs. The next level had a straw mattress and rugs on

the floor. There was a hat on the mattress – John Johnson's hat from the 17th century.

There was one more level above them. John Johnson had to be there. Will peered past his shield as he climbed, and he kept his sword ready. As he put his foot on the third-last step, something lunged at him over the low wall at the top of the stairwell. He swung his shield around, but the blade was past it. It slashed his sleeve, raking over the armour plates as he fended John Johnson's arm away.

He overbalanced, hit the wall behind him and almost fell. Al caught him, steadied him, and pushed him up the final stairs.

John Johnson backed away across the room, his knife still in his hand. His skin was pale and the veins on his face and hands looked blue through it. His cheeks were hollow beneath his black glasses and the muscles on his neck stood out.

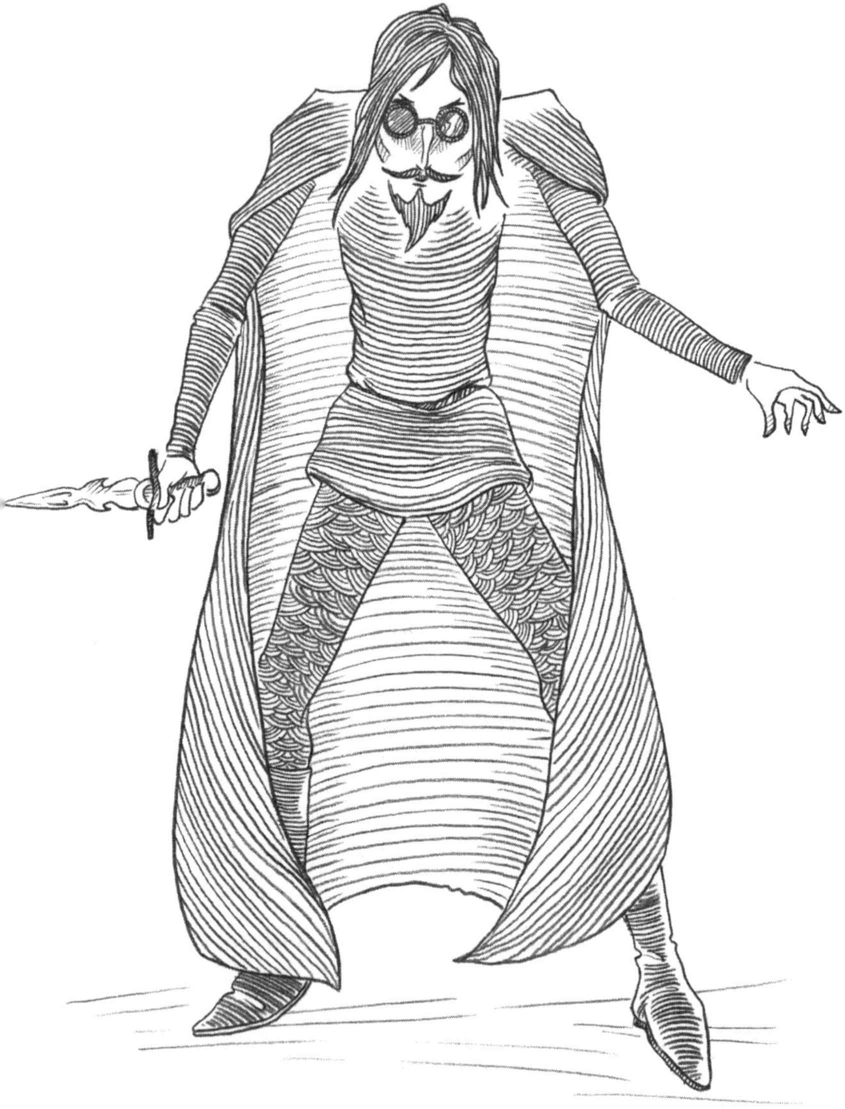

There was a table between him and the word hunters, with a pile of books and scrolls on it. Behind him, Grandad Al's megaphone was on the ledge of the window facing the valley.

John Johnson picked it up with his free hand and raised it to his mouth.

'That's mine,' Grandad Al told him, before he could use it. 'Your men took it from me. You're not going to frighten us with that.'

'I have two kinds of flash and fire, and will destroy you.' John Johnson was going to play every card he had. He lowered the megaphone.

'We're from the 21st century,' Grandad Al said calmly. 'We're not local. We use more than what you've got for entertainment at a party.'

The word hunters spread across the room, tracking John Johnson's every move. Even if he had a bomb, there was no sign of the fire to light it.

'How did you do this?' Will asked him. 'Why did you do it?'

John Johnson smiled. 'Do this? Here? Scare these suspicious people and start work on a castle? Look out the other window. That fjord'll make a great port. It's only the start. But you know that. England begins here. My England. My Europe.'

Will ignored the window. 'How and why did you start attacking us? Why did you have to turn it into this?'

'I'm attacking you because you're in the way. I have a much better Europe planned, and it's only word hunters

who can stop me. It was one of you who got me started.' He
looked at each of them in turn, as if he was sizing them up.
'Your cousin Lemuel's not too bright. Lemuel Hunter? When
I met him in a tavern he was selling objects from the past. I
asked him where he'd dug them up, but he wouldn't tell me.
I thought there'd be good money in it, and there was no need

for all of it to go to someone who was drunk and stupid. So I became his friend. And one night he let slip that he was travelling to the past to get them himself. I followed him to his house and took his daughter as security to make sure that he would help me. I went with him on several trips. I gathered some of the means of travel. I'd send Lem Hunter into that hovel in Norwich to lure your man outside to talk about his pigs. Then I'd go in and take myself back to Alexandria. He'd taken Lem there once, so I knew where he kept the pegs for it.' He watched the word hunters for a reaction. 'He had to make the Alexandria pegs when you turned up, didn't he? He worked out something was wrong and he stopped making them in advance.'

He took a step to the left and ran the point of his dagger along the table.

'He made his hovel more secure too.' John Johnson seemed to be enjoying the chance to tell his story. 'In ways no one can see. But I had most of what I needed by then. I was ready to take the book for myself and to be rid of Lem Hunter. That's when I got my timing wrong. He'd hidden it, and nothing would make him give it up. But I already had what I needed to travel in a rough sort of way and I've made do with that. It's taken its toll on me, but it's worth it.'

'Lemuel Hunter,' Al said as he worked it out. 'LH. You hunted "tawdry" with him.'

'You've done "tawdry"?' John Johnson's face gave nothing away, though he sounded surprised. 'And you're still here? Well done.'

'What did you do with Lemuel Hunter?' Lexi almost didn't want to know the answer.

John Johnson gave a thin smile. 'That hardly matters. Don't you see? Don't you see what this travel allows you to do? I was close to a plot to bring down the king, but this was much better. I could stop the king ever existing. I could be the king. I could be anything. The man they killed as Guy Fawkes was Lemuel Hunter.'

It was a shock to hear it.

'So you're—' Al started.

'I'm not anyone. I've learnt that trick from your friend who sometimes calls himself Caractacus. Don't go assuming I'm Guy Fawkes just because it amused me as a way to get rid of Lem Hunter. You're wasting yourselves, you know, running that book's errands.' He shook his head, as if he was almost sorry for them.

In the distance, they could hear explosions and the scramble of noises that made up the battle. John Johnson took another step to the left and Lexi wondered what they would do next. They had him cornered and outnumbered. She hadn't imagined this moment. Would they take him back to Caractacus?

'How did you recruit an army?' Grandad Al had wanted to know that for a long time. 'What did you do to persuade them?'

'That was the easy part. I did the opposite of stupid Lem Hunter.' He said it as if it should have been obvious. 'I bring them things from the future. They think that, if they're with me, they'll live a thousand years. More. They think I've already lived that long and I've got more ahead of me. The "magic" I can do is good—' he said 'magic' scornfully, as though no one smart would fall for it '—but this is better than your volume instrument and the bombs. It looks like the promise all great religions make – eternal life.' He set his dagger down on the table. 'But that's not the question you should really be asking. How am I here today? How am I going home? That's what you should be wondering.'

He threw himself to the left, and landed on the floor next to a leather satchel. He wrenched at the buckle.

'It's a portal!' Al shouted. 'He's got a portal in there!'

John Johnson shoved the table at them with his boot and reached into the satchel. The table thumped into Will's thigh. Al scrambled to climb over it, but the armour made it difficult.

At that moment, Doug shot across the floor, weaving among word hunters' feet and table legs.

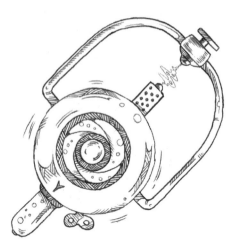

John Johnson pulled out a metal device the size of his palm. He pressed a button in the centre and it started to glow and hum. The glow shivered and widened. He went to take a step towards the window that looked out to the fjord and reached for the key that was on the sill, next to a plate of bread and cheese.

With the smell of cheese in his nostrils, Doug leapt for the wall, ready to scramble up it to get to the plate. He hit John Johnson knee-high.

John Johnson stumbled and overbalanced. His glasses fell and the brightness seared his damaged eyes. The hand with the portal in it hit the wall and he reached with the other to steady himself. But it passed right through the open window and he toppled, rolling over the ledge and out.

The portal crashed to the floor.

There was a scream from outside as he fell, and then nothing.

The ring of portal light shimmered and blinked and went out.

Al got to the window first. He leant out carefully, but the cliff was overhanging the water below. He could see waves coming in and could hear them beating against rocks. There was no sign of John Johnson.

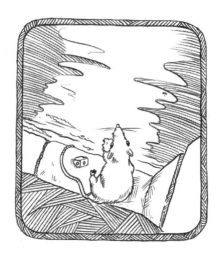

Lexi joined him and looked down. 'There's no way he could have survived that. I'm glad we can't see.'

Doug sat on the windowsill in the sun, holding the cheese with both front paws and gnawing at it.

With that, their job was done.

From the other window they could see the battle was being won. They packed up John Johnson's books and instruments and loaded them onto their horses.

They went to search the building next to the tower for more, but discovered seven sacks that turned out to be full of gunpowder and, beside them, the cast metal parts of an unfinished cannon.

Will picked up the sack they'd opened and emptied some of the gunpowder over the other six. He walked backwards out the door, running a trail of powder along the ground until it ran out.

They called their horses over and the other four word hunters mounted.

'Be quick,' Grandad Al said, as Will crouched down with his box of matches.

He struck one and touched it to the end of the gunpowder trail. It fizzed and smoked and started spluttering towards the tower.

They sent their horses galloping down the trail that led to the valley, swords back in their hands in case there were any grey-robes still planning to fight.

Lexi turned to look as the gunpowder ignited. The smaller building tore apart and stones were flung into the sky. The shock wave hit the word hunters with a physical force and the boom echoed along the valley. The tower buckled and collapsed off the edge of the cliff.

When they reached King Hrothgar the battle was over.

'The tower was the monster's lair,' he told them, as he pointed at the smouldering ridge. 'He's destroyed now. You must have heard it.'

That night he held a banquet in the Hall of the Hart and brought in eight horses with gold headgear and breastplates, and presented them to the word hunters. He gave Wolfgar a golden helmet that had once been his father's.

As the party continued, the word hunters rounded up Aethelbert, Osric and the rest of their berserkers and quietly left.

By starlight, they found the path they'd arrived on and rode along it to the beach.

'Hey,' Lexi said, as she dropped back to ride next to Al. 'You've just got one more peg, right? After the one for the boat—'

'Yeah.' It was the final thing he'd checked in his sack before mounting his horse. 'Just one. The home peg. I'm figuring the portal's at Caractacus's place. Or hoping it is, anyway.'

'There's plenty there that fits with "weird". As long as he didn't set it off by saying it before we left.'

'If he did, he can keep it going.' Al didn't want to contemplate the possibility that there might be any problems ahead – that the portal might flicker and disappear, or might be anywhere but Northwic. 'We've done the job. You, me, Grandad, a guy from World War I, a 3,000-year-old librarian and a pack of dogs just killed a dragon, defeated an army and kept the future intact. I think the least we deserve is an easy portal.'

'Yeah.' She could smell the sea on the breeze now. 'Yeah, we did all that. I'm so ready for the portal.'

In the future she had a warm bed in a peaceful country. She had food when she needed it, and science and knowledge in place of superstition. She had days that felt much less important than this one, and a chance to be 12. Reasons enough to become a warrior, but now she needed to go home.

The boat was where they had left it on the beach and it was now lit by a low full moon. With the peg in place and locked, the sails filled and they slid from the sand.

Lexi sat and gazed up at the stars, wondering if they'd ever look this sharp and clear to her again.

Al put his head down on his sack and the next thing he saw was daylight and the English coast, and Doug curled up under the jaw of Osric the wolf.

Caractacus had another soup ready when they arrived at Northwic.

He heard the horses from a long way off and went outside. As they rode through the trees he checked that each word hunter was there and sitting high in the saddle, and he counted the war dogs.

'I'm not sure you'll fit those extra horses through the portal,' he called as they rode up. 'But you can try.' He reached out and took Lexi's reins. 'Just tell me it's over.'

'It's over.'

He smiled in a way she hadn't seen him smile before. 'Good news.' He patted the neck of her horse. 'Good news for years to come.'

They stayed for soup. They wanted to leave that minute, but Caractacus wanted to hear the story. All of it.

They were almost at the end when Lexi realised what the battle meant. The *Curious Dictionary* would do what it would do – she would be a word hunter for a while longer, or she wouldn't – but there would be no more John Johnson, no more army raised against them. The job might again be the straightforward job that had once seemed close to impossible, back in New Jersey in 1877, when she'd dropped from the sky in a skirt that went all the way to her boots.

If there was more action ahead, she could handle it. And if there wasn't and her time as a word hunter was over, that was fine, too. Caractacus, as always, had made it clear that it was up to the book and to chance, and to the future to deliver what it would.

But it would be different if she went on. In the future there would not be five of them.

She reached out and touched Will on the sleeve. 'You're going, aren't you?'

'Yes.' He looked sad and happy at the same time. He glanced down at the dirt floor and then back in Lexi's direction. 'This time I'm going home.'

'Ah, yes,' Caractacus said. 'I'd forgotten that. Separate peg for you.' He stood up from his stool and walked off into the dark. 'And the librarian?'

'No way.' Mursili had made up his mind long ago. 'Will gets to go to the Moulin Rouge when he's 18. I'd be getting the Bronze Age Collapse. Assuming you didn't send me right back to be trapped in the fire. The empire goes, my language goes, the city burns down and I can't change any of it.' He tried not to think about the people. They were already lost, before he barricaded himself in. 'I'm going to the 21st century. My library needs me. My Cubberla Creek library. Some days now I'm acting head.'

Caractacus brought a peg and some tools back into the light and went to work on the table.

'Now, 1618 then?' he said, tightening something. He glanced up at Will. 'Just my little joke.'

'1918,' Will said, since it was better with Caractacus to leave no room for doubt. 'Fourth of October 1918, just after three in the afternoon. And I'm 15. Soon to be 16.'

Caractacus lifted the lens from his eye so that he could look at Will. 'By just after three, do you mean four minutes or five?' He swivelled the lens down again and poked at the peg. 'I have no idea how to do that. I'm just sending you home. Right back to the spot you left. This should take you there. But leave the key in when you lock it. Other than that, it's business as usual.'

With one final poke it was done. He handed the peg to Will.

'I suppose you'll be wanting a portal, then, all of you.' He stood up. '"Weird". First appearance of "weird". Right.'

He shuffled off again, this time towards his scrolls and manuscripts. He bent down and rummaged through a pile of books that had been stacked on the floor. When he stood up he was holding one, with a familiar golden glow pulsing from the front page. He brought it back and placed it on the table.

Lexi read the title aloud. '*Leofwine and Aelfrices Boc be Aelwihtas?* I'm assuming that's "boc", if that was an "o" before it became the portal.'

It was now a glowing button that read 'home'.

Caractacus flipped a lens down again to read it. 'Yes, that's right. "Leofwine and Aelfric's Book of Monsters". It's from the future. Not your future, obviously. A bit before then. I got someone to bring it back for me.'

'Right,' Will said and stood up. 'This is it, then. Let's do what the button says.' He fiddled with the levers of his peg. 'Thanks. All of you. Thanks for finding me. And everything else. I'm going to miss your century.'

Lexi could feel that she was about to cry, so she grabbed him, hugged him and pressed her face into his shoulder. He put his arm around her and hugged her back.

He was about to reach out to shake Al's hand when he remembered how things worked in their time. 'Sorry, very 1918 of me.' He pulled his hand away. 'You'd think I'd have learnt after all the group hugs at the youth hostel.'

So the others hugged him, too, and then stepped back as he pressed the button, drove his peg in and locked it down.

They felt a wind tear past them as the door blew open and fog poured in. Once it cleared, Will was gone.

Caractacus unlocked the peg and pulled it out. He rubbed it and checked the side of it.

'If you get them out in time you can—' he thought carefully about the language '—reinstall the software and use them again. If you don't get them out, they're gone in seconds.' He set the peg down on the table, held the book up close to his face and said, 'Weird.'

The 'o' instantly became a gold button again.

Al pulled his peg from his sack. 'Go on, Lex, you press it.'

She stepped forward, then hesitated. She wondered if she'd ever be back in this room again. She wanted to say something to Caractacus, but she wasn't sure what it should be.

'You've done well,' he told her. 'You've done your job. You five did a job no one else has ever done. There was never this much at stake. If it was up to me, you'd have done enough. If it was up to me, we all would have. I have the *Curious Dictionary*, somewhere just over there.' He pointed off into the dark. 'It's still in pages. It's just the start. I've a few more years work to do yet. But I'll get it finished now. And English will be English and will keep becoming and becoming. That's what you've made sure of while you've been across the water.' He smiled. 'And what a great story. Not one for you to tell, but a great story nonetheless.'

He took her hand and guided it towards the button. She pressed it and he stood back.

'Goodbye,' he said, as he stepped away into the dark. 'Or see you next time. We'll know when we know. Go home and I'll write you a dictionary.'

He lifted his hand to wave, as Al pushed the peg into the hole in the book and turned the key.

The room shook, the fog returned and the four word hunters lifted above it, above Northwic, above the land that would become England.

Words came and went, and alphabets did, too. Monks toiled by the light of candles, writing and illuminating. Mills rolled paper, type was boxed and ink pressed onto sheet after sheet. With a clatter of keys and then no more than a click, words passed through space and landed. Everywhere on earth.

The word hunters dropped from an evening sky over a street in the suburbs and, with the smallest correction to their flight, landed outside the carport next to Grandad Al's car.

Upstairs, utensils clattered and Lexi and Al's father said, 'No, seriously Mum, where's the bottle opener?'

'Well, that was weird,' Mursili said, as he picked up his phone from the bonnet and saw his notes on it about the word. 'That was the weirdest one yet and we didn't even get back to its origins. I'm sure it's Proto-Indo-European.' He slipped the phone into his pocket. 'Good job, though, everybody.'

'Nice bruise.' Al had noticed it on Mursili's arm. It extended below the short sleeve of his shirt most of the way to his elbow.

Mursili pulled up his sleeve. 'I know. I'll change my shirt.' Where the edges of the armour plates had pressed in, there were black lines, as if he'd drawn dragon scales on his skin.

'Before you go, Mursili,' Grandad Al said, 'I've got something to show you all.'

He led them past the car and through the open door to his study. He searched the bookshelves until he found what he was looking for. It was an old paperback with a battered black spine.

It was *Beowulf*.

'First book in English,' he said, as he handed it to them. 'Well, not the first. The oldest surviving.'

'*Beowulf*?' Lexi tried out the sound of it. 'Did you do that when you got those people to chant "be a wolf"? Is that seriously how the oldest book in English got its name? That is very cheesy. And also excellent, obviously.'

He laughed. 'I have no idea. I'm sure if you look up the orgins of it you'll find a different story. Some people think a man called Beowulf existed, though a few years after we were there. Maybe we moved forward in time in the boat. I really don't know. Maybe Sean Connery made me do it.'

They read the back-cover blurb about the warrior of the title, who crossed the sea to fight a monster for King Hrothgar and who then fought a dragon.

Al flicked through it and read parts of it as he went. He found the voyage and the meeting with Wolfgar, but other sections were completely unfamiliar.

'The monster's eating people here. Look.' He pointed to the page. 'He's got into the hall and he's eating people. That's crazy! The monster was made up.'

'Not for those people.' Grandad Al laughed. 'The moment we left the hall, that story started being told. And it was told by people who believed there was a monster. Knew there was a monster. Even if some of them had attacked the onagers with us.'

'Al, you have to dial it back a few years,' Mursili said. 'In Hattusa, we would totally have gone for the monster. That or a vengeful god. Not all this modern chemistry and loudhailers.'

Grandad Al took the book and started looking through it himself. 'It's been a while since I've read it, but I actually think it's surprisingly close for something around 1,500 years old that passed through a lot of hands and got added to and subtracted from before ever being written down – and written down in another country.'

'Probably closer than Egyptian reports of the Battle of Ashkalon,' Mursili added. 'Finally we Hittites are getting our due for that one—'

'That's Caractacus's point,' Lexi said. 'The one he made first time we met him. It's only once you write a story down that you don't lose it. It's the way to remember and pass things on and build on them. It's the difference between monster stories and knowledge.'

'"*Hie wyrd forsweop on Grendles gryre.*"' Grandad Al had found the section he'd been looking for. '"Fate sweeps them away into Grendel's clutches." It looks like it's about Hrothgar's soldiers before we arrived. And it's the first appearance of "weird". We got ourselves a good story. Not an entirely true one, but a good one. And we sorted Grendel out properly.'

'Alan!' Grandma Noela's voice shouted down the stairs. 'What are you three doing down there? How long does it take to check a few backpacks?'

'Coming,' he called back. 'Just a couple more things to do.'

'I'd better go,' Mursili said quietly. 'Don't want the number two librarian from school turning up out of the blue. That'd be, to use today's word, weird.' He picked up his pack and moved to the door. 'See you two at school on Monday.'

It was the most normal thing to say and, yet, having just visited early 19th-century London with him, dropped in on Shakespeare in 1606 and fought a battle around 492 in a place that might end up as Denmark, 'see you two at school on Monday' was the thing that sounded weird.

As he stepped out into the dark and made his way past the cars towards the gate, Lexi said, 'What about Will? What do you think happened to him?'

Grandad Al put his hand on her shoulder. 'You're too small to remember, aren't you? He stopped being a hunter, as we all do eventually, but he was unique. He'd come here. He'd seen the future. That's so much harder than seeing the past. He knew what he'd learnt in our time about the 20th century, but he couldn't change the bad bits. If you start making predictions and they all come true, well, that's a power. A dangerous power to have. It makes you a target. So you can't be public about it. He tried to change things quietly, but it's hard when you're one unknown voice. He went to Germany and Austria in the 1930s and tried to talk the Jewish leaders into getting their people out, but he couldn't make one person believe that a government could do what Hitler's government eventually did.'

'How do you know that?'

'I got a letter from him in late 1982, when he was 79.' Grandad Al looked over towards the shelves. 'We kept writing after that. Noela and I visited him a few times. He was a history teacher. I told her he was a fourth cousin. Something like that. Easy to believe, since we were both called Hunter.'

'Did he warn you about Colchester?' Al said. 'That the grey-robes would get you there?'

'No. And nor should he have.' He walked over to the shelves and pulled out a photo album. He opened it and then put it back. He took out the next album along. 'You undid Colchester when you rescued me, and you only found him because you were looking for me. It was all for the best.' He turned the pages of the album until he came to a loose photo, which he lifted out. 'Will outside the Moulin Rouge in 1921.'

'Why's it in there?' Lexi said. 'With that photo of Al and me sitting on that old man's lap?'

The man had no hair, bright new false teeth and a checked waistcoat. He was grinning and had an arm around each of them to keep them on his lap.

'Because that's at his 100th birthday party, when you were two. Better than the telegram from the queen, he said it was, having you two there.'

Lexi felt the tears roll down her cheeks and she took in a sharp breath. Al stared at the photo and told himself he remembered it.

'Salads are ready,' Grandma Noela said from the kitchen. 'That's my none-too-subtle cue to you to leave those backpacks and start barbecuing, Alan.'

Lexi and Al took one last look at the photo before their grandfather put the album away, and together they climbed the stairs back to the present. To salads and barbecues and the C soccer team and movies, and all those things that had once been their entire lives, before they had become word hunters and lived across centuries.

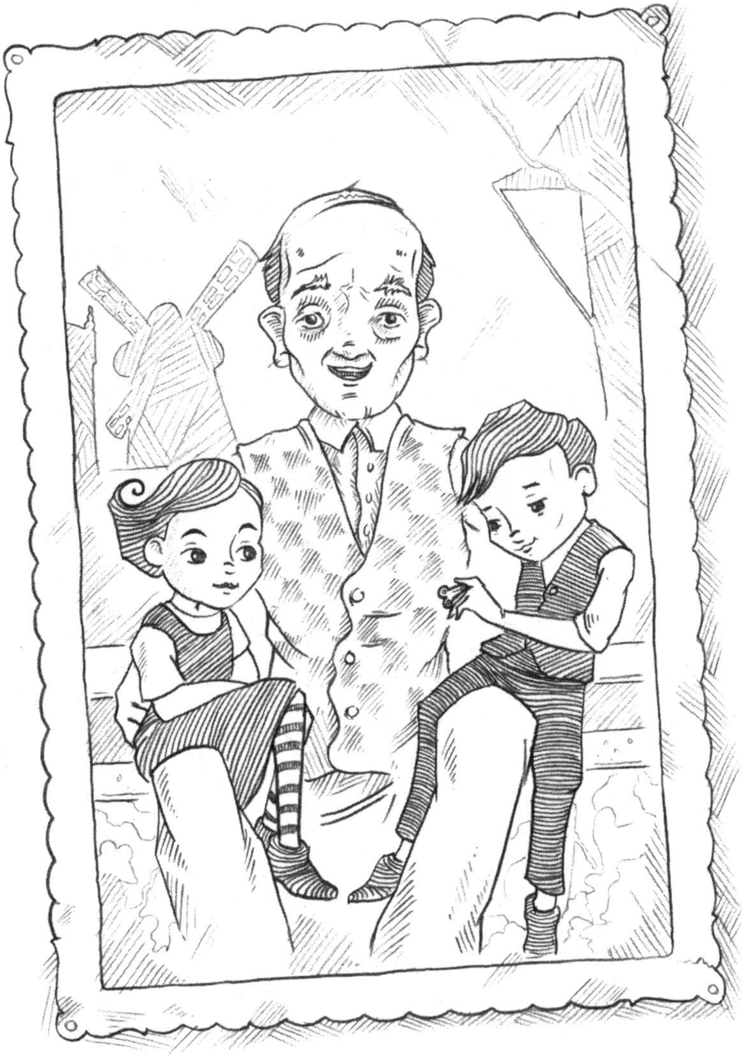

Don't miss the first two action-packed books in the Word Hunters series!

Word Hunters: The Curious Dictionary
ISBN 978 0 7022 4945 7

Word Hunters: The Lost Hunters
ISBN 978 0 7022 4958 7

'All-round fun and a little bit irreverent, Earls and Whidborne have created what is sure to be a favourite.' *Books+Publishing*

'An intriguing series.' *Magpies*

'An action-packed adventure story filled with humour, excitement and mysteries to solve.' *Kids Book Review*

'Young readers will readily suspend disbelief as the twins and their pet rat are transported into other worlds.' *Courier-Mail*